HONEY

Also by Jenna Jameson and Hope Tarr:

Sugar

JENNA JAMESON

and HOPE TARR

HONEY

Skyhorse Publishing

Skyhorse Publishing books may be purchased in bulk at special discounts for
sales promotion, corporate gifts, fund-raising, or educational purposes. Special
editions can also be created to specifications. For details, contact the Special Sales
Department, Skyhorse Publishing, 307 West 36th Street, 11th Floor, New York,
NY 10018 or info@skyhorsepublishing.com.

Skyhorse® and Skyhorse Publishing® are registered trademarks of Skyhorse
Publishing, Inc.®, a Delaware corporation.

Visit our website at www.skyhorsepublishing.com.

10 9 8 7 6 5 4 3 2 1

Library of Congress Cataloging-in-Publication Data is available on file.

Cover design by Brian Peterson
Cover photo credit Thinkstock

ISBN: 978-1-62873-713-4
Ebook ISBN: 978-1-62914-059-9

Printed in the United States of America

Authors' Acknowledgments

Our sincere gratitude to Dr. Danielle Friedman and Lisa Davila, RN for their immeasurable help in clarifying the morass of medical terminology and sharing their expert knowledge of healthcare providers, procedures, and practices. Any errors made, or creative license taken, are of course entirely ours.

—Jenna Jameson and Hope Tarr

Chapter One

"I don't want to own anything until I find a place where me and things go together. I'm not sure where that is but I know what it is like. It's like Tiffany's."—Audrey Hepburn, *Breakfast at Tiffany's*

February, Emergency Room, Bellevue Hospital Center

"Let's go through this again, shall we?"

Dr. Marcus Sandler surveyed the female patient perched on the edge of his exam table, a standout in an ER otherwise flooded with victims of the flu. Honey Gladwell, if that was even her real name, which he seriously doubted, didn't have so much as a sniffle. What she had was a whole lot harder to fix.

Someone, an *intimate* someone, had battered her. Even coming up on the end of a twelve-hour shift, not the eight hours standard for third-year residents, except when your intern was felled with flu, there was no mistaking a textbook case of domestic violence such as this.

Ms. Gladwell had been lucky—this time. The X-rays and MRI results revealed a radial wrist fracture and a blow to the left eye so severe she was lucky the orbit hadn't splintered. Those were the worst of her injuries, the physical ones anyway. Assessing the psychological trauma of being used as a punching bag wasn't Marc's bailiwick, but it couldn't be good. Whoever had done this to her was one sick son of a bitch.

Beneath the patchwork of cuts and bruises, she was probably pretty, though her face was too swollen for him to say for certain. What he could tell with certainty was that she was small, one hundred and five pounds according to her triage vitals, and five foot six without the ridiculous pencil-thin heels she'd hobbled in on. The one-size-fits-all hospital gown swam on her. They might as well have given her a tent to wear. And she was young—twenty-seven as of last week, based on the birth date she'd given. Without a driver's license or photo ID of any kind, he was left with having to take her word on it.

Looking up from the chart he held, he tried again. "Can you walk me through how you got hurt?"

She lifted her heart-shaped face, a classic symbol of defiance even if, like her loyalty, the ballsy attitude was badly misdirected. "Darling, as I told the nurse already, I fell. Down some stairs," she added, her stilted speech carefully modulated, borderline British.

Falling down the stairs—talk about your clichéd cover-up. Marc would have laughed if he wasn't so fucking sick of the same old story. Growing up in Harlem, he'd dealt with domestic violence victims aplenty, including his own mother. Why couldn't these women see that covering for their abusers was as good as giving the sick sons of bitches a license to kill—*them*?

"Where?" he asked, his fingers firming on the clipboard.

Twirling a hank of honey-colored hair, waist-length and tangled beyond the retro beehive, she bit her bruised bottom lip. "At home."

He glanced from her ringless left hand back to her chart. Forty-One Park Avenue, one of those overpriced midtown high rises that invariably announced itself with a water feature in the lobby and boasted a crap-load of amenities that hardly anyone ever used. Her apartment was likewise easy to picture: a featureless one bedroom or junior efficiency with nine-foot ceilings and a private terrace with a partial view. It was the sort of building where a man who could afford it put up his mistress. The wife, if there was one, would be ensconced in a "classic six" in one of the esteemed prewar buildings above 61st but below 96th Streets. Go even a block higher and you were in Upper Manhattan, including the once dreaded Washington Heights neighborhood where Marc lived. Real estate really was all about location. Nowhere was that truer than in Manhattan.

"Forty-One Park, huh? Sounds like an elevator building to me. Standards must be seriously slipping." He softened the sarcasm by shooting her a wink.

No dice. She glared. Her eyes were medium brown, judging from the one not swollen shut. The gold flecks crowding the iris told him she was angry—and that for now it was easier and infinitely safer to focus that emotion on him.

"The elevator is being replaced . . . I mean, repaired. We . . . I had to take the stairwell. It's a whole . . . thing."

Whatever else she was, she was a terrible liar. His God-fearing, church-going, bible-quoting Aunt Edna could spin a better yarn than that without so much as blinking. In contrast, this poor kid was somewhere between twitchy and imploding. The nervous fingers of her unhurt hand twirled the ends of her hair. The one with the wrist fracture was encased in a cast.

"Hmm, I'll bet. You should demand the management company return your monthly maintenance fee."

No response. She pressed her lips together, and he had a fleeting wish to know what they looked like when they weren't cut and puffy, raw and red. Right now her mouth looked almost as if it was turned upside down, the top lip fuller and wider than its bottom mate. Intriguing.

Not yet ready to give up, Marc asked, "Do you live with a . . . roommate, someone who can help you out for the next few days?"

She stopped playing with her hair and shook her head. "No, I don't have . . . It's just me."

The best lies were half-truths. He'd bet his precious vacation leave she was a kept woman, a mistress, her rent and other living expenses picked up by a man who breezed in and out of her life on a whim—his—and who apparently got off on brutalizing women.

"Who did you say brought you in?"

His question prompted more glaring. "I didn't say."

He couldn't help but smile. She hadn't given an inch or shed so much as a single tear since he started treating her. She was totally brave and mind-numbingly stubborn. He couldn't help admiring both, even if they were summoned for all the wrong reasons.

"I'm just trying to make sure you get home safely," he said more gently.

Her slender shoulders slumped as though she were finally succumbing to the exhaustion. "My . . . boyfriend, but he . . . had to go."

"He left you . . . in this condition!" Whatever slim benefit of the doubt he might have been prepared to tender evaporated in that instant.

She shrugged, wincing as if the minor movement hurt, which he was sure it did. "He has a very important job . . . in finance," she added with obvious pride.

So the culprit was some single-malt-swilling hedgie or Wall Street trader, a suit who vented his frustrations with the recession economy by pummeling little girls. Ms. Gladwell wouldn't be the first woman to bear the brunt of a money man's high-stakes, high-stress lifestyle. Nor, unfortunately, would she be the last.

"I can take care of myself," she said suddenly, defiantly, her shoulders straightening.

Obviously that wasn't the case, but as his attending was forever reminding him, he was a doctor, not a social worker, and most definitely not a cop. Rather than refute her, he focused on her chart. The head wound would justify a full admission if he chose to go there.

Who knew, maybe the down time would give her the space she needed to rethink her story—and her life choices.

Pulling the ballpoint from behind his ear, he said, "You sustained a nasty head wound. I'd like to keep you overnight for observation."

"I have to stay here overnight?!" The way she said it made it sound like he'd sentenced her to Sing Sing.

"A twenty-three-hour observational period," he corrected. "That way the hospital won't charge you for an overnight stay." Despite the couture clothes and full-length fur she'd come in wearing, she hadn't listed having any insurance.

Her good eye shuttered. "That would be okay, I guess."

A nurse pulled back the curtain and poked her head inside. "Dr. Sandler, dispatch just called in a notification: nineteen-year-old male, GSW to the chest, intubated in the field, hemodynamically stable but might have a developing pneumo from a cracked rib."

Marc sighed. A gunshot wound—yep, typical Friday night. And he still had an ER packed with puking patients. As much as he might like to linger, he didn't have that choice. He had to move on.

"Okay, I'll be there in a minute." He waited for the curtain to close again before glancing back at the girl. "So, we're set. We'll get you into a room as soon as possible. It's a little intense right now with all the flu sufferers, so hang tight and try to rest."

"Rest? In this madhouse?" She rolled her eyes, the unhurt one conveying a droll amusement that, under the circumstances, was unexpected—and hugely appealing.

She also had a point. Neon lighting, nonstop scuttling back and forth from the various medical staffers, and callouts from the ubiquitous intercom hardly made it a napping zone—unless, of course, you were an exhausted intern. Back then, Marc could have slept standing. Once or twice, he had.

For the first time that night, he felt a smile tugging at the corners of his mouth. "Right, I know. Do your best."

The next several hours whizzed by. The gunshot victim from Spanish Harlem with the gang tats was joined by a NYU student goaded by his buddies into sticking a light bulb up his butt, and a fast-food worker burned by boiling cooking oil when the deep fryer malfunctioned. By the time Marc took a breather, it was nearly 1:00 a.m. Hoping Ms. Gladwell might have had a change of heart—and story—he grabbed her chart and went to check on her.

Only she was gone. Shit! Marching over to the nurse's station, he demanded, "Who discharged this patient—*my* patient—without my knowledge?"

The nurse behind the desk looked up from the computer screen and shrugged. "She AMA-ed."

Left against medical advice, fuck! Incredulous, Marc revved up to rip into her. "And nobody came to find me?"

"It's okay, I signed off." Dr. Denison, his attending, walked up. Dropping his voice, he added, "Let it go, Marc." He wrapped a fatherly arm about Marc's shoulders and steered him away from the station. "You're an excellent clinician, Marc, one of the most gifted trauma interns I've had in some time, but if you don't monitor your intensity you're going to burn out."

"Yes, but, sir—"

"To make it in medicine, emergency medicine especially, you need to accept that you can't save everyone. The sooner you make peace with that, the greater an asset you'll be to me, this hospital, and above all, your patients."

Knowing he was beat, Marc backed off with a nod. "Duly noted, sir. Thank you for the feedback."

Thank you for the feedback—Jesus, what a brownnoser he'd become. He was attracted to trauma as the area of medicine where he could do the most immediate good, help the most people, but the past several months had punctured all kinds of holes in his dream bubble.

"You're welcome." Denison dropped his arm, muscular and dusted with white hairs, and stepped away. "Do yourself and everybody else here a favor and go home and get some sleep. You'll need it. You've got to be back here in nine hours."

Marc nodded. "I will. Thanks."

Watching Denison turn away, he raked a hard hand through his hair. He couldn't save or even help everyone—he got that. But he might have helped her, Honey Gladwell or whatever her name was, if only he'd had more time.

Then again, maybe he did. Forty-One Park Avenue wasn't more than a few short blocks from the hospital. And he had, if not all the time in the world, at least the next nine hours.

✻✻✻ ✻✻✻

Honey hobbled into the apartment, vintage mink coat draped over her shoulders and beaded evening bag tucked inside her sling. She slipped off her satin-covered slippers, maneuvered herself free of the fur, and reached out with her good arm to close the door. Stepping back, the silence struck her like another fist in the face. A few quick glances around confirmed that Drew wasn't there, not that she'd expected him to be. The last time, he'd stayed away five days and then come back bearing a freshwater-pearl bracelet from Tiffany's. She wondered what his apology present would be this time—surely a broken wrist merited something with diamonds?—and how long her reprieve would last. A full week, maybe even two?

Setting her keys in the decorative escargot-fashioned catchall, she surveyed the wreckage. Drew's latest rampage had taken its toll not only on her person but also her treasures. Her vintage Danish-modern table lamp, one of a pair, lay on its side on the floor, the fiberglass shade cracked but the ceramic base miraculously unbroken. Most of the contents of her corner curio shelf, bric-a-brac from the fifties and sixties, had been cleared out and used as missiles, the Melamine turquoise divided "fin" dish and one of a trio of glass cat figurines the sole survivors. The circular wall mirror hung at a drunken tilt, a smear of dried blood marking the spot on the beveled glass where her head had hit. Reaching out to right it with what in the past several hours she'd come to think of as her "good arm," she caught her reflection and gasped. Aside from the short bangs fringing her forehead and the lack of lines bracketing her mouth and eyes, she might be looking at her mother's face, mottled and misshapen from years of serving as her husband's punching bag. After her own nose had run afoul of that same flying fist, Honey had fled, not only her stepfather's house but also her hometown of Omaha. It had taken a progression of Greyhound buses, more odd jobs than she cared to recount, and nearly four months before she finally reached New York City. Ironic that after 1,148 miles and six years, she'd spiraled back to almost the same spot. Despite the icepack the nurse had given her, her left eye was still mostly swollen shut, her mouth so split it would be at least a week before she could even think about picking up a lipstick. The cream-colored complexion she took such pride in preserving, washing off her makeup every night no matter how tired she was, and slathering on sunscreen even in winter, was blotched black and blue. An abused woman. Somehow she'd devolved into that thing, that person, that *statistic* she'd sworn never to be.

It—they—hadn't started out this way.

She'd met Drew six years ago at an after-hours party at the Ritz sponsored by his private equity firm, the sort of sleek yet slightly sleazy corporate setup from which wives and significant others were unofficially barred. All the women there were either mistresses or professional escorts, Honey among the latter. Beyond the inevitable end to the evening, she hadn't set out to meet anyone. Scoping out the crowd, she dodged the wolfish stares of several senior executives, their paunches and wrinkles and balding heads all unappealingly familiar. Not that she got to pick—she absolutely didn't—but just once she wouldn't mind going to bed with someone under fifty with a nice smile and a full head of hair and an erection that didn't rely on Viagra. In the midst of her musings, a champagne cork went flying. The partygoers darted left or right, leaving Drew standing in her direct line of sight. He was just thirty and goldenly beautiful, if a bit short, a dead ringer for the late actor George Peppard, not in his cigar-munching *A-Team* days but when he'd played Paul in her favorite Audrey film, *Breakfast at Tiffany's*. She spent the next hour watching him work the crowd, oozing quick wit and debonair charm, his thick sandy blond hair clipped short and combed smoothly back, his well-built body sheathed in a custom-tailored suit, and his blue eyes clear and bright, not fogged as they so often were now. Somehow he managed to make the simple act of lighting his cigarette, from a personally engraved lighter no less, seem like a sexual act. Finally he forded his way to her, the fresh glass of champagne in either hand sufficing to claim her as his for the night. Accepting the flute with a smile, she'd felt more like a prom queen than a prostitute. Ending the evening in his hotel room had felt both natural and inevitable. The next day he called her agency and booked the first of several months of solo "dates." By the time he'd gotten around to asking her to leave that life and let him take care of her, she was too giddy to give any answer other than yes.

That first year he'd been endearingly polite and boyishly romantic, making her feel more like a fiancée than a mistress. Yes, of course, there was the issue of his wife and young son to surmount, but when he swore he'd ask Katharine for a divorce when the time was right, Honey persuaded herself he must be sincere. In the meantime, every "date" was a delightful adventure, another page added to their unconventional fairy tale. Caviar and vodka at the Russian Tea Room, intimate late night suppers at Balthazar, shopping sprees to Tiffany's and Bergdorf's, carriage rides through Central Park—it was as if Manhattan was their personal playground, as if the gloriously Happily Ever After vision of the future she'd once conjured to keep out the fighting was finally hers, bestowed by a charming if not wholly available prince.

The crash of 2008 had changed him, or at least it had justified his changing. He started drinking more and more, even dabbling in drugs. And he was angry, always so angry—at the clients, the market, the federal government and, most of all, her. The thoughtful scheduling of their "dates" stopped. A text message was the most warning she could hope to get. She couldn't ever know when he might show up—or what mood he'd be in when he did.

But whether he was jubilant or brooding or furious, whether it was a bull market or a bust, whether he'd made or lost millions for his latest top-tier client, he was always, *always* in the mood for sex. Not the gentle passion he'd shown her when they still "dated," when she was self-sufficient in her way, when she'd still had other men and other options. Now all he wanted was to take her roughly, bend her body and will to his. Forcing her down on her knees to suck him off had gone from occasional "play" to their standard scenario. The way he held her head, her long hair balled into his fist, his cock jamming down her throat until she could barely breathe beyond the gagging, always with him fully dressed except for his open trouser fly, made her feel less like a mistress and more like a slave. And not even a *cherished* slave, which since coming to New York she'd learned existed, but a piece of dirt stuck to the sole of his Prada wingtips, something he might decide to scrape off at any time on a whim.

As the scenarios in Drew's playbook got progressively more brutish and one-sided, there were no more safe words, no more beforehand discussions to ensure that whatever happened was consensual. And if she let on how much she loathed it, all of it, he would punish her, not in play but for real. Hiding what she was thinking and feeling wasn't about being mysterious, not anymore.

It was about self-preservation.

But so long as she bore it, so long as she pleased him, he'd still sometimes be tender afterward. He'd scoop her off the floor and sit her on his lap in the vintage modern wingchair that only he was ever allowed to use. At those times, he'd take out his carefully pressed and folded handkerchief and use it to dab cum from the corners of her mouth.

"So long as you keep taking care of me, I'll keep taking care of you, got it baby?"

After six years together, their tainted fairytale was finally reduced to its rancid essence: a business deal, a transaction. He wasn't ever going to leave Katharine, not when the time was right, not ever. He'd given up the pretense years ago just as Honey had given up first the hope and eventually the desire. So completely had she sold herself, she might as well be walking the streets. At least whoring that way would be honest. At least then she'd get to choose. "My ass is my own," or so the sex workers' slogan said. She'd believed that once, had murmured it beneath her breath like a mantra. But she gave up that right, *any* right to dignity and self-determination the day she accepted Drew as her exclusive, the day she'd quit the agency and stood beaming smiles as he signed the first of six one-year leases on "her" apartment. The posh Park Avenue co-op had started out as a castle-in-the-air but these days felt more and more like a gilded cage—a prison.

By a fluke, she'd found FATE—Faith, Acceptance, Trust, and Enlightenment—an informal meet-up for former adult entertainers living in New York City. Through the frank, nonjudgmental sharing of their struggles and triumphs, members strove to make peace with their pasts and "write" their unique new life stories. The weekly coffee klatch met from 6:00 to 8:00 p.m. every Monday at the Soho walkup of their group leader, Liz.

At first, Honey had been skeptical. She was never much of a joiner, preferring solitary pursuits such as journaling to sharing her thoughts and feelings face-to-face. But what had started as a social outlet had quickly become a lifeline. Liz, Brian, Peter, and now Sarah had become more than friends. They were her people. With its salvaged furniture and strewn-about kid's toys, Liz's felt far more like home than her own place did. And yet even there, with them, she couldn't be totally truthful, didn't dare let down her guard. The secret that was tearing her apart inside was the very one that she couldn't admit, not without getting thrown out of the group.

She hadn't really left the life.

She might not work for an "agency" any longer, but she was still accepting money in the form of apartment rent and clothing and jewelry in exchange for sex. And that ongoing choice had brought her to . . . *this*.

Moving into the main room, silent except for her soles crunching on broken glass, the stillness seemed to resonate with the echoes of their earlier one-sided argument.

"Who the hell have you had in here?" Drew demanded, sniffing the air as if catching a whiff of contraband cologne. "Who have you been fucking?" He slammed his scotch glass down so hard on the side table it was a marvel the vessel didn't shatter.

"No one, no one's been here but you, darling," she'd answered, modulating her voice to come off as calmly as she could, even as her heart threatened to hammer a hole through her chest.

Barring the housekeeper, who popped in for two hours every other week, and the super, who'd recently repaired the dripping kitchen faucet, leaving a cloud of Old Spice in his wake, it was the truth. She hadn't even had her FATE friends over. When Liz had asked if they might move the weekly meeting elsewhere while she was having her apartment painted, tempted though Honey had been to volunteer, she knew better. Drew liked things a certain way—the towels folded and draped over the bath rack just so, the decorative pillows on the loveseat and bed plumped and prettily arranged—and the single malt sitting out on the bar amidst freshly washed Lalique cut-crystal glasses.

"Don't *darling* me, you fucking cunt," he spat, closing in on her, the liquor on his breath combining with fear to flip her stomach. "I know when I'm being bullshitted. It's my *business* to know."

She shook her head, vehement in her denial, frightened and yet furious at the unfairness of it all, that she was once again being falsely accused and punished for something she'd never come close to doing. Times like this carried her back to Omaha, to her stepfather, Sam, with his beer breath and blow-dealing backhand. No matter how closely she watched, searching for warning signs, that flying fist had always managed to appear as if out of nowhere. If she lived to be one hundred, she'd never understand how such a big, sloppy man had managed to move so swiftly.

Drew wasn't big or sloppy. Even wasted, he had a fencer's light-footed grace. Despite his regular drinking and more than occasional cocaine use, he somehow managed to stay in shape, sweating out his hangovers in workouts with his personal trainer.

She let out a manufactured laugh, mostly to hide how frightened she was. "Drew, darling, please, you're being perfectly silly. In six years I haven't so much as looked at another man."

Honey paused, momentarily pulled back to the present. Had she really said that just last night? The testimony, true at the time, was true no more. With his tall, broad-shouldered body, closely cropped dark hair, mocha-colored complexion, and thickly lashed hazel eyes that seemed to see straight through her, the ER doctor who'd patched her up was nothing if not easy on the eyes, even if, in her case, she'd only had the one able to open. Firm yet softly spoken, caring yet exuding an aura of command, he struck her as the polar opposite of Drew. The contrast carried her back to the previous night's argument-cum-fight.

Drew answered her heartfelt declaration with a disbelieving snort. "It's not the looking I'm worried about."

"Then what are you worried about?" she asked, gingerly taking a step toward him, for a split second thinking that, this once, she might smooth things over before everything fell to pieces. "I've never given you any reason not to trust me, and I never will."

The lips she once hadn't been able to get enough of kissing curled into a sneer. "You're forgetting how we met," he said, flinging her away from him.

Before last night, his booze-fueled fury hadn't taken them beyond bruising, the marks sufficiently noticeable to call for wearing elbow-high evening gloves and long sleeves no matter the season or time of day. But until now, he'd never hurt her so badly that she couldn't camouflage the aftermath with clothing and makeup, so badly that she needed to go to the hospital. Until now he'd never actually broken—fractured—anything, at least not beyond her heart, which felt as if it must be sutured and scarred, callused and numbed, only not quite numb enough.

Blaring from the house buzzer bumped her out of her morbid musings. Her heart rate ratcheted. Drew, back so soon! But no, he would never buzz into their—his—apartment, not even if he'd forgotten his key. A spare was kept at all times by the doorman. If Drew wanted in, he only needed to walk up to the lobby desk and have Freddie, Carlos, or Joey turn it over. Even if the neighbors had called the building superintendent to complain of the noise from their arguing—again—the hefty holiday tips Drew doled out to the building staff assured blind eyes and deaf ears year-round.

She reached out and pressed the intercom button, her hand, like the rest of her, shaking. "Y-yes?"

Joey's Queens-accented voice cut through the crackle of static. "Ms. Gladwell, there's a guy—gentleman—here to see you."

So she wasn't to have any reprieve after all. Honey stuffed a fist—the fist of her "good hand"—into her mouth to muffle any sobbing.

"Ms. Gladwell?"

Deep breaths, take deep breaths . . . What would Audrey do in such circumstances? Mix martinis? Pop on a pillbox hat? Flutter her doe-like eyes and explain, albeit apologetically, that this simply wasn't a convenient time?

Only Audrey would never find herself in such circumstances, not on-screen or off. Not even her supposedly Svengali-like first husband, Mel Ferrer, had gotten the better of her. Being the biddable wife had merely been another part to be played, Honey was convinced of it. Even as Holly Golightly, one of her many iconic screen roles, she managed to convey the sense that she was the mistress of her destiny, a gamine-like goddess having a marvelous time making fools of all the mortal men.

Honey dropped her hand and found her voice. "Yes, yes I'm listening. If it's Drew . . . Mr. Winterthur, please tell—ask—him if he'll please be so good as to come back another time. I'm not feeling terribly well at the moment and—"

"It's not Mr. Winterthur, it's . . . He says he's your doctor."

✳✳✳ ✳✳✳

"Are you stalking me, Doctor . . . ?" Ms. Gladwell asked him, her one slender arm draped along the doorframe. The other arm was in the soft cast and sling that he'd prescribed.

"Sandler," Marc supplied, more miffed than he cared to admit.

Had he really just risked his professional reputation and possibly his medical license for someone who couldn't be bothered to take note of his name? Of all the foolhardy and self-sabotaging things he'd done in his thirty-three years, trailing Honey Gladwell home from the hospital ER might well top the list.

Her good eye flashed, whether with humor or annoyance he couldn't yet say. "Well, Doctor *Sandler*, this certainly is a surprise."

"Think of it as me resurrecting the time-honored tradition of the house call." He looked past her and into the apartment, preparing for the possibility that the bastard who'd battered her might have returned, literally, to the scene of the crime. "Can I come in?"

She shot a nervous look over her shoulder before turning back to him. "I'm not really in a position to receive guests."

"I'm not a guest. I'm your doctor. I only need five minutes, ten tops. C'mon, what do you have to lose—unless, of course, you're afraid to let me in?"

The dare worked like a charm. "Don't be absurd," she snapped, backing up to make room for him to enter.

Not giving her time for second thoughts, Marc planted one Skechers on the other side of the threshold. Inadvertently he brushed against her, catching a whiff of shampoo and shower gel, all overlaid with what was likely some ungodly expensive perfume.

The apartment was almost exactly as he envisioned it would be, down to the sliding-glass door opening onto a communal, wrap-around balcony, the partial park view, and retro-inspired furniture that was altogether too stylized and sleek to be comfortable. There was, however, one glaring detail that had been missing from his mental picture: it was a wreck. An overturned lamp lay sprawled across the Berber wall-to-wall. A half-open door showed a mussed bed and clothes spread over it and the carpet. The empty shelves and shattered glass suggested that Ms. Gladwell must have made a doomed but spirited attempt to fight back—good for her.

"Maid's day off?" he quipped, turning back to her.

She lifted her swollen chin. "The politically correct term is *house-keeper*, and as a matter of fact it is. She only comes every other Tuesday."

Framed prints lined the far wall, movie posters of the same dead white screen actress, the one who starred in *My Fair Lady*, *Gigi*, and a slew of others from the fifties and sixties that were now relegated to Turner Classic Movie fare. For the moment, Marc was blanking on her name. No doubt it would come to him, but for the time being the scarlet stain smudging the glare-free glass covering *Breakfast at Tiffany's* reminded him that he had more important matters on which to focus.

"I'm sure she'll be happy to know that the elevator's fixed. Hoofing it all the way to the ninth floor carrying a mop and broom must wear on a body."

She didn't answer that, not that he expected she would. Dropping her gaze to his full hands, she asked, "Have you come bearing gifts, doctor?"

He hesitated, looking down at the bags he'd as good as forgotten, one white paper from the hospital pharmacy with the prescription information stapled to the outside, the other plastic bearing carryout and the Mendy's logo. Looking back up, he said, "You ran . . . left before I could write the script for your meds."

He held out the pharmacy bag, but she drew back as though he'd offered her meth. "I don't take drugs."

Marc stifled a smile. "Again, good to know, but you might want to make an exception for the next day or so. One is an anti-inflammatory to reduce the swelling—"

"I know what an anti-inflammatory does."

"And the other is to help manage the pain. Take it on a full stomach and avoid alcoholic beverages."

She hoisted her chin. "Other than the occasional glass of champagne, I don't drink."

He couldn't help it. He glanced over to the Art Deco cocktail cart. Prominently positioned, it was as well or better stocked than most commercial bars. "Someone here does, though I'll admit you don't strike me as much of a scotch drinker." He would have pegged her as a Veuve Clicquot girl, though when she first came into the ER last night he hadn't detected so much as a whiff of alcohol on her breath.

Her swollen face flushed. "I entertain frequently. A good hostess anticipates the desires of her guests."

"Who do you party with—Guns N' Roses?"

Her unhurt eye narrowed. "Any other prescriptives before you go?" She wasn't only being rude for the sake of it. She was frightened.

"Yeah, this." He handed her the carryout.

"Is that—"

"Chicken soup. It's good for the soul, or hadn't you heard?" The side trip to Mendy's on Park and 34th Street had taken him several blocks out of his way, but it was worth the walk. The celebrated kosher deli made some of the best chicken soup in the city.

She tilted her head as though making a study of him when, really, it was the other way around. "Are you quite certain it's my soul you came here to check up on? I'd thought it was my body."

Improbably, he felt himself flushing. Seeing her in her own clothes and environment, rather than swathed in the hospital gown in a cur-tained exam room beneath neon lights, was a different experience entirely. Any previous pretense to detachment flew out the goddamned window—or in this case, sliding-glass door. Even dangling a broken strap and denuded of beads, her floor-length evening gown was unmis-takably couture—and she wore it like a queen. But then she had the sort of body his mother would call "neat"—small breasts, small waist, slim hips, long slender legs. There wasn't an ounce of extra body fat on her, and yet he couldn't say she was skinny, at least not unhealthily so. Marc ordinarily went for fuller-figured women and yet suddenly, improbably, he found himself fantasizing about what it would be like to settle his hands on her buttocks and bring her gently but firmly against him.

Good thing his hands were full.

Swallowing against his mouth's sudden dryness, he held out the takeout bag. "You need to eat. I would have picked up a prime rib but biting into beef with a swollen jaw isn't fun."

She hesitated and then reached for the bag with her unhurt arm. "Thanks." She looked inside to the plastic container. "Goodness, that's a lot of soup." She crossed to the open kitchen and set the bag on the breakfast bar.

Watching her walk away—if he wasn't careful, the sway of those hips would hypnotize him like a pendulum—he answered, "I figured I'd better pick up enough for two."

She whipped around, wincing as if the abrupt movement must hurt her. Or maybe it was his question, and the truth, that brought the real pain. "I told you last night, it's just me." Wide and frightened, her unhurt eye met his.

"Is it?" He started toward her, stopping when his rubber sole came down on something more substantial than slivered glass. He lifted his foot and his gaze caught on the object in question: a gold cufflink. Like the scotch, it was expensive—and a dead giveaway. He bent and picked it up, taking note of the monogram, AW, before straightening. "You don't live here alone." This time it wasn't a question.

"Whether I do or not, it's none of your business." She shoved away from the counter and came toward him. Reaching him, she held out her hand.

He handed the cufflink over. "When your *roommate* lands you in the ER, *my* ER, it kind of is."

She slipped the male jewelry inside her sling. A bruise, yet another one, had begun blooming atop her bared and otherwise milky shoulder.

Resisting the insane impulse to close the gap between them and press his lips to the wicked mark, he focused back on her face.

Looking up at him, she asked, "Do you follow all your patients so closely?"

"Not all, only the ones whose accident stories don't hold water." Hers had more holes than the suspected Mafia hit who, riddled with bullets, had DOA'd the month before. "Or who run off before I discharge them."

"How much do I owe you for the prescription? I'm afraid I don't keep much cash lying about."

"Consider it on the house." He reached into his pocket and pulled out his card.

She stared at it as though it was a spider. "Your card? Seriously?" She looked at him askance.

He felt his face burn. She obviously thought he was hitting on her. Under other circumstances, non-medical circumstances, she might not be far off. "With the website and phone number of a women's shelter written on the back."

Her shoulders dropped as though someone had dumped invisible weights on them. "I know what you're thinking . . . what this must look like, but it was just a silly spat that got out of hand."

"I'll say." And by the way, who under the age of sixty used words like "spat" anymore?

She shook her head. "Drew loves me, and I . . . love him. He's really a marvelous man. It's just that he's been under so much stress at work."

Drew, a common nickname for Andrew—the "A" in the "AW," it had to be! So that was the sadistic son of a bitch's name. Filing it away for the future, he said, "Spare me the excuses. I'm under stress at work. Most people I know are under stress at work, either logging in crazy hours or holding down multiple jobs to make ends meet, and yet they find ways to deal with it that don't involve knocking around their women."

"I'm not anyone's woman." The remark was made with another lifting of that stubborn little chin, a chin that despite its swollen state would fit neatly in his hand.

He locked his eyes on hers. "Aren't you?"

She swallowed, hard, sending a ripple down the length of her throat, which was just long and elegant enough to be considered swan-like. A throat that begged a man to lay his hand on her nape, not in violence but as a prelude to drawing her into his kiss.

"Doctor Sandler, please . . ."

Her voice trailed off, but not before it pulled him out of the fantasy and back to the present—winter 2014, doctor-patient, all strictly above board. Sure, he was human. He was allowed to feel concern for her, *clinical* concern, nothing more—because feeling anything more, even an iota more, would buy him more trouble than he could handle right now, possibly ever.

"You must believe me, it's never . . . happened before. It won't happen again. It—"

"Stop!"

He recognized a lie when he heard one—and the one she was feeding him, and herself, was supersized, what his ma and Aunt Edna and those of their era called a *whopper*. He had no intention of swallowing it or even pretending to. He reached out and took her hand. Small surprise, her fingertips felt frozen, her palm clammy. He pressed the paper into her palm and gently furled her fingers into a fist, the slightness of her small, slender hand—of her—making him feel protective, even tender. Rubbed raw.

Lifting his eyes to hers, he said, "Do us both a favor and keep it. Put it in your shoe, so in case you ever need it—"

"I won't."

"Good, I hope you don't, but just in case you do."

"Very well, thank you."

For whatever reason, her thanks, sincere-sounding, embarrassed him. He shrugged it off. "Head trauma can be unpredictable. If you need medical advice or someone to talk to or . . . whatever, call me. My pager number is on there, too."

She hesitated. "Will that be all, or is there something more you wish to lecture me on, some other inappropriately personal remarks you wish to make?"

"Just one."

She lifted her face to his, waiting, and Marc suddenly felt as if he were diving headfirst into the deep end of the pool, that first surreal rush when you lift your face to the surface and remember that it's okay to breathe again.

"Whoever he is, whatever it takes to get out from under him, this life, do it. Ditch him."

She shook her head, vehement and stubbornly loyal. "You don't know him."

"Maybe not," Marc conceded, "but I know this much—he doesn't deserve you."

She lifted her face to his, pinning him with her stare, the unhurt eye large and luminous, dark and angry. "It should take you exactly four seconds to cross from here to that door. I'll give you two."

As dismissals went, hers was kickass, especially considering the circumstances. Honestly, he couldn't help but admire her moxie, misdirected though it was. "Suit yourself," he said and started to say more, stopping himself when he saw her stare pointedly to the door at his back. That look left him little choice but to make his exit or risk trashing his life, or at least his career.

It wasn't until much later, when he was back at the hospital working on his third cup of coffee and about to start his shift, that it struck him.

Her signature sendoff was taken verbatim from an old movie.

Chapter Two

"True friends are families which you can select."—Audrey Hepburn

Two Weeks Later

"And then this rat of a doctor—and not only ratty but overbearing—showed up at my door refusing to leave until I let him in. Apparently he was miffed that I dared to leave *his* ER without *his* permission. Can you imagine? All in all, it was a great deal of drama for a tiny tumble down the stairs." Honey paused, gauging her "audience."

The other members of her FATE group stared back at her, rapt—worried. Liz, their founder, formerly the porn star known as Spice, now a self-employed graphic designer raising her son as a single mother in the aftermath of breast cancer. Peter, a recovering alcoholic who'd left prostitution to pursue his passion for interior decoration and now worked as a window dresser for Ralph Lauren. Sober for several years, he'd married his Irish husband, Pol, in a fairytale ceremony at Alger House, a historic West Village venue. Missing was Sarah, best known as the international adult film sensation, Sugar. A newly minted bestselling author and wife of society scion Cole Canning, she was at home counting down the days to delivering their first child. What could these intrepid souls possibly know about fear, not only of the next fist to come flying, but also of failing to measure up?

"I thought it was an elevator building?"

The question came from Brian, the former adult film videographer who now clocked in at his other dream job as a mechanic for classic cars. The same Brian they all teased for his habitual single-word sentences, his taciturn brevity set aside in rare exceptions such as now.

Honey hesitated. She tried for the sort of trilling, devil-may-care laugh her idol, Audrey, would almost certainly have summoned. "Really, darlings, elevators do break down."

Peter leaned toward her. "It sounds to me like this doctor was concerned about you." He reached for her hand, her "good" one, his earnest blue eyes delving into hers. "We're all concerned about you, sweetie."

More silence and charged looks and then Liz stepped in. "That guy you brought as your date to Pete's wedding—"

Honey had been strung tight as piano wire since she crossed Liz's threshold twenty or so minutes earlier, and the well-intentioned grilling was sufficient to send her springing to her feet. "I'm not sure I care for what you're implying."

Liz's eyes widened as if . . . as if Honey had slapped her, something Honey had never done and would never do, and yet lately, or rather after this last time, she'd begun wondering . . . what would it feel like to wield all that power, to harness all that fear?

"Honey, I'm not implying anything. I'm asking you outright. Are you okay? Because if you need anything, any kind of help—"

"Don't be absurd, darling. I'm marvelous, never better."

Scanning their circle, she acknowledged that she'd been a fool to come, an even bigger fool to imagine she could brazen things out beneath these eagle eyes. Not that her group mates had left her with much of a choice. When first Peter and later Liz had called yet again, each threatening to come over to Forty-One Park and carry her out bodily if she missed even one more meeting, she'd caved. Feeling naked without her liquid eyeliner and false eyelashes, still she'd showed up that Monday, grateful that the pillbox hat from the sweet little second-hand shop in Gramercy retained its netted face veil. Though she looked much improved from two weeks before, it was her friends' first time seeing her. Predictably they'd freaked. Warmed as she was by their concern, seeing their horrified faces carried her back to that awful night. As much as she disliked drugs—the painkillers the snoop doctor had dropped off were still untouched in their bottle—if there was a pill she could take to forget that night, a sort of pharmaceutical Men in Black clicker, she would reach for it without reservation.

What was the use in replaying the past, especially as Drew had returned not a week later but on her first night home, more sincerely sorry than she'd ever seen him? Lifting her gently into his arms and laying her carefully onto the bedspread, he'd actually *cried*. Later, he texted an excuse to Katharine about having to pull an all-nighter and stayed with Honey into the next morning, waiting on her hand-and-foot, heating up the Mendy's chicken soup lying fallow in its plastic container in her refrigerator and serving it in the pretty bowls she especially liked. Other than the bottle of Moët they shared—beginning with his teary-eyed toast to turning over new leaves and embarking on new beginnings—he hadn't drunk anything. The bottles of Laphroaig and Macallan and Glenfiddich had remained safely capped on the cocktail cart. Peace had prevailed. He was so bent on pleasing her that he even suggested watching a movie, *Breakfast at Tiffany's*, her favorite. Cradling her champagne flute in her "good" hand, watching the beloved film while Drew gently cuddled her and did his level best to look interested, Honey had almost believed it was the old days—almost.

The old days—how far away they now seemed. She'd just turned twenty-one, the adored mistress of a dashing and devoted lover who swore that if she'd only be patient, someday soon he'd leave Katharine and make her, Honey, his wife—only "someday" never arrived. Despite his insistence that they kept separate bedrooms, Katharine had become pregnant with a second child. Josh, their firstborn, had had a bad bout of the chicken pox. Then Drew was simply too swamped at work to "get into anything right now." A divorce would devastate him financially, especially in the current downward spiraling economy. Why should he hand over fifty percent of his net worth to someone who, beyond pushing out two babies, had sat on her ass for the past seven years? Surely Honey saw how his hands were tied? Surely she understood that her perpetually bare ring finger didn't mean he loved her any less? What was marriage anyway but a piece of paper and a whole lot of headaches? Couldn't she see how lucky they were to be free of it all—the routines and ruts, the lackluster sex and confines of convention?

Honey had protested, cajoled, and even threatened to leave him, but she had nowhere to go and no one to go to, and they both knew it. Slowly, gradually she'd surrendered the fight, surrendered altogether, and slipped into acceptance that her lot in life was to spend birthdays and holidays alone.

Unbidden, another face intruded—one from which hazel eyes stared knowingly out from a strong-featured face, not smoothly shaven as Drew's always was, even on weekends, but darkened by more than a day's growth of beard. Dr. Marcus Sandler—and yes, she hadn't forgotten his name, not after his oh-so-memorable visit.

Sure, he was good-looking—okay, *very* good-looking—and smart—okay, *very* smart—but living in Manhattan she'd met her fair share of handsome, intelligent men, had even had a few of them as clients, though her bookings had run to the fifty-and-over set. Beyond being annoying and sanctimonious and nosey, why had Marc Sandler made such an impression on her?

Probably because he'd gone out of his way for her. Despite her earlier remarks, he wasn't a rat, not really. With his earnest eyes and misplaced insistence, he was an anti-rat, a postmodern Prince Charming, the sort of straight-up guy who'd likely head for the hills if he so much as suspected all the truly ratty, not to mention stupid, things she'd done.

Had she really left Omaha and come all the way to New York only to end up with an alcoholic, a mean drunk, just like her stepfather, Sam? It seemed that history, and family patterns, repeated, no matter how many miles you put between yourself and your past. Given how things had turned out, she might as well have saved herself the trouble and stayed put, gotten a job bagging groceries at the Piggly Wiggly, joined a bowling league, married a mechanic, and otherwise lived her mother's life. Who knew, she might actually have been better off.

The weight of her many misjudgments and mistakes suddenly descended, an icy avalanche from which she couldn't see any way to dig out. Feeling buried, overwhelmed, she got up to go. "Everyone, I'm so dreadfully sorry. Please forgive me. I'm being beastly. I suppose I'm not quite as recovered as I'd thought." She looked to Liz. "This was splendid, really lovely. I'll just be going now, but I will see everyone next week. Ta."

I'll see everyone next week. Reaching for her purse, Honey owned the promise was yet another lie.

✳✳✳ ✳✳✳

The annual hospital gala, the dog-and-pony show put on for board members and high-end donors, had Marc feeling as though he'd landed in an alternative universe, one in which he was very much an alien. Pulling at his cuffs, he tried telling himself he should feel honored to be asked to attend as a representative of Emergency Medicine. He *was* honored and yet . . . Jesus, how he hated all of it: the bite-sized morsels of finger food that whetted an appetite without satisfying it, the socialites with their stiff smiles and even stiffer helmet-head hairstyles, the obligatory pianist pounding out show tunes. Most of all, he hated having to dress up, on a weeknight, no less.

He owned two ties and a single suit, all bought from Men's Wearhouse and usually only brought out for weddings, baptisms, and the occasional family funeral. But even in his "Sunday best," he was woefully underdressed for this black-tie crowd. Not for the first time, he slid a finger beneath his shirt collar. Used to living in hospital scrubs at work and T-shirts and jeans on days off, he felt as though he was wearing a noose.

He certainly felt trapped and out of his depth. Hospital bigwigs, including the administrator and chief of staff, circulated the room glad-handing and courting high-end donors. Bellevue might be the country's oldest public hospital, but like every such medical facility, it relied on community support to keep running, never more so than in a recession. The closing of the venerable St. Vincent's in the West Village still hung over them all like a ghost, a grim reminder that prestige and a legacy of stellar care and community service were no longer any guarantees of survivability. To survive, flourish, an institution needed big bucks.

Wearing a penguin suit that was probably custom tailored, Dr. Denison sidled up to him, gin and tonic in hand. "Having a good time?"

"Yes, sir," Marc dutifully replied.

The senior physician cracked a laugh. "Better work on that poker face."

"Sir?"

"At least try and *look* like you're having a good time. These fundraisers are a necessary evil, in this economy more so than ever."

"I know that, sir. I'm sorry. I guess I'm not much of a schmoozer."

"Then you'd better work on faking it. You could take some pointers from Vandeveer."

Following Denison's nod, Marc looked over to the lanky, red-haired attending chatting up Mrs. E. L. Elmhurst, a prominent social-ite and professional do-gooder. Too bad Vandeveer hadn't pursued his true calling: PR. Jared Vandeveer was a malpractice suit in the making. Just the month before, he'd botched a simple percutaneous tracheot-omy and the patient had nearly hemorrhaged to death. The next time they—the hospital and whatever ER patient was unfortunate enough to come under his care—might not be so lucky.

He turned back to Denison. "But he's—"

"Tut, tut, when it comes to your attending, hear no evil, speak no evil. Say what you will about Jerry, he's a hell of a fundraiser. Do you want that expanded trauma unit or not?"

"Of course I do, sir, but—"

Denison's hand descended on his shoulder. "We're all on the same team, Marc. We just have different roles to play. Now go do your part in pitching us."

"But sir, I'm not sure I'm cut out for—"

"Stop being so goddamned modest. You're one of my most promis-ing protégés to come along in the last decade. We need you front and center, not hanging back in a corner like some goddamned wallflower waiting for someone to ask you to dance."

"Yes, of course, sir." Marc shifted toward the party in progress and that's when he saw her—*her*—Honey Gladwell, breezing in on the arm of her date.

Jesus fucking . . .

Marc might not give a shit about clothes—he didn't give a shit—but not caring wasn't the same thing as being an ignoramus. His mother and aunt both had watched "What Not to Wear" religiously for a decade. He'd studied for his boards with Clinton and Stacy tsk-ing in the background. It was inevitable that something had rubbed off, if only by osmosis. The LBD—Little Black Dress—was widely considered to be a female wardrobe staple, but Honey Gladwell wore hers, a strapless floor-length sheath, like she'd invented it. Fitted black evening gloves reached above her elbows, accentuating the opalescent creaminess of her pencil-thin arms. A triple collar of pearls wreathed her slender neck and her hair was swept away from her face and piled high, no doubt to show off the caramel-colored highlights. She looked stunning and expensive and untouchable, though Marc suddenly wanted to touch her, and not in a doctor-patient kind of way.

But even amidst the rush of blood to his penis, which wasn't only standing at attention but growing in girth, his brain still managed to work. Gorgeous though she was, something still felt . . . off. The look she pulled off wasn't only styled—it was carefully, even meticulously *curated*. Seeing her here like this, in a social setting rather than a clinical one or, God help him, her wrecked apartment, Marc felt as though several pieces to the jigsaw puzzle of "Who is Honey Gladwell?" fell prefitted into his palm. Seeing her styled to near air-brushed quality, the bruises faded without any discernible trace, the arm freed from its cast and sling, all the framed film posters in her apartment made sudden, stunning sense. Audrey Hepburn. The legendary film actress was more than an idol set upon a pedestal and worshipped from afar. Honey was channeling her in a big, *big* way. Chic short bangs and piled high hair, liquid eyeliner, and that artfully modulated accent that bordered on British—it was all a put-on, an act. Well, maybe not entirely. That reed-slender body, that confident carriage, that pearlescent complexion that seemed almost to shimmer—those traits could be helped along but not outright faked. And though both women had big, brown eyes, Honey's standout feature was her "upside down" mouth, the top lip extending beyond the bottom. Barring cosmetic surgery, those distinctive lips would always keep her from pulling off clone status. Any plastics guy who so much as considered messing with that mouth deserved to have his license yanked—and his scalpel-hand severed.

It should take you exactly four seconds to cross from here to that door. I'll give you two.

He'd Googled her comeback line. Sure enough, it had turned up on a site of famous film quotes, in this case *Breakfast at Tiffany's* starring Audrey Hepburn as Holly Golightly, a young country girl who decamps to New York City, where she reinvents herself as a stylish party-girl pseudo escort. Marc recalled seeing the movie poster hanging in Holly's apartment.

Holly Golightly, Honey Gladwell—could it be coincidence that "Honey's" name was so similar to that of Hepburn's signature screen character?

Marc didn't really believe in coincidence.

He darted Denison a swift, sideways look but fortunately the senior physician didn't seem to connect the battered young woman of three weeks ago with the self-possessed stunner who strolled in on the arm of her date dressed as if she'd just come from the Met Ball and carrying herself as though she owned the room and everyone in it.

His regard veered to the sandy-haired WASP in Brooks Brothers by her side, and he felt his smile slip. "Who's that?"

"Andrew Winterthur, senior partner in a private equity firm, Hamptons set, old money, comes from a cadet branch of the Carnegies."

Andrew . . . Drew. The owner of the castoff cufflink and, it seemed, of Honey Gladwell's hide. Not a hedgie but near enough; otherwise Marc had been right on the (old) money, straight down to the single-malt swilling.

The dude might have the blood of robber barons coursing through his veins, but Mendel's Black Box had gotten in at least one good shot. He was short. Maybe not Tom Cruise or Mel Gibson short, maybe not exactly a lawn ornament, but still short. Marc guessed five foot eight, tops, and likely that owed to his shoes having lifts. Despite all the patients Marc had seen since, he could rattle off Ms. Gladwell's triage vitals as though they were his own. She stood five feet six inches in her bare feet and her current stilettos must jack her up another three inches at least. The result brought her about an inch—or two—taller than her date. For an egomaniac like Andrew—Drew—Winterthur, being surpassed by a woman, especially *his* woman, even in such an inconsequential physical way, must really rankle.

Marc's attention swung back to Honey Gladwell, specifically to the slender stem of her very elegant, very kissable, very snap-able neck. Imagining the well-heeled dirt bag's milk-white mitts wrapped around it sent a rush of adrenalin shooting through him, raising every primal protective instinct he'd carefully buried to Code Orange. His heart rate ratcheted. His palms dampened. And his cock—God, his cock was so full and thick, so hot and hard, so aching and thrumming he felt like it might defeat his zipper and burst out of his pants at any moment.

Before he knew it, he heard himself blurt out, "I've got this one."

Denison's tanned face registered surprise. "Are you sure? He's a big fish, and you haven't gotten your feet wet yet. Maybe Vandeveer would be a better—"

"I've got it."

Leaving Denison in his dust, he pushed a path toward Honey and Winterthur, grateful for his unfashionably baggy suit pants with their pleated front—someday he'd remember to take them in for altering—which hopefully hid his boner.

Reaching them, he pasted on a smile. "Good evening, I'm Marc Sandler, one of the ER doctors here." He stuck out a hand in Winterthur's vicinity, mentally replacing it with a fist. Towering over the punk, he'd never been happier about being six foot two.

Even though his overt focus was on Winterthur, he managed to steal a sideways look at Ms. Gladwell. He wasn't the only one who needed to work on a better game face. A hotspot of pink appeared on both her cheeks. Her lower lip quivered ever so slightly and her breathing hitched, bringing the tasteful glimpse of creamy cleavage into greater prominence. Was she really so surprised to see him here? Certainly she must have known running into him tonight was a distinct possibility.

"Whassup doc?" Winterthur finally reached for his hand, enfolding it in a ridiculously crushing grip. Or at least it was probably meant to be crushing. Little dude always trying to measure up—Marc knew the type.

"I was on duty three weeks ago." He paused, waiting for recognition, and shame, to dawn.

It didn't. Bleary eyes met his. "Expecting a medal?"

Jesus, what a jerk.

"Drew!" Honey gasped. Swiveling to Marc, she sent him a pained look of apology.

Only she wasn't the one who should apologize. The way she jumped to take responsibility for her boyfriend's in-your-face rudeness galled Marc, but then again her behavior fit the profile. Like so many women in her situation, she'd probably been browbeaten, not to mention beaten-beaten, into believing everything but the weather was her fault.

He focused on Winterthur. "A medal, hardly, certainly not for doing my job." Not even when that job involved patching up women in the wake of their men's meltdowns.

For the first time since walking up, he looked Honey Gladwell over, a direct, headlong stare, no subterfuge. The eye was healing nicely, the bruise on the cheekbone beneath cleverly concealed with cosmetics. The classic red lipstick she'd selected must mean her mouth had returned to its normal size; that it really was that lush and wide and wonderfully shaped with a top lip slightly longer than its mate. That sexy mismatched mouth sealed the deal. The prettiness he'd suspected weeks ago wasn't prettiness at all. It was beauty.

Marc switched back to the son of a bitch, sizing him up. The clammy handshake, heightened color, and perspiration filming his upper lip all suggested an addict looking for his next fix. Given the frequency with which his focus seesawed between the two service bars, Marc would bet that his drug of choice was alcohol.

A moment later Winterthur confirmed it. "Jesus, who does Honey here have to fuck to score us some beverages?"

"Drew!" she said again, this time in a high whisper, her mortified gaze flying to Marc's and then falling to their feet.

The asshole chuckled, confirming that his penchant for torturing came with a verbal component as well. After several scotches there was no telling how raunchy—or violent—he might get. Unfortunately sons of bitches like this one had too much savvy to blow up in public. They did their damage behind the scenes where the only witness was too beaten down and scared to talk. Conjuring scenarios for how the evening might end sent ice water shooting through Marc's veins, the psychological equivalent of throwing ice water on his erection. Crazy as it was, he couldn't keep from fantasizing about scooping up Ms. Gladwell and carrying her away. She was only a hundred pounds and change. He'd bench pressed that much plenty of times.

But women like Honey Gladwell didn't let regular guys like him go all Neanderthal on them. No, you'd better have an expense account in the high six-figures and the right address if you expected to fuck, or fuck up, a woman like her. He thought of his Washington Heights two-bedroom and choked back a bubble of sour laughter. Women like Honey Gladwell might take a walk on the wild side from time to time, they might live on the edge somewhere between perennially and occasionally, but they absolutely did not venture above 96th Street—never, no way. Born and bred in New York, Marc knew the score. Women like Honey Gladwell weren't looking for white knights.

They were looking for sugar daddies.

"Sorry, Honster, but I'm running low on patience. That server I saw earlier must be taking the biggest dump of his life." He turned back to Marc. "Mind entertaining my friend for a few while I score us some drinks?"

His friend, not even his girlfriend, but then again he was, technically speaking, married, judging from the hammered gold banding his left ring finger. "It would be my pleasure," Marc replied, fastening his focus on their mutual "friend."

Seemingly satisfied, Winterthur turned back to Honey. "Want anything, babe?"

She hesitated. "Champagne, please."

The server Marc had earlier seen butlering glasses of sparkling wine and chardonnay did indeed seem to have vanished. Snaking lines had formed in front of both service bars. With any luck, Winterthur had a substantial wait ahead.

He snorted. "I'm guessing this is more of a Cava crowd, but I'll see what I can scare up."

She waited for Drew to move beyond earshot and then leaned in to say, "So, doctor, we meet again."

Marc started, belatedly realizing she'd beaten him to breaking the ice. He hadn't figured her for the initiator, especially considering the circumstances of their first meeting. But that glowering gaze left no doubt that Ms. Honey Gladwell was not about to stand for being compartmentalized into the narrowly circumscribed role of "victim." That she actually was a victim, both of Winterthur and of her own dubious life choices, suddenly seemed, if not beside the point, certainly tangential to it. Honey Gladwell was a victim—but the stubborn tilt to that chin and the sparks shooting from her brown eyes assured him she was a hell of a lot more.

"Look, about the other day—"

"You should know I hate snoops."

Jesus, she'd done it again, not just preempted him, but cut him off. What was next? Pull the knife out of the Brie and brandish it to his balls? Shove a discarded champagne cork up his ass? And seriously, *snoops?* What was up with the vintage vocabulary?

"I wasn't . . . that is, I'm not a snoop. I'm a doctor." At this rate he wouldn't be one for much longer. "I was concerned for your well-being. If I gave you the wrong impression or made you feel uncomfortable in any way, I'm sorry."

The look she sent him could have frozen water. "I suppose this is the point at which you're going to ask me not to say anything. Don't worry, I'm not planning to . . . so long as you let it go. Understood?"

It really was true. No good deed went unpunished. He'd tried to save her and because of it she had him by the balls.

"Okay, deal."

He had no choice. She was an adult woman, apparently fucked in the head but technically of sound mind. If she wanted to stay with someone who periodically pulverized her, neither Marc nor anyone else could make her do otherwise. As Denison repeatedly pointed out, he couldn't save everyone. For now he changed the subject—sort of.

Jerking his head toward the bar, he said, "So that's him, huh? Mr. Single Malt?"

She cast a disparaging downward look at the Stella in his hand. "If you mean my boyfriend, then yes, he is."

Marc took another swallow—from the bottle—the warm beer sliding down his suddenly dry throat. What was it about Honey Gladwell that had him feeling as though he was once more that awkward sixteen-year-old trying to strike up the courage to ask one of the popular girls to the junior prom?

"Finance guy, huh?"

She lifted her chin, swollen no more but delicate and softly rounded. "Drew manages one of the highest yielding hedge funds in the city."

She made the pronouncement with obvious pride. The bastard might have beaten her badly enough to land her in the ER, but it was obvious to Marc that she was still a long way from cutting him loose, if indeed she ever did.

"Good for him." He slid his gaze over her, not overly long but long enough. "You look nice, by the way."

That was a lie. She didn't look nice. She looked amazing.

The compliment won him a small smile and a flash of dark, doe-like eyes. "Thank you, by the way."

"Your arm should still be in the soft cast, though. You shouldn't stop wearing it until you're fully healed."

"I do wear it, just not . . . tonight."

"Doesn't really go with the dress, I guess."

She sent him a fleeting smile. "No, it doesn't."

"Hey, you wouldn't want to grab a cup of coffee sometime, or maybe a cappuccino? You look like more of a cappuccino drinker." Whoa, where had that come from? So much for playing things safe.

"Tea, actually."

"Okay, tea then. What do you say?"

She sent him a suspicious look. Dropping her voice, she said, "If you think you can persuade me to file some sort of . . . report, you're—"

"Barking up the wrong tree, sure, got it. Let's just say I don't feel like we ever got to finish our conversation the other day." Given how skittish she was, the soft sell was definitely the way to proceed.

"Oh, I assure you, Dr. Sandler, I finished."

He thought again to her snappy comeback and found himself fighting a smile. "Okay, in that case, let's start a new topic thread: art, music, film—your pick."

"Do you really expect me to believe you want to go out to just . . . talk?"

"It's coffee—okay, tea—not a marriage proposal, and why not? You'd be doing me a favor. Other than blood relatives, everybody I know works in some capacity in this hospital. You'd be helping to broaden my horizons."

She cast a quick glance across the room to Winterthur, thankfully still stuck in line. "Does it somehow escape you that I have a boyfriend?"

"A boyfriend with a wedding ring and an itchy backhand—yep, I totally see where you're coming from. You wouldn't want to let a gem like him get away."

"If you're going to simply insult me—"

"I'm not insulting anybody. Okay, well maybe the sadistic cheater you're seeing, but otherwise we're good. So what do you say to coffee—oops, I mean tea? Think of it as striking a blow for independence. If he asks who you're meeting, you can say I'm your very good friend, Marcie."

Dark brows drew upward. "Marcie?"

"What, I don't strike you as a Marcie? C'mon, you're hurting me, girl."

Her full mouth twitched. "A Marguerite, maybe, but you're definitely no Marcie."

"Marguerite, I can live with it. So it's settled. You and Marguerite are meeting up for your weekly tea talk . . . say, tomorrow at two?"

She hesitated. Considering the circumstances, anything other than an outright refusal had to be a positive sign.

"The Starbucks on Park is pretty close to you."

What looked a lot like fear flared across her face. "Not there."

Had he been alone, Marc would have taken the opportunity to thump himself on the forehead. The venue he'd suggested was more than nearby. It was a stone's throw from her building, which made it too close for comfort—or safety.

"I prefer Tea &—"

"Miss me?" Drew broke in, coming up beside them.

Honey started.

"Jesus, you look like you saw a ghost." Drew passed her a fluted champagne glass. "Am I interrupting something?" He darted a suspicious look between her and Marc.

Taking the drink, she shook her head. "Of course not, darling. We were just making small talk."

Winterthur divided his attention between them, his upper lip curling. "Small talk, huh? How's that going?" His stare stopped at Honey, and though she stayed rooted to her spot, Marc sensed her inwardly shrinking away.

Clearly the clichéd excuse wasn't cutting it. As was often the case in the ER, a bold, split-second decision was called for—and he was the only one of them in a position to make it. "Actually, we were catching up."

Drew slanted him a puzzled look. "Catching up? I don't follow."

"We met before," Marc answered, "a few weeks ago."

Beside him, he heard Honey's sharp intake of breath.

The son of a bitch slugged back his drink. "Really, how's that?"

"I treated Miss Gladwell after her fall."

Four sheets to the wind though Winterthur might be, still he stiffened. "Small world."

"I know, right?" Marc shifted to look at Honey. She might not have seen a ghost but she'd gone as pale as one, her red painted lips the only discernible color in her blood-drained face. "You're obviously recovering beautifully, though I do urge you not to abandon the soft cast too soon. We want that fracture to heal cleanly so you have full mobility in the future."

"Y-yes, doctor, I will. Thank you." The smile she sent him expressed genuine gratitude.

Winterthur knocked back the remainder of his drink. Chewing ice, he said, "In that case, I should thank you for taking such good care of my girl."

Marc forced a shrug. "All in a day's work." It had been a long time since he'd wanted to hit someone this bad but unlike the impetuous, angry boy he'd once been, he'd learned to rein in his temper—most days.

Winterthur slipped a hand inside his suit jacket's inner pocket. He pulled out a pre-written check. "I was going to give this to my man Vandeveer on our way out, but on second thought I think I'll let you do the honors." He handed Marc the check.

Marc glanced down long enough to glimpse a seventh zero, then slipped it into his pocket. "This is very generous of you. I'll pass it on to the Powers That Be and make sure you get a tax receipt."

A shrug met that assurance. "You can tell the big dogs that you wooed me."

"Thanks, but that isn't necessary."

"No, I insist. In fact, you call the administrator over here right now, and I'll play along and make him think you laid it on thick."

Marc bristled. For guys like Drew, everything was one big Monopoly game and everything—and everyone—a commodity for sale. "Thanks, but I don't need to lay on anything. I believe in this program and its mission."

"Easy, doc, no need to get your blood pressure up. Shit, I hear that's all kinds of bad for you. Chill out and have another drink—a real drink—with us." He gestured with his glass, empty now except for melting ice. "C'mon, what do you say?"

"I'll stick with my beer, thanks."

"Suit yourself." He swiveled to Honey. "What about you? Ready for round two?"

Ms. Gladwell—Honey—glanced down at the champagne glass in her hand, still half full, and shook her head. "Thanks but no. I'll have a headache if I have any more after this."

He jabbed an elbow into her arm, the one that was still healing, and smirked. "Honey here is a lightweight. On the bright side, that makes her a cheap date . . . or is it just cheap?" The laugh he let out, and Honey's flushing face, had Marc yearning yet again to pound him. "Seriously, babe, don't be a buzz kill. Have another drink. It's not like I'm not paying for it."

This time Marc couldn't help himself, or at least he chose not to. He reached out and laid a "friendly" hand on Winterthur's shoulder. "It looks like we're both set on drinks, but don't let that stop you."

"Don't worry, I won't." Drew dropped his gaze to Marc's hand, and Marc let it fall away—for now. Flicking his gaze to Honey, he added, "Hang tight. I'll be back." He wheeled away and walked off, only slightly swaying.

Ms. Gladwell—Honey—turned back to Marc. "Tea & Sympathy on Greenwich and 11th. I'll meet you there at two."

❋❋❋ ❋❋❋

Sprawled atop the bedspread, propped against the banked pillows, and cradling a glass of scotch, Drew remarked, "So that black doctor tonight was kind of a tight ass."

Honey froze, her deer-in-the-headlights look staring back at her from the maple and mahogany dressing-table mirror. With his luminous eyes, full lips, and body that might have belonged to a fitness trainer—or a statue of a Greek God—Marc Sandler was almost too beautiful to be a doctor. Strike the "almost," he was too beautiful. Back in Omaha, her childhood physicians from dentist to pediatrician and everyone in between had been liver-spotted and balding, not to mention sporting a substantial spare tire. Marc Sandler was none of those things. Along with his . . . hotness, he apparently was caring and kind, dedicated and funny. Not laugh-out-loud funny but more like . . . ironic. More than once she found herself losing the battle against smiling—and smiling too much wasn't a "problem" she usually had, not anymore at least.

Unfortunately he was also nosey—and persistent. In a weak moment, she'd agreed to meet him for tea. What had she been think-ing? Manhattan was one big small town. The odds of running into someone who might know her and Drew were not as remote as she'd like to believe. She must need her head examined. If Drew found out, she likely would.

"Was he?" she asked, striving for a bored tone. "I hadn't noticed."

What a whopper. She'd noticed everything about him, from the amber flecking his irises to the cheap lace-ups he'd paired with his poorly fitting suit.

A "humph" was all the answer she got. Unsure of whether she should be relieved or worried, she reached up to unclasp her earrings, part of Drew's apology present from a few weeks ago.

You can always tell what a man thinks of you by the kind of earrings he gives you. Or so Audrey's Holly Golightly announced with such stir-ring self-confidence in *Breakfast at Tiffany's.*

The clusters of glass pearls and cut crystals were vintage costume jewelry Drew had picked up at Pippin on 17th Street, pretty enough and yet a definite step down from previous pampering. That they came with the Marchesa cocktail dress she'd coveted, and a pair of black Valentino Intrigate pumps, more than made up for the price differen-tial of real stones versus paste, she supposed. Still, considering he could have killed her, he'd gotten off cheaply—too cheaply.

Honey swallowed hard. Earlier at the hospital fundraiser he joked that she was cheap. It was horrid enough to be spoken to so in private but being badmouthed in public—and before the delicious doctor with the earnest hazel eyes and bulging biceps, no less—had taken horrid to new heights. Several hours later, the remark still stung every bit as much as a physical slap.

The brooding silence was broken once more. Drew called out, "And yet you met him before—in the ER."

Take a deep breath. You can manage him. You simply have to stay calm and centered. If you don't lose control then neither will he.

Imagining herself as a clock hand, she turned slowly to face him. As she did, she deliberately let one shoulder of her cream-colored silk robe slip. "I thought we made a pact not to bring up that night, not ever again. New leaves and new beginnings, remember, darling?" She softened the scold with her best Audrey smile.

His gaze veered to the dipping silk just as she'd intended. "Yeah, sure, still . . . . You never did say what you told him."

She sipped on her bottom lip, not a lot, just enough to get him good and horny. "I told him the truth—that I fell down the service stairs."

See, this is what happens to trash. To trash, trash, trash . . .

Staring at her mouth, he hesitated, and then asked, "What else did you say?"

You fucking piece of garbage, this is where you belong.

Despite her freezing heart, she forced her gaze to stay warm. "Nothing, I swear it."

It was, strictly speaking, the truth. She'd plunged down the service stairs, a full flight to a cement landing, the dark plastic Glad garbage bags breaking her fall. What she hadn't added, what she'd give almost anything to be able to blot from her brain, was that she hadn't tripped and lost her footing. She hadn't simply stumbled and spiraled downward on her own steam. She hadn't merely met with a mishap as a normal person with a normal life might.

She'd been dragged into the stairwell by the hair and thrown. By Drew.

Seemingly satisfied, he beckoned her over, scotch from his glass slopping onto the clean sheets. "So long as you stuck to the story, we're good. Are we good?"

Honey released the breath she hadn't realized she'd been holding. Every iota of self-preservation she still possessed urged her to flee—the bedroom, the apartment, the life—but to where? Until she figured that out, hadn't she better stay put?

Resigned, she forced herself to take a step and then another and another, closing the precious gap between her and the bed. Reaching it, she untied her robe, letting the front fall open.

Swallowing a sob, she nodded. "Yes, Drew, we're good."

Chapter Three

"Everything I learned I learned from the movies."—Audrey Hepburn

Marc pulled back on the red door of Tea & Sympathy and stepped inside, the sudden rush of heat making his nose run. The West Village British-themed tea shop and restaurant was crowded despite its being past lunchtime, the floral-print-covered tables packed sardine-style even by Manhattan standards, the patrons uniformly female, which made a certain sort of sense, he supposed.

She wasn't here yet, not that he expected her to be. From his years of sporadic dating, Marc had observed that Manhattan women were not known for their punctuality, and he had no reason to believe Honey Gladwell would prove any kind of exception. Fifteen minutes late was as good as on time. On time was, well, early.

He used the spell to settle in, take stock of his surroundings. Shelves lined with bric-a-brac, framed restaurant reviews, and tea paraphernalia covered the walls. A chalk board announcing the day's specials—spotted dick, seriously?—took up valuable real estate near the open kitchen. There was absolutely no standing space for waiting. Because of the tight quarters, the venue had a strict policy of not seating anyone until the full party arrived. Fortunately two o'clock was past primetime so far as lunch went and the taken tables were already showing signs of clearing out. The occupants of one of the two-tops were making a move toward the bill, their lacquered fingernails inching ever closer, their cell phones at the ready to calculate the tip. The women rose to leave and in short order the table was bused and reset. Marc had always held to the old saw that it was infinitely easier to ask for forgiveness than permission. Testing it now, he slid into one of the still warm seats, nearly knocking out a neighboring table's tiered tray of finger sand-wiches and miniature scones.

"Ladies, so sorry," he said, feeling hulking and clumsy and alto-gether out of place.

The door opened, admitting a gusty chill that stirred the table lin-ens and won patrons' scowls despite everyone else, including Marc, having recently done the same. Glad he hadn't yet managed to remove his overcoat, he looked up.

Enormous sunglasses, a white scarf wrapped movie-star style about upswept hair, perfectly painted lips—it was her, Honey Gladwell, no later than a fashionable five minutes. Mesmerized, Marc watched her breeze in, her camel-colored overcoat classically cut, the wool so soft-looking it must be cashmere. Standing inside the closed door, she untied the belt and slipped it off and—wow!

A little black dress, classically simple and flawlessly elegant, skimmed her litheness in all the right places, nipping in at a tiny waist that Marc could likely span with his two hands—and God how he really wanted to test out the theory! Elbow-high black gloves banded slender arms. Black stockings, the kind with a seam in the back that required actual—gulp—garters, sheathed her long, slender legs. He hadn't seen anyone so tricked out in the middle of the afternoon since the days when he'd gone to Sunday service with his mother and auntie.

"Wow." It had been a long time since a woman had made him feel more than a tepid interest, let alone wowed him, but the wow factor on this one more than made up.

Remembering his manners, he slid back his chair and rose, too caught up to care that he clipped the side of the adjacent table yet again, this time sending dainty china cups teetering in their rose patterned saucers.

As if mesmerizing men must be her métier, Honey laughed, a musical trilling that brought to mind champagne glasses tinkling in toast. "Is that a good wow or a bad wow?" she asked, effortlessly slipping into the empty seat opposite him.

Marc sat as well. "It's just that you're . . . You're so dressed up."

Clothes made the man, or so his mother never tired of telling him. He'd stalwartly rejected that sentiment on both principle and practicality—until now. Staring across at his chic companion, it struck him he'd better get busy. No brown socks with black shoes around this lady, ditto for sneakers sans socks—or sneakers period. For now, the smartest thing he could do was keep his coat on. Beneath it he had on a faded sweatshirt with the logo from his undergraduate alma mater, well-worn jeans, and Nikes. His right Nike, he just now remembered, had a hole topping the big toe. It was a lucky break he'd gotten himself seated first. This way she'd likely never see it.

She answered with an airy wave. "I believe in overdressing. I believe in primping at leisure and wearing lipstick." Another Audrey quote? It kind of had to be. Real people didn't speak this way, at least not any he'd ever met before now.

He opened his menu and made a pretense of perusing it. Bangers 'n' mash, shepherd's pie, Welsh rarebit, roast beef with Yorkshire pudding—Jesus, who ate this stuff?

He ventured a glance up. "So I can't help but notice you seem to be really into Audrey Hepburn."

Over the top of her open menu, her dark eyes met his. "Audrey Hepburn was—is—a sublime human being. I don't only respect her. I *adore* her."

O-okay then. Everyone had their quirks, he supposed, and her "girl crush" on a woman who, had she lived, could be her grandmother's age caught his curiosity. "Why are you so hung up on her specifically? I mean sure, she was pretty and glamorous I guess, but so were a lot of other female actors of her era—Marilyn Monroe, Elizabeth Taylor—"

"Monroe and Taylor aren't even in the same league!" Judging from the black look she gave him, you would have thought he'd just suggested slaughtering kittens or detonating a nuclear bomb. "Audrey was talented, deeply and importantly talented. And it's not only her acting and fashion sense that set her apart. It's her *soul*."

"You sound like she's a personal friend. You must have been a little kid when she died." He couldn't recall her exact birth year from her chart but a cursory eyeballing put her around twenty-six, no more than twenty-seven. Her sudden expression of raw yearning made her seem even younger.

She gestured with her gloved arms in evident exasperation. "I was but . . . Oh, never mind. It's obvious you aren't inclined to understand."

Attracted to her though he might be—okay, was—Marc didn't take kindly to condescension. Sure, he'd grown up pretty poor and was laid back about what he put on his back, but those things didn't make him a Neanderthal. "Why not try me? I might surprise you."

She paused, scanning his face as though attempting to take his measure. "Oh, very well," she said, around a puff of breath, apparently irritated at being called upon to explain herself. "I feel as though I know her. Watching her films as a kid got me . . . got me through a lot. I wanted to grow up to be just like her—beautiful and brave, witty and accomplished."

From where Marc sat, she had three of the four checked off, not a bad score in his book, although breaches in the bravery department likely had cost her a lot, February's ER visit included. How did a girl who put such stock in bravery justify staying tethered to a brute?

"Did you know that during the Second World War, Audrey served as a courier for the Dutch resistance?" she rhapsodized. "And that she suffered malnutrition that left her with lasting health problems?"

He hadn't known, but then tracking the travails of dead white film starlets wasn't something he'd ever gotten into.

"And then there's all the amazing work she did later in life with UNICEF. She went on a humanitarian mission to Somalia just four months before she . . . passed." She looked away but not before he glimpsed the sheen in her eyes.

Tears, seriously! It was one thing to be sentimental, but the way she spoke about Audrey Hepburn made the actress sound like a glammed up Mother Teresa. All in all, her devotion struck him as a little . . . extreme.

"Ready to order?" an Anglo-Irish accented voice broke in.

The server's interception prompted Honey's look of relief. Jesus, he hadn't meant to grill her. Why had he? Why couldn't he ever just . . . go with the flow? Let a conversation unfold without turning it into a structured Q&A or, worse yet, nitpicking it apart? On or off duty, he always seemed to be searching for clarity—answers.

"I am." Dabbing a gloved finger discretely to the corners of her eyes, Honey closed her menu and looked up. "I'd like a pot of Darjeeling and—" She hesitated, glancing over to Marc. "Am I correct in assuming this is your treat?"

"Of course, I invited you," he answered, hating that she'd thought for a minute he might mean to make her pay for her portion.

Her question rattled him and not only because it showed she wasn't one hundred percent certain he was a gentleman but because of the disparity it pointed out. Since when did someone who carried a designer handbag have to worry about splitting the lunch check?

"In that case—" Relaxing visibly, she shifted back to the server, to whom she sent a dazzling, dimpled smile. "I'd also like the BLT with

English bacon and a side of . . . " She paused, dipping her head to peruse the menu. "Mashed potatoes—with gravy, please. Oh, and the peas—are they the mushy kind like they eat in the UK?"

The server lost her harried look and smiled. "That they are."

Honey beamed back at her. "Marvelous, then I'll have those as well."

Stunned to speechlessness, Marc could only stare. Where in that size zero body did she plan to fit all that food? Afterward would she excuse herself to the bathroom and puke it all up as one of his dates from Match.com had done? God, he hoped not. As a doctor, he knew that bulimia was a disorder. As a guy who'd grown up seeing his mother scrimping to stretch the grocery money to feed the five of them, he was short on sympathy.

The server's gaze flickered to Marc. "And what will you be having, sir?"

Go with the flow, Marc. For once, go with the fucking flow.

He didn't have a clue what "mushy peas" were—if they were anything like the parboiled "soul food" his older relatives had tried turning him onto, he was pretty sure he'd hate them. Sushi, Thai, and northern Italian were his dietary staples. But then he hadn't come for the food. He'd come for Honey Gladwell. The prospect of getting to know her better, maybe even winning her trust sufficiently so that she'd let him help her before she got the crap beat out of her again—or worse— eclipsed his culinary preferences.

Finding his smile, he closed his menu and handed it off. "I'll have what she's having."

✳✳✳ ✳✳✳

Marc had to give Honey credit. Girlfriend could put some food away. Not only did she clean her plate, not only did she not rush to the restroom afterward, but she did yet another thing that played against type and surprised him—pleasantly. She ordered dessert.

"I'd adore the crumble—provided Himself can be persuaded to share it with me," she said to their server, her adlibbed Irish accent winning her yet another smile.

She was a natural mimic. In the course of their lunch, her vaguely British accent had morphed into one that was nearly as Irish as their server's.

The girl divided her gaze between them. "You seem like such a nice couple," she remarked and rather than correct her, Marc took a sip of tepid tea. "If you don't mind my asking, how long have you been together?"

Marc nearly spat the mouthful of tea. Throat burning, he finished swallowing, then said, "We're not—"

"Officially engaged yet," Honey slipped in smoothly, sending him an overtly adoring look. "Marc is the traditional sort. My mum's been ill, and he insists we wait 'til he can ask her permission proper-like."

"Ah, but that's lovely," the girl chirped, looking Marc over with approval. "But don't mind me, standing about jabbering away. I'll be back with your crumble in a jiff." She turned to go.

Feeling as if most of the oxygen had been siphoned from his lungs, Marc waited for the girl to step away before leaning over and asking, "What was that about?"

Honey shrugged. "Just having a bit of fun is all—good *craic*, as they call it. You must admit it makes for a good—grand—story. That girl will likely go about wearing a smile for the next half hour."

Marc stared at her, equal parts charmed and disturbed. He was no psychiatrist, but he couldn't dismiss his sense that something was . . . off. He'd asked Honey here with a mission in mind: to discover who she was—*really* was—so that he could help her. From what he'd so far seen, she was whatever and whoever the people around her wanted her to be.

"But what you told her, it's a lie."

Her gaze shuttered. She shook her head. "No, it's not. It's more like . . . a fairy tale."

Marc opened his mouth to debate that but before he could, their dessert arrived.

"One crumble, two spoons," their server announced, setting the food between them and the check by Marc.

"Oh, lovely!" Honey enthused, picking up one of the spoons and tucking in.

Considering the Manhattan culture of calorie-counting women, the unbridled, guilt-free pleasure she took in eating, seeming to savor every mouthful, not only with her sense of taste but also with her eyes, was more than unusual. It was damned refreshing.

She ate her half and most of his, as well as lapping up every lick of the clotted cream. When no excuse came to visit the restroom—she rolled on her red lipstick at the table in front of him—he decided she either must work out like an Olympian or be blessed with a teenage boy's fast metabolism.

She dropped the lipstick and tortoise shell compact back into her bag and clamped it closed. "Thank you ever so much. Lunch was lovely, but I should be going."

"Home, you mean?" Marc asked, feeling as though they'd just sat down though according to the clock, lunch had lasted longer than an hour.

She hesitated, eyeing him. "I'm not sure my next engagement is any of your concern, but yes."

"When can I see you again?"

She glanced away. "I'm not sure that's a good idea."

"Does this mean the engagement's off?" he joked, taking the opportunity to study her profile, only her small smile was about as telling as the Mona Lisa's.

She turned back. "I'm afraid I'm serious."

Shit, she was serious. Sobered, he asked, "Why is that?" Was he so wishful and rusty that he'd misread her playful flirting as "signals"?

She toyed with the teaspoon. Eyes lowered, she answered, "You know the answer as well as I. I'm . . . with someone."

Right, the prince who hit her—God forbid she should break whatever commitment she'd made to that sick son of a bitch. Rather than say so and risk driving her away, he set aside his sarcasm and said, "And yet you're here with me now."

He'd only pointed out the obvious, but the dagger look she shot him demonstrated she didn't at all appreciate being brought to the mat on a topic that likely wasn't only sensitive but painful. "I *was* here with you. Now I'm leaving." She pushed away from the table and started up, the back of her chair ramming the empty table behind her.

"Wait." Half-rising, he shot out an arm, catching her gloved wrist.

She stared down at his hand covering hers and then back over at him. Her darkening eyes dared him to hold on, to prove himself as bad a brute as the man he meant to try talking her into leaving.

"Sorry," he said, withdrawing immediately and slipping his offending hand out of sight beneath the table. Resuming his seat, he added, "It's just that having a whole day off is kind of a big deal to me. I hate for the afternoon to end." Heart hammering, he waited.

She sat back down. Dark doe-like eyes met his. A smile trembled over her freshly painted lips. Out of the blue, Marc found himself fighting the urge to lean across the table, this time to cover that crazy sexy upside-down mouth with his.

Lightly penciled brows lifted. "What do you usually do when you have a whole day off?"

Was she only casually curious or was the question as leading, as flirtatious, as it sounded? There was only one way to find out. Trouble was, he had no idea where or what to suggest. He was really that rusty.

Whatever "game" he'd once laid claim to had gone by the wayside, a casualty of medical school and then internship and now residency. Other than out for a meal, which they'd already had, where did you take a woman on a daytime "date"? A walk was casual and noncommittal, plus it would give him more time to get to know her. They could continue their quirky and fascinating if not exactly illuminating lunchtime conversation. Washington Square, Union Square, Sheridan Square and several other public parks were all nearby. Only it was fucking freezing outside and he'd bet her fancy cashmere coat didn't come with much of a liner. He paused, willing his brain to work. Going with the flow was all well and good, but it couldn't begin to trump old fashioned skullduggery. Honey Gladwell had managed to be a delightful lunch companion without revealing so much as an iota more about herself beyond her Hepburn obsession. He was no closer to breaching that barricade than he'd been weeks ago.

Maybe casting their meet-up as something more, as a date, was putting too much pressure on him? If, say, they were just hanging out, what would he suggest? Better yet, where would he want to go? As a kid he'd spent every spare coin and moment he could scrape up on one pastime: the movies.

"The IFC Theater isn't far from here," he heard someone, himself, say. "You seem like someone who might be into foreign films." Marc wasn't into foreign films, not in the least, but he suddenly felt supremely grateful to Gina, the thirty-something trauma nurse with the nasally voice who was always going on about some highbrow flick she'd seen there.

She nibbled her lower lip, which did all kinds of crazy things to Marc's mind—and his muscle. "I adore foreign films, only . . . "

Her voice trailed off, and he wondered if maybe, unlike him, she didn't have the whole day off. If maybe she had a schedule to keep— and a sadistic tyrant to please. The last thing he wanted was for her to get hurt again. He was supposed to be figuring out a way to help her, not endanger her.

"Look, if you really need to . . . get back, I'll understand."

She bit her bottom lip. "N-no, at least I don't suppose I do. And there is a film I've been dying to see."

Marc felt his mood lighten. "Great, then come to the movies with me. I'll buy you all the bad-for-you movie popcorn you can put away."

***

The popcorn sold at the IFC concession counter wasn't bad for you. In fact, it was organic. That Marc hadn't known that was probably a pretty good giveaway that the foreign film theater wasn't his regular hangout—oh well.

Likewise, *Blue is the Warmest Color*, or *La Vie d'Adèle*, wasn't the kind of film he would ordinarily have picked. Actually he hadn't picked it. Honey had. Whether spooning up mushy peas for him to try at lunch or suggesting they see a lesbian coming-of-age love story, she seemed to enjoy coaxing him out of his comfort zone. Who knew, maybe she saw it as expanding his horizons. Ironic that someone he'd initially intended to make his mission had somehow managed to turn the tables on him. But they could figure out the dynamics of their emerging "relationship" later, assuming it did indeed . . . emerge. Right now he felt happy just to be spending more time with her.

On the middle of a weekday, the theater was deserted except for two teenage girls in the front row. Like the film, Marc let Honey choose their seats. They settled into the center section toward the back. They'd missed the previews, not that he deemed that much of a loss. Ordinarily watching the movie trailers was a big part of how Marc unwound, but seeing as how all the films shown here were foreign, he was happy enough to save his subtitle reading for the main event.

"So what exactly is this film about?" he whispered into Honey's ear as the opening credits rolled.

She turned to face him. "Love."

A chick flick—Marc bit back a groan. "Great, I mean it's what makes the world go around, right?"

"I used to think so." She reached over, snagged a piece of popcorn, and popped it into her mouth.

Training his tone to sound casual, he asked, "But not now?"

He could see how being battered would sour someone, anyone, on love and romance. What he couldn't begin to comprehend was why she didn't just take herself out of there. She must have some means at her disposal. Everything on her back was either vintage or designer or both. Unless maybe the deal was the dude gave her a credit card to use and had the monthly statement sent to him. If that were the case, Winterthur would be able to track not only her spending habits but also, retrospectively, her whereabouts.

Mulling over the possibilities, he focused on the film—or tried to. After the characters' initial meeting and the ubiquitous "relationship building" scenes, things heated up quickly. The two women locked lips. The soft gazes and coquettish looks they'd been trading up to this point had left no doubt where things were headed and yet when they finally kissed it seemed to come out of the proverbial blue, striking almost as a complete, joyous surprise.

Beside him, Honey sighed. Her snacking stopped and her breathing picked up audible pace. Her tightly laced legs relaxed. She'd taken off her gloves to eat the popcorn and now she traced a single finger across her collarbone, slowly back and forth, again and again. No doubt about it, she was turned on. So was he. He wouldn't have thought two French lesbians going at it on-screen, the one seriously butch with blue-tinted hair, would have gotten him going but it did.

That was bullshit. The screen actresses weren't responsible for the boner concealed beneath the coat across his lap. Honey was. In his mind's eye, she was the one naked and being backed onto the bed, he equally naked and coming down on top of her.

Easing back into the seat beside him, her light perfume mingling with the buttery aroma of the theater popcorn, she was completely irresistible, utterly edible. Add to that, it was dark, movie-theater dark, and every dirty fantasy he'd had since the age of thirteen about pulling down a girl's jeans' zipper pretty much sparked to full-throttle life.

Only Honey wasn't wearing gender-neutral jeans. She had on a dress—a sexy, sophisticated dress. And black stockings. Not pantyhose, but actual stockings, the kind that required garters. Whatever else she had or didn't have going on under there, Marc could only imagine— and badly wanted to find out. Mentally slipping down her body-cinching black dress, unsnapping those gartered hose, and peeling off those silky stockings, he sent a sideways look her way—and saw that she wasn't watching the movie either. She was watching *him*.

Through the darkness, her eyes anchored to his. She moistened her lips, that crazy upside-down mouth that always brought his mind back to kissing—and fucking. Imagining those sweet lips cinching about his cock, he felt himself further thickening.

There was no getting around it. Marc absolutely had to kiss her. He reached for her, slipping one arm beneath her back. With his free hand, he touched her cheek. If foreign films had this kind of effect on him, he'd be better off going cold turkey—*after* today. For once, *this* once, he was completely caught up in the moment.

She could have moved away but instead she came closer. Leaning over, he angled his face to hers. Their mouths met, matching as if drawn by magnets. He slid his tongue along the seam of her lips, back and forth, teasing her there until she opened. Once she did, he touched his tongue to the tip of hers, and then swirled it about. She tasted of cinnamon from the crumble and butter from the popcorn and, like some crazy Ben & Jerry's flavor, the combination worked. And so, it seemed, did they. There was no first kiss fumbling or awkwardness, no inadvertent clinking of teeth or salivating of spit. They kissed as though they'd been doing it their whole lives, as though kissing each other was what they'd been born to do, what they'd been made for. Kissing Honey wasn't any kind of prelude to better things but its own thrilling journey, one he was satisfied to savor, not rush.

He settled a hand on her knee, leaving it there to give her ample opportunity to push it away. She didn't. Instead those gorgeous long legs of hers did something much better. They opened. Not wide, not spread eagle—she was too ladylike and subtle for that. More like a gentle easing apart as though gifting him with access to her private place was the most natural of acts.

Her slim-fitting skirt didn't give him much room to maneuver. Rather than raise it, he slid his hand underneath, gliding along silky stocking-sheathed thighs to where those stockings ended—and her satiny flesh began. She was wearing panties, which for some reason surprised him, and garters, which didn't. Mired in murky darkness, still the contrast between the black banding her milky thighs was unbelievably erotic. Fuck blue hair and baggy boy clothes, neither chick on-screen had a snowball's chance in hell of holding his attention, though their moans were definitely fueling his desire. Whatever moves he'd amassed in the last two decades of adulthood, whatever expertise he might boast, now existed solely in the service of bringing Honey pleasure. He honestly couldn't remember the last time he'd wanted to satisfy a woman this much, to make her moan and pant, cream and come. Maybe never.

A slit bisected her panties' crotch; for a second or so he indulged in the fantasy that she'd slipped on the sinfully sexy undergarment with him in mind. Not that it much mattered. He had her full attention now. The silky fabric wasn't only damp—it was soaked through. His stroking exploration revealed she was waxed, not shaven, scoured bare and silken smooth. Musk drifted up, teasing his nostrils, whetting his palm and his appetite. He worked a finger inside her, damning the darkness that kept him from seeing every desire-drenched fold.

Honey moaned and fitted herself against his hand, her mouth ever so slightly parted, her slim hips lifting. If someone, an usher or the theater manager, were to discover them, he most definitely had something—a lot—to lose. But it was midday in the middle of the week. Anyone who came out to the movies to watch lesbians fuck, even in the name of art, was likely inclined to make allowances. To be safe, he checked in on the teenage girls in the front row, but by now they were too busy swallowing each other's tongue to complain about what he or anyone else might be doing.

Relaxing, he turned back, covered them with his coat, and slid a second finger inside her. Warm and wet, her body seemed almost to inhale him. He followed with a third digit, and Honey began to move, grinding against his cream-coated fingers as though they were a cock she couldn't get enough of. Seeing how into it she was almost sent him over the edge—almost. Pulling out, he found her clit and swept his thumb over it in deliberately slow circles. As if she was an instrument he strummed, her whole body seemed to vibrate. She came, shuddering, her release flooding his fingers, her sharp cry joining that of the women on screen.

She lifted her face from where she'd buried it in his neck and smiled over at him. "That was lovely, thank you," she said, as though not speaking of sex at all, as though expressing gratitude for some innocuous gift or treat. A pair of gloves, a sweater—a lunch.

Beneath the cover of his overcoat, she drew down his zipper. Marc sucked down a deep breath as her hand slipped inside his open fly and freed him from his briefs. Deft fingers took possession, a sweet vise he had no desire to escape. Her slender hand encircled him, glided back and forth along the length of his shaft. Teasing her thumb over the slit bisecting the sensitized head, she tested his wetness and his willpower.

A bead of semen leaking from his slit filled him with sudden alarm at the realization that he was precariously close to coming. And that he was sitting with his dick hanging out of his pants in a movie theater. With a woman who was a former patient. No matter how you looked at it, the view was all kinds of bad. He was a physician, for chrissake, not some horny teenager.

Snapped back to reality, he moved her hand away and zipped himself up, albeit with some difficulty. Covering himself with the coat once more, he shifted over, putting as much space as he could between them. "I'm so sorry. I . . . we . . . This is so . . . wrong."

"Wrong?" she echoed as if the thought hadn't occurred to her, as if giving hand jobs in public places was a routine part of everyone's day.

And yet she didn't strike him as slutty, more like a child of nature— a wild child but a child just the same. It didn't help that part of her hair had come down, the stray strands spilling free from their pins, loose waves framing a face that suddenly seemed achingly young, heartrendingly lost.

Averting his gaze from her wounded one, he reached into his pocket and handed her a paper napkin. "Yes, wrong—on my part, not yours."

Averting his gaze while she made herself as presentable as possible, Marc raked a hand through his hair. Now that his erection was easing, he was thunderstruck by the enormity of what they—he—had just done. He'd set out to help her, not screw her. For someone who prided himself on being a straight arrow, who'd colored inside the proverbial lines even as a kid, who almost never went with the flow or lived in the moment, he'd bulldozed through a hell of a lot of boundaries today. He only hoped that Honey, once she gave some greater thought to what had just happened, could find it in her heart to forgive him and trust him to help her.

God knew it would be a good long while before he forgave, or trusted, himself.

✳✳✳ ✳✳✳

Standing alone in her bathroom several hours later, combing out her hair at the mirrored vanity, Honey admitted she felt different, or at least more like herself than she had in some time—years. Climbing out of the cab in front of her building, the cab for which Marc had insisted on paying, she'd caught herself humming—actually *humming*.

Her first year in the city she'd hummed a lot, danced in her underwear, and sang in the shower. Sure, there'd been scary stuff to sort out, the basics of food and shelter, but once she'd nailed those down, everything else took on the sheen of an adventure.

That she was harkening to her escort service employment as "the good old days" was nothing if not a statement. At least she'd had some degree of self-determination, if not exactly power.

Most of her "dates" had taken place in the evenings, leaving her mornings and afternoons free, solid blocks of time to do whatever she wished. As soon as she could, she'd cut out of her crazily crowded apartment and hit the streets. Between the Angelika in Soho, the Paris Theater in midtown, and the IFC in the West Village, she'd seen nearly every foreign and indie film in its first week of release. That aspect of her former lifestyle had been rather glorious.

She and Drew had a few movie outings during their first few years but their tastes were so divergent she soon gave up. Finding a film that satisfied his desire for ample sex and gratuitous violence that she could also watch without having flashbacks or flinching had proven somewhere between difficult and impossible. Added to that, he absolutely refused to see anything with subtitles. It was so much simpler to do something else or stay home.

Her earlier impromptu movie "date" with Marc was nothing if not memorable. Despite all the fantasy scenarios she'd enacted for clients, making out in a movie theater was a personal first. Of course she'd have to re-watch the film at some point, not that she was complaining. They'd parted ways more than two hours ago, and her body still hadn't stopped tingling.

That meant masturbation. She had a goody drawer chock-full of toys and various vibrators, but while she'd always appreciated novelty, no battery-operated device had ever been able to trump the temporary bliss brought on by her own deft touch. No matter how difficult or outright awful her life ever got, she was fortunate in always being able to bring about release by her own hand. Self-pleasuring was a salvation of sorts; her body a temple where she took care to worship on a regular basis. Alone, she could indulge the fantasy that she belonged to no one but herself.

But of course that wasn't so. She belonged to Drew—for now. As content as she'd be to curl up in bed cocooned in her and Marc's comingled pheromones, she couldn't take that risk. She was going to have to bathe. Not because she felt dirty—she didn't—but because she never knew when Drew might decide to drop by. If he caught so much as a whiff of another man on her or her sheets, he'd either kill her or make her wish he had.

Not that the issue had ever come up before now. Once she'd left the escort industry to be with him, she'd been entirely faithful. Sex with his wife aside, she doubted he could say the same. Still, she wondered that she didn't feel even the tiniest twinge of guilt about what had happened earlier. She really must not love Drew anymore. Was that progress, one small step toward a brighter, freer future, or had she finally become that numb?

Either way, her exit strategy, studying for and taking her GED exam, was still some months away. Without that all important certificate, she was more or less unemployable for much beyond flipping burgers. In the interim, she'd have to suck it up, bide her time, and play Drew's game.

Resigned, she set the brush aside, slipped off her robe, and stepped inside the shower. In the spirit of multitasking, she might as well get clean and get off at the same time. To help move things along, she envisioned Marc joining her beneath the jets. How might he look with warm water sluicing over him? Amazing, she felt sure of it, even if so far his lean, powerfully built body had been only hinted at, mostly hidden by his horrible clothes.

She turned the warm water up a notch and shifted away, wetting her hair and back in the steaming stream. Lathering herself with shower gel, she let the fantasy unfold. In it, she stood spooned against him, his erection pressing into her backside, his big hands bracing about her. Hmmm, lovely. Closing her eyes, she cupped her breasts, gently rolling her nipples between her thumb and forefinger as Marc might. The thought of being with him again, *really* with him, only this time fully naked and at their leisure to make love any way and anywhere they wanted, resurrected the throbbing between her thighs. She trailed a light hand lower, sliding it along the curve of her soap-slick stomach, tracing the periphery of the bared triangle with the pads of her fingers. A gentle raking of fingernails over her unbuffered flesh drew goose bumps. She hadn't had a bush in years. Paying clients, most of them married, preferred baby smooth genitals. Honey had long hypothesized that they must see so much untrimmed "topiary" and unshaven legs at home that they were desperate for a contrast. And then there was the disturbingly popular fantasy of fucking a prepubescent girl that got so many of them off, even the fathers. For whatever reason, the girls sans bushes always got more bookings and bigger tips than those who went au naturel. The decision to go with a full waxing wasn't about personal aesthetics. It was a simple matter of economics. One day when Honey "retired"—if indeed she could find a way to support herself that didn't involve slinging hash or fries—she meant to let it grow back in, not unlike men who experimented with beards or left off shaving on vacations and weekends.

Trailing a finger along her crevice, she wondered which Marc preferred. Full bush—she'd swear on it, though she couldn't quite say why she was so certain. He just seemed like the sort of man who would want his intimacy served up no muss, no fuss in accordance with the KISS rule of keeping things simple.

Earlier they'd broken not only KISS but a whole host of other rules, too. She only hoped neither of them lived to regret it—or were stupid enough to try and repeat it. Their sexy movie date was best kept as a cherished memory, fodder for innumerable fantasies she might roll out as needed—as in now.

She traced the cleft partitioning her pussy with a single soapy finger, imagining Marc watching her. Reliving how he'd touched her there, his finger-fucking firm yet gentle, making her hotter and wetter than she'd been in . . . a very long while, suddenly she couldn't put off her needs any longer. She faced back to the showerhead, reached for the hand held shower massager—and turned it up to the turbo setting. Widening her stance slightly, she brought the pulsing jets down to her—

"Honey, baby, where are you?"

Honey froze. The voice, Drew's, had the effect of dousing her with ice water. Quickly she replaced the showerhead, rinsed, and shut off the water. With no time to make herself presentable—unlike a lot of men, he preferred her to apply plenty of makeup—she grabbed a towel from the rack, wrapped herself in it, and stepped out.

Standing in the bedroom doorway, he dropped his briefcase when he saw her.

Wincing at the thud, she tightened the towel around her. "Drew, I—"

"Wow, you look . . . amazing."

Her second "wow" of the day, not a bad record. Seeing the approval in his eyes, hearing it in his voice, she relaxed marginally. "T-thanks."

He was on her in an instant, tugging off the towel, pulling at her breasts, smothering them and her with soul-sucking, scotch-drenched kisses. The room was on the narrow side, the bed but a few feet away. Maneuvering them over to it, he turned her around and bent her over the edge.

Honey had come to hate being taken from behind, mostly due to the stinging spankings that often accompanied the position, but after making out at the movies with Marc that afternoon, not having to look Drew in the eye seemed a blessing suddenly. Not because she felt badly about the day's events but because facing him would destroy the fantasy that her eager lover might be Marc.

Drew reached around to her front. A dry finger thrust into her pussy, but fortunately she was still moist. Still, despite the shower she'd just taken, and the sexy self-stimulation she'd begun while in it, she tightened as soon as he touched her.

Behind her, he barked, "Relax."

"I am. It feels . . . good," she lied, relieved that for now at least he wasn't deliberately hurting her.

She closed her eyes and turned her thoughts inward, back to the movies and Marc. The washboard flat belly she'd felt beneath his T-shirt. The shape and breadth of his no-doubt beautiful cock that, incredibly, she'd wanted to lick and swallow and suck. The deft way he'd known exactly where and how to touch her. It had taken him all of two minutes to bring her to climax. Again she asked herself what it might be like to repeat the experience with him, only in private, somewhere secluded where they could take their time in learning each other's boundaries and bodies.

Absorbed by the fantasy in the making, she suddenly realized that Drew's dry finger was dry no more but coated in her cream. Though he hadn't an iota of Marc's finesse or patience, amazingly whatever he was doing began to feel . . . not so bad. In casting caution and conscience to the wind, had she stumbled upon a way to make the following months, if not pleasurable, certainly more endurable?

He pulled out. Though he wasn't particularly well-endowed, she knew the exact moment when his penis replaced his fingers. For once he slid inside her without her needing to lube herself first. Again, the sensation of him battering her backside wasn't exactly exquisite but it was bearable. She closed her eyes, hands bunching in the thick comforter. She must really be a cheap whore to get through sex with a man she feared and loathed by thinking of another whom she liked, but there was no arguing with success. So far it seemed to be working. To help herself along, she slipped a hand around to her front, reached down, and touched herself as she hadn't had time to do in the shower. Her clit was sensitized from the earlier make-out session with Marc, slightly, deliciously tender. Circling it with her thumb brought her back to her happy place; steadier strumming carried her to the cusp. Holding the image of thickly lashed hazel eyes, a square jaw softened with a day's beard growth, and moist, sensuous mouth in her head, she let herself slip over the side. Honey came, not the swift, sweet release she'd experienced earlier but release, orgasm, all the same.

Behind her, Drew pulled out and drove back into her. Despite her being damp, the piercing thrust was painful. He let out a groan, withdrew—and blew his load on her back.

For the next few minutes his heavy breaths and dripping from the bathroom shower were the only sounds in the room. Honey counted to ten, then twenty in her head, willing him to get up and off her.

She was almost to twenty when finally he did. "That was incredible, just like old times," he said, giving her butt a soft slap. He straightened and moved away from the bed. The sound of a zipper sliding up confirmed that, for the time being, he was done with her.

Careful not to get cum on the comforter, Honey pushed herself up on her elbows. At the very least he could have offered her a tissue, used the towel he'd torn off to wipe her, or stepped into the bathroom to wet a wash cloth, but it seemed that even those small civilities were too much trouble. Perhaps it was only Marc's lovely manners that made Drew's selfishness seem all the more egregious, but regardless, the contrast struck her. And while wrapping herself in bedding marked by a certain sexy doctor's spunk was an undeniably dirty-sexy thought, the prospect of lying in Drew's drippings disgusted her.

"You know," she said, reaching for a pillow and tucking it beneath her breasts, "you don't have to do that. I'm on the pill."

Coming back to the bed, he leaned over and bit her shoulder. "Sorry, babe, but you can't be too careful." He smoothed his hands over her buttocks, spreading them slightly, and despite knowing that he wouldn't be ready again for at least another hour, Honey tensed. "Now if you'll stop being such a prude and let me fuck this tight little butthole of yours, I promise I won't go anywhere. I'll come right inside you."

"Drew, please—"

He leaned in and gave her crack a lingering lick, fluttering his tongue over the puckered flesh. "Hmm, sweet as . . . honey," he said, framing her with his mouth, his words buzzing against her butt, and suddenly she was reminded that he hadn't always been such a selfish lover. He pushed up from the bed and straightened. "Chillax, you're off the hook for tonight. Kathy's mother's in town and we have an eight o'clock dinner rez."

Honey sagged into the mattress, glad she faced away so he couldn't read her relief. "Okay, well, I don't want to make you late."

"I'm going to grab a shower first. The old bitch has a nose like a bloodhound. Join me?"

She shook her head. "No thanks. I'll . . . rinse off later."

He shrugged. "Suit yourself."

Reaching for her childhood stuffed animal cat, Mr. Pinky, set atop her night table, Honey buried her face into the worn terry cloth, wondering how she'd ever got so lost. She'd left Omaha for New York with Mr. Pinky, a suitcase crammed with cheap designer knockoffs—and a whole lot of big-city dreams. Most of those dreams, she now acknowledged, had revolved around meeting a man—the man—who would take care of her.

Eight years later, her version of Happily Ever After looked a lot different. It wasn't about finding love, marrying, and having children, though she hoped to someday have all of those things.

It was all about freedom.

Chapter Four

"If I'm honest I have to tell you I still read fairy tales and I like them best of all."—Audrey Hepburn

April, Union Square Park

Weeks slipped into months. Banked snow, blackened by vehicle exhaust and plowed by pedestrian feet, slowly melted away. The thermometer inched upward. Trees and bushes budded. Public green space became green again. Before Marc knew it, they were into April. Making out at the IFC seemed more like something he'd fantasized about, not actually done. And yet, paradoxically, Honey had become a very real presence in his life.

Amazingly they'd found a way to be friends. By mutual agreement, the movie make-out episode was never brought up—or repeated. If Marc had his way, and he meant to, it never would be. As much as he'd loved kissing and stroking her, and having her do those things to him in return, the shitty feelings that followed had taken too great a toll. He might have stopped before going all the way, but that didn't excuse going as far as he had. He wasn't her doctor anymore, but he'd started out that way. Initially he'd sought her out solely to try and help her out of her situation. That was still his hope. Good intentions were great, but on the downside, hell was paved with them. Action was needed to back them up. Being "just friends" wasn't always easy on him—it was hardly ever that—but given that was the only way he could stay sane and still see her, the struggle was worth it.

They settled into a pattern, meeting weekly, more often when his ever-shifting work schedule allowed it. Either way, he made it a point to touch base once a day, preferably by phone but at least by text, not only to say hi but most importantly to make sure that she was all right, that Drew hadn't hurt her again. So far as Marc knew, he hadn't. According to Honey, who was still infuriatingly tight-lipped on the subject, Drew was slammed at work, including managing a new private investment pool he'd set up for middle-income people to have access to making money in the market. Marc was happy to hear it. Hell, he'd welcome another crash if it meant keeping Winterthur occupied and away from her. Every time he watched her walk off, he wondered if their next meet-up would be in the ER or worse, the morgue. Until she decided to leave—and it was, he reluctantly admitted, her decision, not his—they would play things as safely as possible, including steering clear of any place in the vicinity of midtown or Wall Street.

With the weather warming up, more and more their clandestine catch-ups occurred outdoors in public parks, or at least they started there. Sometimes their rendezvous segued to brunch or dinner. When that happened, Marc always paid. Along with being raised by his mother to be a "gentleman," he'd noticed that Honey didn't carry much cash, though she did have a credit card, which she very rarely used, at least not in his presence. It might or might not be in her name, but he bet anything the monthly statement went to Winterthur. He wasn't a psychiatrist but he'd seen and read enough to know that control was a big-driver issue for most abusers. Keeping Honey on a short leash financially was likely one of the ways Winterthur exerted his.

Still, despite his "friendship" with her, little had changed. She was still living in Winterthur's Park Avenue apartment—and under his thumb. Knowing the bastard must make at least occasional love to her, if you could call using someone's body for sport, and occasionally as a punching bag, "making love," had him seeing red. The thought of Honey in the bastard's bed and at his mercy made Marc want to punch things—starting with Winterthur's face. But since doing so would bring on all kinds of trouble for Honey, he settled for a substitute. Going back to boxing at his local gym wasn't going to move any mountains, but at least the workouts helped him release the tension and anger in a safe, healthy way. Too bad Winterthur didn't try it.

The tension wasn't only anger; it had a strong sexual component as well. Honey might be just his "friend," but the desire to be more to her hadn't gone away just because he'd found his mislaid morals. If anything, it was stronger than ever. But right now she didn't need a second lover complicating her life. What she needed, *all* she needed, was a friend who had her well-being at heart. Marc focused on being that for her.

That didn't mean it was easy.

He descended the curved steps from the statue of Mahatma Gandhi to where Honey had finally stopped snapping pictures of him with her iPhone camera. Situated on the periphery of the park's southwest corner, the bronze depicting the renowned Indian leader was set against a backdrop of magnolia trees in full blossom. Eyeing the stalls of the green market, where not only fruits, vegetables, and meats were sold but also an array of artisanal cheeses, wines, and baked goods, all of them locally sourced, Marc heard his stomach rumble. Earlier he'd suggested they put off picture taking, pull up a bench, and make a picnic of the goods they'd bought.

But Honey could be stubborn when she felt something to be sufficiently important, a character trait that gave Marc hope that her days as an abused kept woman might well be numbered. Noting the fire in her eyes and the firming of her mouth, he recognized this was one of those times—and that he didn't have a chance.

Those blossoms, she pointed out, flinging a slender arm back toward the tree, were as fragile and fleeting as they were beautiful. One good rain would send most of the petals dropping. A slightly overcast sky and the weather forecast calling for midday thunderstorms bore her out. Marc resigned himself to more posing.

"You must be the worst model ever," she declared, softening the complaint with a smile. "Besides being a fidget, you're a blinker."

Marc admitted to both. "I've singlehandedly managed to mess up every family Christmas and Fourth of July photo for the past two decades. My mother says I was drawn to emergency medicine because it always keeps me in motion. I've never admitted it before, but I think she may be right. A desk job would kill me. Unless I'm reading, I seriously hate sitting still. Even then I'm more likely to pick up my tablet and start pacing."

He paused there, belatedly wondering what had started him babbling. Honey was incredibly easy to talk to. Over the past months, he'd probably strung more words into sentences with her than he had in the last five years of dating. And she was fun, seriously fun. Be it something as simple as strolling through the city on a quest for the perfect angle, light, backdrop—whatever—she was a great companion, a great friend, a great . . .

Rather than go "there," he glanced down at her hands. "Can I see?"

"Sure, but remember to be gentle. I'm still . . . learning." She held out the phone.

He took it from her, flipping through the last few photo frames. "Whoa, these are really good. You have a real eye." The compliment wasn't only intended to boost her self-confidence. He meant it.

She dismissed his praise with a shrug of her slender shoulders. "I'm just an amateur."

Not for the first time it struck him how often she prefaced her passions and accomplishments with "just," as if by getting the jump start on minimizing herself, she might divert some knockdown blow.

"Everybody starts out that way. You think the Sistine Chapel was Michelangelo's first time picking up a paintbrush? That Frank Lloyd Wright started out with Fallingwater as his inaugural project? That he didn't maybe, you know, try designing something simpler like a tree house first?" He would have referenced a famous photographer too, but off the top of his head he couldn't come up with any.

But he had her laughing, and that was something. Shaking her head, she shot him a smile. "You really are sweet, but I'm hardly in the same league."

At times like this, Marc could have shaken her—gently, of course. "My point is to stop being so hard on yourself. How do you even know what league you're in until you try? Why not take a class, *one* class, and see how that goes? There's the New School or SVA or . . . " He stopped when he saw her gaze glazing over.

"Classes and camera equipment cost money," she said, looking beyond him toward the green market which showed signs of winding down.

So do shoes, Marc felt like saying, but for once kept his mouth shut—sort of. "Why not make like the Nike ad and 'Just Do It?'"

She slid the phone back into her purse and looked back up at him. "Maybe I will . . . someday."

In Marc's assessment, someday usually equated to never, but tough as it was, he kept his lip buttoned and his judgments to himself—for now. Instead, he said, "You know I may still be a lowly ER resident, but I do okay for myself. I have some money set aside, and I'd be happy to—"

"I will *not* take money from you." Her fierce look took him aback. He hadn't seen anything like it since that first day, the morning when he followed her back to the Park Avenue apartment.

"At least hear me out first before deciding."

"I've already decided," she said, her expression softening, though her voice held firm. "Besides, you disapprove of me. Don't trouble yourself to deny it. It's true."

"I do not . . . well, who cares what I think? I just—"

"I do not accept money from disapproving gentlemen," she answered gamely.

Mark bit back a groan. Another Audrey quote! From *Breakfast at Tiffany's*, he believed. In the spirit of being a better . . . *friend* to her, a couple of weeks ago he'd streamed it from Netflix and watched the whole thing through. Though he'd never been a fan of old films—the whole "Sally Tomato" subplot was supremely silly—this one was more entertaining than he had reason to expect. Or maybe it was his knowing how much the movie meant to Honey that had made it of interest to him.

"Consider it as a loan if that makes you feel more comfortable," he conceded, though he never meant for it to be anything but a free-and-clear gift. That Honey wasn't prepared to accept it in that way called for some creativity on his part. He paused to regroup, an idea tickling the corners of his mind. "Or maybe we could work out some sort of barter agreement."

Her gaze narrowed. "What kind of barter?"

Her suspicion was as apparent as her uniquely pretty mouth. A few months ago he might have been offended, but not so now. Now he got it—her. It wasn't that she distrusted him specifically. It was men as a whole. Not for the first time, he wondered what relationships might have preceded the one with Winterthur. Though he couldn't put his finger on exactly why, he was starting to suspect she hadn't ever had a real adult boyfriend.

Marc circled back to her question. What could he reasonably— and respectably—have her do for him that, above all, wouldn't get her into hot water with Winterthur? Jiggling his knee, he thought for a moment. Eureka—he had it. His mother, when she visited, was always on his case about his apartment. Not only was it a "wreck" so far as mess went, but apparently it was so uninviting as to merit being called Spartan, or so she complained. Along with being low on time and patience for fixing it up, Marc was afraid he didn't have the taste. Fabric swatches, paint chips, draperies, and home décor items—it was all part of a foreign world he couldn't begin to figure out.

But he bet Honey could. He thought back to his first, and only, time inside her apartment. Despite her "boyfriend" busting the place up along with her, he remembered it as sophisticated but also charming. Someone had obviously taken considerable time and care in searching for unique, not cookie-cutter, furnishings and pieces. Marc seriously doubted that person was Winterthur.

Hoping he could sell her on the idea, he steered them over to an empty bench. Settling onto it, he shifted to face her. "I bought my place a few years ago. The building is early twentieth century and doesn't have all that much in the way of amenities, but it gets great light and it still has most of the original features."

Her face lit. "I love prewar apartments. They have such great bones."

"Yeah, well the problem with my place is that it's so *barebones*. It still looks like I just moved in and with my work schedule—"

"I'd love to help you redo it."

"You would?" Could convincing her really be this easy?

She nodded. "I'm no expert. Whatever I know is completely self-taught. But I do have a . . . friend with a background in interior design. He works in Manhattan as a window dresser for Ralph Lauren."

Until now, Marc hadn't heard her mention having any friends of either gender. For a fleeting, not very self-flattering moment, he felt a twinge of actual jealousy. Tamping it down, he nodded. "Ralph Lauren, wow, that's great." To Marc, one designer was the same as another; still, the Ralph Lauren brand was so strong, even he knew the name.

She nodded. "It really is. He has all sorts of imaginative ideas. Who knows, he might even lend us his employee discount. I'd have to ask him about that, of course."

"That'd be great, but no pressure. I mean I don't want to put anyone on the spot." He hesitated. "When uh . . . do you think you might want to come by and, you know, have a look?"

She hesitated. "I'll have to check my . . . schedule. Can I let you know tomorrow?"

By her schedule, what she meant was Drew's. But it was what it was—for now.

"Sure," Marc forced himself to answer. Pulling one of the croissants he'd bought earlier out from the white paper bag, he handed it to her.

"Yum, thank you," she said, taking a big bite.

For the next few minutes, they ate in companionable quiet. Feeling a drop on his nose, Marc looked up. Clouds were moving in, no doubt about it. "Looks like we're getting rained on after all," he observed.

Honey sent him what he now recognized as her *I told you so* look but otherwise she refrained from rubbing it in. "The wind is picking up," she said, reaching up to deal with the loosened hair lashing her face.

Marc couldn't resist. He reached over and tucked a thick caramel-colored lock behind the shell of her ear, his hand lingering on her jaw.

"Thanks," she said, looking down—looking shy. "I should go back to wearing hats."

Marc dropped his hand. Drinking in the sweet silhouette of her downturned face, he felt a pang of real regret. Had he been too quick to jump to "just friends" as their only solution? Once Winterthur was out of the picture, and Marc hoped to God that wouldn't be much longer, might it be time to revisit what he'd already come to think of as their relationship?

"You look great in hats, only maybe not the really big ones. They hide too much of your face."

"Maybe sometimes I like hiding."

Marc swallowed hard, his throat knotting. "You shouldn't have to."

She looked up at him, smile fleeting, eyes not so much sad as . . . wistful. "What next?" she asked, changing the subject. "Or do you have to get back?"

"I have some time." Actually he had a thousand things on his plate—errands to run, cleaning chores to do (his apartment might as yet be no showplace but that didn't mean it had to be filthy), groceries to buy—but none of them seemed anywhere near as important as spending this precious one-on-one time with Honey. "I know it's supposedly spring but how would you feel about heading across the street to Max Brenner's for a real, non-Starbucks hot chocolate?"

Brightening, Honey smiled, this time without reservation. "'Chocolate by the bald man'—how can I possibly resist? So long as you don't mind making a fast stop first, that would be divine."

✳✳✳ ✳✳✳

Leaving the park with Marc, Honey crossed 14th Street and headed for the vendors lining the sidewalk from Designer Shoe Warehouse to Juicy Couture. Only it wasn't knockoff handbags or sunglasses or any of the sundry New York-themed tchotchkes sold with tourists in mind that drew her. It was the rescue cats and kittens displayed for adoption.

Six days a week, rain or shine, the weathered African woman with the brightly colored head scarves and weary eyes set up her folding table, pet cages, and supplies in the same spot of sidewalk across from the park. Since discovering her by chance almost a year ago, Honey had made it a point to stop by at least once a month, more if she could manage it. Regardless of the season, the rescuer always had a new supply of cats and kittens in desperate need of homes, always a new heartbreaking true story of cats that had been abandoned or otherwise abused, not just in Manhattan but throughout the five boroughs. Honey had a hard time hearing those stories, but because she felt it was important, deeply important, neither to turn her back or close off her ears to animal suffering, she made a point of listening for as long as she could. Welling tears were her signal to herself that she was approaching the limit of what she could bear. Then and only then did she make her excuses and move on. Hearing the hard-luck stories was the difficult part; cuddling one of the kittens was a delight to which she looked forward all month.

The visits always ended the same way, with the woman holding out a sweet-faced kitten and imploring, "Please, won't you give this baby a home?" And each time Honey would shake her head and explain that she didn't have time to take care of a pet, her building didn't allow them, her roommate was allergic et cetera. Whatever her fib du jour was, seeing the woman's look of disappointment slashed at her heart. Feeling the telltale prick of tears, she'd hurry to hand over whatever spare money she'd mustered and make her getaway before she might weaken.

Drew might not be allergic, but he detested cats. He wasn't particularly fond of dogs either. He was always complaining that the Yorkie for whom Katharine had paid top dollar to a breeder upstate was a farter. But cats he truly hated. He barely tolerated the stuffed animal, Mr. Pinky, Honey kept on her nightstand.

She glanced to Marc. "I won't be but a minute."

He shrugged. "Take as long as you like."

The way he'd let her lead him over without question or complaint warmed her. Despite his crazy busy schedule, he never acted as though he was in a rush, let alone more important than anyone else. His humility was yet another thing she loved—*liked*—about him. Before meeting Marc, she hadn't acknowledged the extent to which six plus years of stroking and otherwise supporting an epic ego such as Drew's had drained her. And Marc was *soooooo* patient. With all those winning qualities stacking up, it was becoming harder and harder to think of him as "just a friend"—or to want to. Even his helping her with her hair back in the park had sent her senses seesawing, the practical if not precisely impersonal touch tempting her to lean in and claim what she craved—more of those heart-melting, breath-stealing, altogether amazing kisses he was so good at giving.

And he'd been so sweet about the whole photo thing, posing for her even though he admitted to hating having his picture taken. His modesty was yet another endearing trait, especially since he came with chiseled features and a hot body that many a professional model might covet. If she happened to find out he liked cats, too, it might well push her over the edge of reason. As it stood, keeping her hands to herself, meaning "off him," wasn't getting any easier. Her new "gig" as his unofficial interior decorator would likely stretch her self-control to the limit; still, the opportunity to spend more time with him in private was too golden to pass up.

Sitting on an overturned milk crate nursing a tiny kitten with a bottle, the rescue lady looked up. Gaze alighting on Honey, her lined faced lit. "You haven't been around in a while. I've been wondering where you took yourself to."

"Nowhere, just keeping busy," Honey replied, grateful for once to have something to report that was real.

Studying for her GED was challenging her in more ways than one, especially since she was hiding it from Drew for obvious reasons. Her reasons for not telling Marc were subtler but no less real. Admitting you were a high-school dropout was hard enough under the best of circumstances. Making that admission to your highly educated "friend," who also happened to be a doctor, would be a serious hit to what was left of her pride.

Aware of Marc watching her, she took out the five dollars she'd folded into her Prada bag's inner pocket, all the cash she'd managed to squirrel away from what Drew doled out as her "allowance," and discreetly slipped it through the slot of the plexiglass donations container.

The woman's smile broadened. She reached out to Honey with her free hand, the palm cracked and callused, the fingernails clipped short and peeling, no doubt from the bleach she constantly used in cleaning the carriers and cages. "God bless you, God bless you. You're an angel."

Fallen angel, Honey mentally added.

The praise, so undeserved, shamed her. If this God-fearing, animal-rescuing woman knew who, or rather what, she really was, she might well throw Honey's five dollars back in her face.

And Marc? He was so good-hearted, so principled. The severity with which he berated himself over their movie theater make-out, which had been as much her "fault" as his, had made her determined to do nothing more that might drag him down to her "level." It was bad enough he knew she was a kept woman. If he were ever to find out about her escort days, he wouldn't want to be friends with her—or anything else.

Going to work at the agency had been a monumental mistake; leaving it for Drew an even stupider move. Though he lavished her with expensive clothes and jewelry when he was feeling generous or, more often than not, guilty, he gave her very little cash. The apartment rent he paid directly as a debit from one of his many accounts. Groceries and incidentals such as cab fare, mani-pedis, and the occasional tea or lunch out were paid with the credit card he'd set up for her. The bill, however, went to him. At the end of every month, he pored over her statement line-by-line, questioning anything that suggested she might have a life outside their relationship.

"I wish it could be more," she said sincerely. Avoiding looking at Marc, who seemed to be watching her intently, she bent down to peer inside the cage. "Who do we have here today?" she asked, knowing the question would be the lead-in to the most recent heartstring-pulling rescue story.

Only today the cage was empty.

The rescuer held out the kitten she was feeding. "Here, hold him." The towel slipped away, revealing the top of a tiny marmalade-colored head. The kitten yawned—and Honey's heart squeezed in on itself.

"All right, but only for a minute." Honey reached out and took the kitten, whose eyes still had a faintly bluish cast. Poor little mite must not be quite six weeks old. "Where's his mother?" she asked, though she suspected she wouldn't like the answer.

"Taxi," the woman answered with a grim shake of her turbaned head. "Damned fools drive too fast and then they hit something—*someone*—and don't have the decency to stop."

Honey nodded. Homeless *and* motherless; that was a tough path to tread, and well she knew it. She went to hand the kitten back when it let out a loud mew. "Oh my, that's quite an impressive pair of lungs for such a little kitten," she said, cuddling him back against her. He might weigh under a pound, but clearly he had a big personality to grow into along with his paws.

"Do you like cats?" she asked Marc, angling her arms so he could better see the kitten.

He hesitated and then admitted, "I'm more of a dog person."

Finally an actual flaw—thank God! "You have to admit, though, he's adorable, quite the cutie."

"Most baby animals are." Reaching out with his forefinger, he used it to gently rub the crown of the animal's downy soft head.

"He's the last of the litter," the woman broke in, dividing her watchful gaze between them. "It's always that way with the runts."

"Runt, why I never," Honey said, holding up the kitten as though he were speaking, not her.

Out of the corner of her eye she caught Marc smiling. He had the most beautiful smile, his teeth white and straight and banded by lips that she knew for a fact were as soft and kissable as they seemed. A few months ago at Tea & Sympathy, it had seemed great fun, good *craic*, to tease him by pretending to the waitress that they were a couple. Now she found herself wishing that were the truth.

"Take him—*please*," the rescue lady implored. "You seem like you have so much love to give and he needs a home."

A lump lodged in Honey's throat. They were skipping ahead to phase three—the begging portion—not that Honey blamed her. The poor woman deserved a medal—and a break. What an enormous responsibility it must be to nurse a never-ending stream of creatures so cute and needy.

Honey opened her mouth to trot out the litany of well-worn excuses, only she never got the chance.

"My granddaughter in Atlanta is getting married this weekend, and I promised her I'd be there to see her walk down the aisle." She gestured to the kitten Honey still held. "I don't have anyone who can keep him while I'm gone, and I can't take him with me on the bus. If I don't place him today, I'm going to have to give him up to the shelter."

The shelter! "Oh, no! But he's so small."

The woman nodded. "He needs to be bottle fed every two to three hours. Unless they can find a volunteer to foster him, he'll likely be—"

"I'll take him!"

The words were out before Honey even knew she'd spoken them. Both Marc and the rescuer stared at her; the latter with relief—and triumph. "Oh, thank you! Giving a home to this blessed baby, you won't be sorry."

Honey wasn't so certain about that. If Drew discovered her new "roommate," the kitten wasn't the only one of them at risk for being skinned. The saving grace was that he was logging in incredible hours at the office these days, ramping up for a big Investor Day bash he was throwing at the Waldorf for a pool of mostly out-of-state clients. With luck, his work responsibilities would keep him away for at least another few days.

The rescuer was already on her feet and tossing cat care items into a plastic bag. "I'll give you a few of these syringes and his towel to wrap him up in 'til you can pick up a carrier."

Feeling perspiration breaking out, Honey flung her free hand, palm out. "Wait, just to be clear, I'm *fostering*, not adopting him. I need to know that you'll take him back once you're home from the wedding."

The woman waved a hand, dismissing the notion. "Trust me, once you have this sweet baby angel for a day, you won't want to give him up ever."

Honey suspected that was true. Feeling him burrow against her breast, she felt as though she and the kitten belonged to one another already. But she couldn't afford to forget that she was not a normal person with a normal life, not yet anyway. Given Drew's mercurial moods, keeping Cat—she'd already decided on a temporary name, God help her—would only endanger him.

"Do I have your promise or not?" Though it tore at her heart, she was prepared to hand the kitten back and walk away, if need be.

"Yes, yes, all right, you know where to find me if you decide you don't want him—only you won't."

Silent until now, Marc turned to Honey. Dropping his voice, he asked, "Are you sure about this?"

Honey shook her head, vaguely aware that most of her hair was tumbling down her back and her bangs were in dire need of trimming. Since meeting Marc, she'd definitely become a lot more casual about her grooming. Funny thing was she actually felt prettier.

"No, but a few days I should be able to manage. I have a soft spot for all animals but especially cats. The orange tabbies are my favorite. This little one reminds me of the cat in—"

"Don't tell me, let me guess—*Breakfast at Tiffany's.*"

"Why yes, that's right," she said, surprised. "How did you know that? I thought you've never seen an Audrey Hepburn movie?"

Expression sheepish, he admitted, "I maybe saw part of it flipping channels or something."

Honey hid a smile, brushing a light kiss atop Cat's head. Forget not-entirely-perfect. Dr. Marcus Sandler—Marc—was as flawless as mortal men might come.

Chapter Five

"I believe in pink. I believe happy girls are the prettiest girls. I believe that tomorrow is another day, and . . . I believe in miracles."
—Audrey Hepburn

Twenty-four hours later, Honey was a mother—a *cat* mother, and only temporarily. Still, she reasoned, it counted.

Yawning, she drew the feeding bottle nipple from Cat's mouth. "Good boy," she praised, setting him down and giving him a nudge toward the litter box, one of several cat-related Petco purchases she— Marc—had made before leaving Union Square the other day.

Sleeping in two-to-three hour snatches wasn't the same as logging in a solid night's rest, but the sense of accomplishment, not only of doing a "good deed" but of being truly loved and needed, more than made up for any grogginess. Having a pet to care for seemed to really ground her. Tired—okay, exhausted—though she was, she'd made really good progress in studying for her GED exam.

A *ding* announced that a text message had just landed. Assuming it must be Marc, and excited to compare schedules for when she might come over for a look at his place, she hurried across to where she'd left her phone charging.

The text message wasn't from Marc. It was from Drew.

ON WAY, PREPARE TO CELEBRATE.

Oh, no!

She eyed the time. If only she had more of it, she would call up one of the FATEs and ask them to take Cat for a few hours, if not the whole evening. Liz's Jonathan was crazy about cats, seeking out any excuse to go downstairs and play with their neighbor's two. Who knew, maybe after several hours of kitten-sitting, Liz might consider keeping Cat permanently. Now that her chemo treatments were well over, she no longer had to panic about possibly being scratched. At least that way, Honey would get to see him once a week.

But she was getting ahead of herself. There wasn't time and unfortunately there was no one in her building she could call on for a favor. Because of her embarrassment over several loud fights with Drew, she'd made a point of ducking her neighbors. In retrospect, she saw just how isolating being a mistress, and an abuse victim, could be.

Panicked, she paced the apartment, gathering up any "evidence"— cat toys, dishes, and stray tufts of fuzzy orange fur. There was no help for it. Cat and his accoutrements were going to have to go into hiding until Drew left.

Picking up the kitten, who'd just dutifully done his business, she carried him toward the pantry closet, not a walk-in but roomy enough. "Don't take this personally, Cat, but you're going to have to go in the closet for a few. But don't worry. Mr. Pinky will take good care of you."

*** ***

Drew showed up forty minutes later in an uncommonly good mood, bearing a bouquet of calla lilies and a takeout bag of Chinese. Honey had just finished checking on Cat, tummy full and curled up fast asleep around her stuffed animal.

Praying that he would stay that way, she pasted on a smile. "You said we're celebrating. What's the occasion?" she asked, carrying the flowers into the kitchen.

"Can't a man bring his girl flowers without there being an occasion?" he asked, shooting her a wink.

He really was in a good mood. Still, to be safe, she prefaced her reply with an apology. "Sorry," she said. "These are lovely. Thank you. It's just that you texted something about celebrating—or did I maybe misunderstand?" she added quickly. With Drew, she'd learned not to take any chances.

Still smiling, he came toward her, joining her at the sink. "Remember I told you about that Investor Day I wanted to throw? Well, the funding came through and it's happening: a blowout bash at the Waldorf for my key out-of-town investment clients, and I want you there."

Caught off guard, she nearly dropped the vase she'd just finished filling. "Me? Really?"

For years she'd prayed to the Powers That Be to be more involved in his life, not only set on the sidelines of it. Now that it seemed he was prepared, even excited to include her, she wanted no part of any of it—especially him. Arranging the flowers, she only hoped that the date wouldn't conflict with her Monday night FATE meeting. Or the online GED study group she'd joined. Or, above all, her meet-up with Marc. Decorating his apartment was something to which she was truly looking forward. Who knew, maybe she'd even confide in him about taking her GED. She'd recently bit the bullet and told the other FATEs. Predictably, they couldn't have been more thrilled for her.

"You bet, babe." Stepping behind her, he glided his hands lightly up and down her upper arms, caressing her as he'd used to. Still, she steeled herself not to flinch. "I want to show you off. Together we'll show those schmucks what real success looks like."

"That is a lot to celebrate. I'll just . . . pour us some wine."

She turned away and went to the refrigerator, mostly as an excuse to break free and put some space between them. On opening the side door, she spotted Cat's formula—crap! She shoved it into the vegetable crisper and brought out the bottle of pinot.

Carrying it to the counter, she decided she might as well take advantage of Drew's good mood to test the waters on another subject. "So I was thinking of maybe taking a class."

A class would serve as an excellent cover for those times when she needed to spend time at Marc's. Feeling as though she were scheming her escape from Alcatraz, she turned to the cupboard and took down two blown crystal wineglasses. Circa 1960, smoky-hued, and striped with 24 karat gold, the set of six had been a housewarming present picked out by her and paid for by Drew. With his drinking escalated to hard liquor, the glasses hadn't gotten much use these last few years. Averting her eyes, she poured out the white wine and handed him the fuller goblet.

"What kind of class?" he finally asked. He took his wine and the carryout bag and headed into the main room, leaving her to follow.

Passing by the pantry closet, she caught Cat's meow. He must have heard their voices and awoken.

Drew looked back at her from where he'd plopped down on the sofa. "What was that?"

Honey's heart thudded. "What was what?"

Scowling, he tilted his head to the side. "I thought I heard a cat."

"Oh, that," Honey said, striving to smooth out any tremble from her tone. "The neighbor may have mentioned something about getting a kitten."

He turned away toward the TV but not before she spotted him scowling. "Well, she'd fucking better keep it quiet, or else I'm complaining to the management company. With the rent I pay on this place, I'm not going to put up with the building being turned into some kind of pet hotel." He slugged down a gulp of the wine. "A cat, Jesus. Where's the rat poison when you really need it?"

Rushing across the room, Honey picked up the TV remote. "Why don't you relax and watch something while I set dinner out?"

She turned it on and punched the volume-up arrow several times. Takeout dinner with minimal conversation (for them both), scotch (for him), and sex (also for him), Honey had their "date night" drill down pat. If only she could find a way to speed things up. Cat would need to eat in another two hours. She needed to get Drew out in time before hunger prompted the kitten to start crying in earnest.

"Not so fast." Drew swiveled to look back at her. "What kind of class?"

Of all the times, did he really have to pick tonight to finally show some interest in her as a person? She shrugged, as though she was still figuring things out. "Oh, I don't know, maybe something to do with . . . interior design or—"

He rolled his eyes. "Baby, you're hardly Parsons School material."

Once the demeaning comment would have prompted tears, but she was past caring what he thought of her. Used to him beating her down emotionally as well as physically, she sometimes felt as if her soul wasn't only scarred—it had grown calluses.

Modulating her tone to meekness, she said, "Well then, what about photography?"

"What about it?"

She shrugged again. "It might be fun to learn to take better pictures."

One sandy brow lifted. "And who's going to pay for this hobby?"

"I could get some sort of part-time job."

It was ironic how flipping burgers had once been a fate she'd been willing to do just about anything to avoid. Considering all she'd since done to survive, asking "Fries with that?" no longer seemed like such a monumental humiliation. Instead she'd let herself be seduced into taking the ultimate dead-end job: mistress. She had absolutely no security—no medical benefits, no savings, and no job security. At any time, he could announce he'd grown tired of her and turn her out. Just please, God, let her get her GED first.

Finished with the wine, he got up and went over to the bar to pour himself, what else, a scotch. "Just what kind of . . . job do you think you could get?"

Even though she was taking positive steps to fix things, she mentally kicked herself for not sticking around Omaha long enough to complete high school. New York wasn't going anywhere. Another few months of living under Sam's tyranny wouldn't have mattered in the long run. But all the shit going down at home took its toll. Her grades bottomed out. Being held back and made to repeat her sophomore year had badly battered her self-confidence. Instead of finishing, she'd fled, arriving in the Big Apple with no diploma and no job skills. GED or not, she wasn't qualified to do anything lucrative, at least nothing legal. Getting her feet wet in the workforce with a part-time job wasn't just about money. It was about freedom. Like her weekly FATE meet-up, a job would be a safe haven, an outside place where Drew couldn't control or intrude.

"Oh, I don't know, darling, something in retail, perhaps. It would just be a few days a week."

"A few days a week!"

So much for his good mood! Feeling her panic kick in, she hurried to smooth things over. "Drew, *please*, forget I ever mentioned anything."

"I provide you with—" he flung his open arms wide, presumably to encompass the bounty of the apartment "—all this, anything you want, and still it's not enough."

He slammed the glass down, sending scotch lopping the sides. The wet ring would leave a permanent stain on the wood if it wasn't wiped up. Were she a normal woman in a normal relationship with a normal man, she would have whisked away the spillage and reminded him to use a coaster, all without worry of being backhanded—or worse. Her situation was nothing if not ironic. Growing up, she'd yearned for a glamorous life, an existence far removed from the tool-belt-wearing brute her mother had married. Being poor and getting hit had seemed to go together, like Forrest Gump's peas and carrots. Looking back, she supposed it made sense that *Lifestyles of the Rich and Famous* had been her favorite show even if she had watched it in syndication.

But now she knew that brutes came from all walks of life, from those living below the poverty line to others pulling in eight-figure salaries. She no longer yearned for "champagne wishes and caviar dreams," but a normal life where she felt loved and cherished, respected and safe.

Normalcy was what she had with Marc. It was impromptu picnics in the park, and picking out kitten toys together, and squabbling over how long he had to stand posing. Meeting Drew's glaring gaze, she was yet again struck by the contrast to Marc. His eyes were hazel, thickly lashed, and deeply kind—so kind that even after several months, Honey sometimes still found it difficult to meet them. More than anything, those eyes told her what kind of man he was, the kind of man who might have been hers if only she'd had the character and courage to hold out for him.

"If I find that you've pawned so much as one piece of the jewelry I've bought you over the years—"

"I would never part with a piece of it."

That was another lie—a whopper. Though she hadn't sold anything yet, she had gone so far as to take a few of the glitzier pieces to be appraised. High-end jewelry was touted as an investment—until you went to sell it. Once she left, pawning her jewelry would be a stop-gap measure, a way to keep the wolf from the door for a few months at most—long enough to figure out her life?

The house buzzer had Honey whipping around. Who could it be? Other than Drew, no one ever came over, especially not Marc, not after that first day.

Drew followed her to the call panel. "That would be Frank," he said, shifting her aside.

"Frank?"

He nodded. "Frank Dawes, a work buddy of mine who really wants to meet you."

✻✻✻ ✻✻✻

"Honey, meet my main man, Frank. Frank, this is Honey."

Paunchy, red-eyed, and wearing the remains of his dark hair in a Donald Trump comb over, Frank openly ogled her. "Wow, Drew, she's all you said and more."

Honey knew that look—and she knew she didn't like it. Behind the scenes, finance guys, so-called suits, were ruder than any construction worker. Wolf whistles and cat calls were at least honest. Men like Drew and Frank weren't only skanky—they were shameless hypocrites.

"Figures Ole Drew here would keep you all to himself," Frank went on, jabbing Drew with his elbow. "You always were a selfish son of a bitch, Winterthur."

He had that much right.

Drew grinned back. "Consider this me making it up to you."

Honey marveled at the uncharacteristic joviality. Always so touchy with her, Drew certainly seemed to take his colleague's ribbing in stride.

Frank peeled off his suit jacket, handing it to Honey to hang. "You give me this, and we're even."

So they'd struck some sort of deal or, more probably, a bet, and Drew apparently had lost. Stomach sinking, she wondered what he'd wagered. Searching for clues, she glanced over to him, but for once he couldn't seem to look her in the eye.

"I'm going out for a while," he announced, his gaze on the apartment door. "I promised to pick up some . . . stuff for the kids."

"But you just got here. What about dinner?" As much as she wanted to clear him out, replacing him with Frank didn't seem like much of a trade-up.

He shrugged. "You and Frank have it. I'll pick up something on my way home."

"Home" meant Drew's other apartment, the one he shared with Katharine and the kids on West 76th Street. In their early days, Honey had dared to drop by the building once. Lingering at the entrance, all but willing Drew's wife to walk out, she'd imagined living there someday soon in Katharine's stead. At the time doing so had seemed poignant, tragically romantic. Now it struck her as seriously fucked up.

"Gotta go. It's almost eight." He paused to consult his wrist, or rather the vintage Piaget watch banding it. Eighteen karat gold and obscenely expensive, it was an anniversary gift from Katharine from three years ago. Back when Honey had still believed she was in love with him, seeing him wear it had hurt her.

Not so now.

Honey followed him over to the door. "Drew, please, you can't just . . . leave me here alone with him." She gestured back to where Frank stood mixing himself a drink.

"Got any ice?" he called out from the bar.

Honey ignored him.

Drew laid two fingers beneath her chin, lifting her face so that she had no choice but to look at him. "Babe, *babe*, c'mon, we both know you don't need any chaperone. Just be nice to him, show him a good time. He's in the middle of a divorce and needs a sympathetic ear to pour his troubles into. You're always complaining about feeling iso-lated—lonely. Now I finally bring a friend over and you're giving me shit about it."

"I'm not—"

"Just be your sweet self for an hour or two. Can you do that for me?"

"But I've never met him before. What are we supposed to talk about?"

"Talk about?" A smirk suffused his face. "I'm sure you'll come up with something. Tell him you're thinking of taking a class. I'm sure he'd be into hearing all about that. He's all about self-improvement."

She caught at his hand. "Drew, please—please don't leave me."

"I'll be back before you know it. Have a drink for once. It'll loosen you up." He grabbed his jacket and slipped out the door.

Feeling as though she were walking the pirate plank in an Erroll Flynn film, she retraced her steps into the main room. Frank was making himself at home on the loveseat, a gin and tonic in one hand and the remote in the other. He'd loosened his tie and undone his top shirt button. Wiry black chest hairs peeked out from his open collar. More hairs sprouted from the backs of his fat-fingered hands.

"So you're into old movies, huh?" He jerked a chubby hand toward the wall of movie posters.

"I enjoy classic films, yes."

He seemed to find that funny. "I enjoy movies too. Drew mentioned he has quite a . . . collection."

Honey knew all about Drew's porn stash. It wasn't like he made any effort to hide it from her. Watching people fuck relaxed him, or so he insisted. Despite her pleadings, he often made her watch with him. That several of the films featured two of her FATE friends, Sarah and Liz, formerly the adult film actresses Sugar and Spice, made viewing particularly uncomfortable, not that she cared to explain that to him. So far he was completely in the dark about her weekly Monday night FATE meetings. Honey meant to keep it that way.

"Maybe we could watch something together?" Frank suggested with a wiggle of wiry eyebrows.

"You're welcome to watch whatever you like," she said, knowing that if she was rude to his friend, Drew wouldn't hesitate to take it out on her later. "I'll just be in the kitchen." She turned to go.

Frank flung an arm across the couch back. "Aw, c'mon, don't be like that. Make yourself a drink and pull up a seat." He patted the cushion beside him as though he were the host and Honey his guest.

Honey stayed on her feet. "No, thank you."

He took a swig of the G&T and eyed her. "You know, Drew told me all about you."

"Sorry?"

"Don't play innocent with me. I know how you two hooked up."

Drew had sworn never to tell and obviously he had—yet another reason to move forward with leaving him. "We met at a corporate function—a party."

"Oh yeah, you met at a party all right, but you were no regular guest."

That did it. Too furious to be afraid, she strode toward the apartment door. "I think you should leave." She grabbed his coat from the hook and held it out for him to take.

"Yeah, well, it's not exactly up to you, now is it?"

"This is my apartment, and I'm asking you to leave—now."

Smirking, he set down his drink and stood. "This dump and everything in it belongs to Drew—and that includes you." He started toward her.

Honey thought about grabbing her purse and running out, but she had Cat to consider. He would need to eat soon, plus she couldn't risk him possibly crying and being found by Frank who would, of course, rat her out to Drew.

Reaching her, he grabbed her chin, jerking her face to his. "Drew tells me you could suck the cork out of a wine bottle, you're that good. Let's see whether or not he's exaggerated."

"Stop it!" His big, pinching fingers really hurt. She tried pulling away but it was no use.

"Hey, don't get your thong in a twist. I'm just being friendly."

"I thought you were Drew's friend."

He laughed at that. "I am. And friends share . . . lots of things. If he wants my help covering his ass on Investor Day, he knows he has to keep me happy, and right now my happiness hinges on him passing me a key to this place—and 24/7 access to you. But first I want a little nosh."

She jerked back. His sloppy kiss, wet and stinking of booze, landed on her cheek instead. "I don't believe you. Why would Drew need you to cover for him at work? He's a partner."

One ugly, thick brow lifted. "That, sweetheart, is the billion dollar question."

He grabbed her again, pinning her arms and pulling her hard against him. Crushed against his barrel chest, Honey felt as if she couldn't breathe. His erection pushed against her lower belly, and he shifted his hips, making sure she could feel it.

Panic closed her throat, preventing her from screaming. She was about to be raped in her own home, not by some random perpetrator but by a man her "boyfriend" had set her up with. Willing herself to calm down, she considered her options. Her arms might be pinned but her legs were still free. She lifted her right one—and drove her bent knee upward into Frank's balls.

He let her go in an instant and doubled over. "Why, you little bitch," he hissed, cupping his groin and backing away.

Honey eyed her purse and keys, both hanging on the coat rack behind him. She was ramping up to make a rush to grab them when the apartment door opened.

Drew poked his head inside. "I forgot my phone." Entering, his gaze went from Honey to Frank and his brows shot up. "What's going on?"

"You owe me—double." Frank straightened, stalked over to the door, and grabbed his overcoat off the hook. He threw it over his forearm and turned around. "This isn't over," he said, stabbing a fat finger in Honey's direction.

Drew threw an arm about Frank's shoulders as though he, and not Honey, was the injured party. "Don't worry. I'll deal with her later. C'mon, I'll walk you down."

✳✳✳ ✳✳✳

Drew returned a few minutes later. Whatever calm he'd shown in front of Frank was burned away by glowering fury. "Clothes off, on your knees—now."

Sitting on the loveseat hugging her knees to manage the shaking, Honey looked up. "No, Drew, please, you have to listen. He tried to—"

"I don't give a shit if he screwed you left, right and sideways. He's not just my friend. He's my business associate. And thanks to you, he's royally pissed. You need to be taught a lesson—and I'm going to teach it—tonight. Now get undressed."

Honey swiped a hand across her streaming eyes and shook her head. "I won't, not like this. You can beat me, you can kill me, but you can't make me do that, not anymore."

Meow, meow, meow . . .

Honey's heart dropped. Every bit of moisture seemed to be sucked from her mouth.

Drew's eyes widened. A smile twisted his lips. "The *neighbor* got a kitten, huh?"

Be quiet, Cat. Please darling, please . . .

Meow! Meow!

Honey sprang to her feet. "I'll speak to Mrs. . . . to her tomorrow, ask her to put him—it—in another room." The words tumbled out in a flurry, desperate and choppy. For someone who lied with fair frequency, she was truly terrible at it.

The triumph on Drew's face told her that he wasn't buying it. Cat's crying was nonstop now, the sound clearly coming from within the apartment. Like a hunting hound sniffing out its quarry, Drew followed the mewling to the pantry door. Honey rushed after him, tripping over her feet to try to get to Cat's hiding place before he did.

They reached the kitchen at roughly the same time. Any further dissembling was pointless. Drew had found her out. The best she could do would be to swear to have Cat gone in the morning. Wherever she took him, even a shelter that euthanized surplus pets, would be preferable to what Drew might do.

Heart pounding, she said, "Please, it's not what you think. It's not what it looks like."

Ignoring her, Drew pulled back on the bi-fold door, and Cat popped out. He swung around to Honey. "I'd say it looks like a cat."

She eyed the kitten swishing about her ankles. Could she grab Cat and make a run for it? The last time she'd tried escaping Drew had caught up with her in the hallway before she made it to the stairwell. At least this time she wore ballet flats rather than heels. It was a long shot, but it was also her and Cat's best chance.

As if reading her mind, Drew reached down and scooped up the startled kitten before she could. Grasping Cat by the scruff, he left the kitchen area, crossed the living room, and carried the terrified, shrieking animal over to the sliding-glass balcony door.

"Drew, no!"

With his free hand, he drew back on the door and threw one foot over the threshold. Honey tried using her body as a barricade, blocking him from stepping out, but it was no use.

Holding Cat away from him to avoid being clawed, Drew edged over to the rail. "Morris here had better sprout some fucking wings."

Cat's wailing filled the night, eclipsing even the traffic noises below. Tiny orange paws flecked with cream pedaled the air, seeking the security of solid ground.

Honey fell to her knees, the chilly air whipping her hair into her eyes, the cement cutting into her skin. Tears scalded her eyes, slid down her flushed face. "Please, Drew, I'm begging you. Don't do this. He's just . . . a little kitten. Do what you want to me, but leave him alone. He's not . . . he's not even mine. I'm just . . . keeping him."

Drew stilled. "You'll do anything I say."

She turned her face to look up at him. Even in the throes of her fear, Honey acknowledged she'd never hated someone so much.

He turned away from the rail. "I want this . . . thing out of here tomorrow, got it?"

Honey released her held-back breath. "Yes, yes, I'll take him back, I swear it."

And she would. She knew Drew. He never bluffed, at least not with her. The next time she wouldn't be so fortunate, and neither would Cat.

First thing in the morning, she'd call up Liz and beg her to take him, temporarily or, better yet, permanently. Either would solve the immediate problem. If Liz didn't adopt him, then the rescue lady in Union Square would have to honor her word and take him back once she was back in town. Honey had been stupid to bring an animal home in the first place, stupid and selfish to think she could live like a normal person, free and unafraid, even for a few paltry days. She should have known better than to bring a helpless creature into the hot mess that was her life. She *did* know better and yet . . .

Drew tossed the kitten. It was a tough throw but at least Cat landed on the patio on all fours rather than splattered on the sidewalk below. He sprang over the threshold and scrambled inside, slipping beneath the sofa. With luck, he would stay there and out of sight until Drew left.

But he wasn't going anywhere until he had his pound of flesh, Honey knew that. They'd struck a deal, and he would expect her to hold to her end of it. He needed to hurt someone, and that some-one was her. Feeling as though she were living a nightmare version of someone else's life, Honey stood on stiff legs. She wiped a hand across her wet eyes, turned, and walked back inside the apartment. The glass door slammed shut as Drew followed. She didn't bother looking back, nor did she need to. By now she knew the basic drill. She also knew that what lay ahead would be far worse than anything he'd so far done to her. Unlike the night he'd thrown her down the stairs, he was in full possession of his faculties. His quiet, calculated silence was far more threatening, far more terrifying, than a storm of flying fists and shouted accusations.

Coming up on his chair, she began to undress, not neatly as she usually did but letting her clothes fall to the floor piece by piece. Still facing away from him, she reached behind and unclasped her bra. Released from the underwire cups, her breasts felt heavy and vulner-able, the nipples pebbled not from desire but from the chill. Drew stood so close that she could all but feel his hot breath on her back. At some point, she'd stopped crying. She slipped off her panties and toed them to the side, waiting.

He still didn't touch her. Making her stand there and second guess him was part of the torture, she supposed. Finally he rounded her and took his seat, still fully dressed down to his shoes. Honey didn't have to ask what he wanted. She knew. Gaze averted, she dropped to her knees.

"I *own* you. Say it."

Head bowed, she acknowledged she'd been right. This was going to be worse, a lot worse, than any physical pain he'd so far inflicted, harder and more soul-shattering, than she'd imagined.

"Say it!"

She dragged down a deep breath. The sobs she held in threatened to suffocate her. "Y-you o-own m-e."

"Louder."

"You . . . own me."

"Again."

"You. Own. Me!"

"Later you're going to suck my cock like you've never sucked it before, but first . . . " He held out one foot, the wingtip dusty and splattered from walking on the city streets, and jabbed the toe into her crotch. "First you're going to lick my boots, Honey, every goddamned fucking filthy spot."

Chapter Six

"Anyone who does not believe in miracles is not a realist."
—Audrey Hepburn

Marc woke to pounding outside his apartment door and thunder claps outside his window. He'd been in a sound sleep dreaming about Honey. They were back at the IFC, only this time there was no holding back, no stopping, no regrets or guilty feelings. Hating to leave the dream haven, he rolled onto his side, willing the sound to cease. With luck, he could go back to sleep and pick up where they—he—had left off.

No such luck. The pounding persisted. As much as he wanted to blame the din on the storm, he couldn't keep ignoring the obvious. Someone was definitely at his door. He cracked open an eye, mentally reviewing the probable causes for waking him up in the middle of the night. Old Lady Barnes's cat crawled out onto the fire escape—again? A drug deal going down in the hallway—again? One of the older folks falling asleep with the stove on—again? His life was pretty predictable. Or at least it had been before he met Honey. He glanced over to the rain pelting his window and hoped that whatever the problem was, it wouldn't involve going outside.

He pulled on sweatpants and a T-shirt and headed out into the main room. Peering through the peephole, he saw that for once the cause of the late night commotion was nothing he could have foreseen.

Honey!

He unlocked the deadbolt, slid back the chain and opened the door. Soaked to the skin, Honey stood in his hallway leaking rainwater onto the linoleum. "Honey, what are you doing here? It's got to be—"

"Two a.m." She all but collapsed against him, her bulky designer bag poking him in the chest. "I tried calling but you didn't . . . you didn't answer and I-I didn't know where else to go, where to take us."

Her wild-eyed look freaked him out, and he was pretty sure her eyes were wet from more than rain. Fearing the worst, he pulled her all the way inside and kicked the door closed. "You came to the right place." *You came to me.* And then it struck him. "Us?"

She slanted a look to the bag, which he saw was open rather than clasped. "It will only be for a few days until I can . . . return him to the rescuer."

As if on cue, Cat poked his orange head out the top and yawned. Dumfounded, Marc stared.

"I know you don't care for cats, but he really is the best little darling and he's had . . . a really rough night." Her face crumpled.

"I'd say he's not the only one." Marc took the bag, set it and Cat on the floor in case he wanted to explore, and reached for her. Wrapping both arms around her, he tucked her head against his heart.

She burrowed against him. For several seconds they stood like that, wordless and still, Honey heaving silent sobs against him.

"That's it, let it all out," he said against her wet hair.

He took the opportunity to check her out, running light hands along her shoulders, spine, and hips, searching out signs of soreness or damage. When she first entered, he hadn't picked up on any stiffness, though soaring adrenalin might still be masking any symptoms. Obviously some kind of damage had been done, and he had every reason to assume that Winterthur was once again behind it.

She lifted her face and stepped back. Whatever makeup she might have earlier worn had been scoured away. Keeping on his clinical cap, he searched for swelling, but other than puffy eyes from crying he couldn't find anything wrong.

"How did you get here?" he asked, not because it was all that important but because he wanted to satisfy himself that she hadn't blacked out.

"Subway. I've never taken the A train this far before. It was quite an adventure." For the first time since she showed up, she sort of smiled.

"I'll bet." The smile showed no teeth chipped or missing, at least none in the front. Relieved, he searched her red-rimmed eyes. "You need to tell me what happened."

She hesitated, and then shook her head. "I've left him. I've left Drew. That's all that matters, all there is to tell. I waited for him to fall asleep and then I grabbed what I could without having to turn on a light, including Cat, and I left him."

Marc was half-afraid to believe his ears. He'd figured she was weeks, no months, away from making a move, if indeed she ever did, and now suddenly here she was. Whatever Winterthur had done this time, it must be seriously psychotic. And yet other than being upset and wet, she looked more or less all right. "Can I get you something?"

She let out a sharp laugh. "That depends, what do you have? Narcotics, wine . . . "

"I was thinking more along the lines of warm milk. The tryptophan has sleep-inducing properties."

She wrapped her arms around herself as though suddenly registering the draft. "Do you have tea, perhaps?"

"I might be able to rustle up a bag."

If he had any on hand, it was either Lipton or Red Rose, purchased for his mother's last visit and not replenished since. Not the fancy stuff he'd seen her drink before, but at least it would warm her up. Speaking of which . . .

He hesitated and then lifted his arms, pulling the T-shirt over his head and off.

"I'll find you something to wear in a few but for now, put this on." He handed her the shirt, not missing how her eyes widened as they lingered on his chest.

"The shirt off your back even—you are a good Samaritan, aren't you?" she said with a laugh.

"I try." Mindful of how vulnerable she must be despite the stab at humor, he turned quickly away.

She slipped on the T-shirt and followed him into the kitchen. "So this is your place," she said, looking around.

Marc tried seeing his apartment as she must—the herringbone patterned hardwood foyer floor, the broken kitchen tiles and rusted appliances, the temporary blind tacked up to the window in the main room, the adhesive strip on its last leg. Unlike him, Honey was used to "the finer things in life," as his mother would say. Not only finer, but the finest. When push came to shove, would she really be okay with leaving her posh past and Park Avenue apartment to live with him in Washington Heights on a resident's salary? Whoa, that was putting the cart before the horse, more like the whole team of horses. She'd come to him tonight seeking safe haven and not a whole lot else. And yet he could feel her gaze going over his bare shoulders and back, not just curious but almost . . . caressing.

Filling the kettle and setting it on the burner to boil, he said, "Yep, it is. And as you can see, it definitely needs some love." He turned away from the stove.

She managed a small smile. "It seems I may have more time and schedule flexibility than I thought."

Addressing the future, even the foreseeable one, could wait. For now, he focused on the basics. "You need to eat something."

He pulled out a chair for her, one of four set around the oblong table. His apartment was no show place, but it was roomy with an eat-in kitchen, all but unheard of in newer constructions.

Honey hesitated, and then sat. "You sound like my mother."

"Do I? Where are your folks, by the way?"

"My father died when I was six. My mother is . . . back home."

"Where is home?"

Avoiding answering, she gnawed on her lower lip. "Nebraska . . . Omaha."

He never would have guessed. "Nebraska, no shit? What happened to your accent?"

A frown furrowed her forehead. "My accent? What do you mean?"

"You know, how folks talk in *Fargo*."

She rolled her eyes. "*Fargo* was set in Minnesota, not Nebraska."

He shrugged, hiding a smile. "Same difference."

"Spoken like a native New Yorker. All of you act as though this city were the epicenter of the universe. Then again, I suppose it is." She sent him a wistful smile. "So what is on the menu at Chez Sandler?"

"I thought you said you weren't hungry."

"Actually what I said is you sound like my mother—which you do."

He grinned. "She must be a very wise woman."

He said it to be humorous, but she obviously didn't take it that way. Her gaze shuttered. "Actually, she's rather narrow-minded in her beliefs, but otherwise a very nice woman. Oh, and she picks bad men, though considering how I've spent the last six years, I'm not really in a position to be throwing stones."

There was definitely a story there, but like future plans, it too could wait. "So back to breakfast: eggs and bacon, bagels and lox—pick your artery-clogging poison."

"Don't do as I do. Do as I say?" she suggested gamely.

"Something like that."

"I don't suppose you have any peanut butter?"

Peanut butter, that was easy. "I think I have a jar here somewhere, along with some grape jelly." He just might join her. A full belly always helped him to think more clearly. At the moment, he didn't have a clue what to do with or about her.

She made a face. "I don't do jelly."

"Seriously? No PB&J, not ever?"

She shook her head. "Never. I'm quite adamant about it."

He smiled. "I can see that."

"Have you any Fluff?"

"Any . . . Sorry?

"Marshmallow Fluff. It comes in jars, giant-sized jars. It's like biting into a cloud, a sticky, gooey cloud. I love it."

"Where do you buy this . . . Fluff?"

She paused as if considering the question. "Supermarkets, I suppose. I wouldn't imagine most bodegas stock it."

"I can see you're a woman of very . . . discerning tastes, Ms. Gladwell."

For whatever reason, his comment seemed to amuse her. At last those beautiful lips broke into a true "Honey" smile. "You, Dr. Sandler, have no idea." Her gaze skimming over his pectorals left no doubt that she was no longer talking about sandwiches.

"Maybe I don't, but I'd . . . I'd like to. Now that you've left Winterthur, maybe we can take some time and—"

Behind him, the kettle blared. Marc reached around and switched off the burner.

"Don't let's say another word," Honey broke in, her smile gentle. "Right now what I want is to eat peanut butter sandwiches and drink tea and cuddle until we go to sleep. Is . . . is that all right?"

Marc nodded. His unfinished question was way out of line. He had no right to press her. The last thing he wanted was for her to think she had to trade sex for safety. What she needed right now was a friend.

Pouring boiled water into a mug, he watched her out of the corner of his eye. "Yes, Honey, that sounds perfectly fine."

✳✳✳ ✳✳✳

Honey hadn't thought she'd be able to eat a bite, not now or ever again. Her throat still stung from the mouthwash she'd used to gargle. Even with the bottle emptied, she hadn't felt close to clean. But she'd surprised herself, devouring her peanut butter sandwich and most of Marc's, which he'd also made without jelly in deference to her sensibilities. Though not necessary, the sweet gesture warmed her. They were just finishing when Cat found his way into the kitchen and joined them. Because of Drew, he'd missed not one but two feedings, which could be dangerous given how little he still was. Honey had considered grabbing the formula from the refrigerator before going, but she'd been too afraid of waking Drew. Once he'd . . . finished with her, he'd hit the scotch pretty hard, too hard to manage getting himself home. Honey had huddled on her side of the bed, biding her time, waiting for his snoring.

Fortunately Marc came through yet again, this time with a jar of chicken-flavored baby food left over from his niece's last visit. They stirred a little warm water into the mix, and Cat licked it greedily from Honey's finger before falling asleep in her lap. A shallow foil pan and some potting soil hastily dumped inside would serve as a litter box until morning.

Though she was still probably in shock, Honey didn't feel so much numb anymore as she did drowsy. And, against all odds, strangely content. Even though she was seeing Marc's apartment for the first time, she couldn't help feeling as though she'd finally come home. Watching him clear their cups and plates, the low light glinting on the sculpted planes of his breathtaking chest, the same chest that had represented safety and shelter when she'd first shown up, she owned that she wanted to do a great deal more with him than cuddle.

They left Cat snoozing on an old dish towel and got up to go to bed. Slipping her hand into Marc's felt like the most natural thing in the world. Fingers threaded with his long ones, she let him lead her through the warren of high-ceilinged rooms to his bedroom. An antique four-poster sat in its center.

Stopping at the foot of the bed, he slid his hand from hers. Earnest hazel eyes scoured her face. "What I started to say earlier . . . I was out of line. It's important to me that you know you're safe here. I'm not going to force myself on you or press you in anyway. We can get in bed and cuddle if that's what you want, or I can grab a blanket and sleep in the next room. I'm good either way."

"I don't want to cuddle." As soon as her words were out, his face fell. "And I don't want you to sleep in another room, either. I want you to stay and make love to me. That is, if you want to."

"If I want to?" He stared as though he couldn't quite believe her. "I haven't been able to stop thinking about you since I saw you that night at the hospital. I tried, but I couldn't. When I first saw you tonight standing at my door, I thought I might be dreaming."

Honey blinked back tears, happy ones this time. "I feel like I'm the one who's been dreaming, sleepwalking through the last six years. It took you to wake me up."

How could she have known that a night that had held so many horrors could end so sweetly? In the midst of it all, envisioning Marc was all that had sustained her. Wearing his too-big T-shirt, she slid into his open arms. Despite the difference in their heights and sizes, they fit like two halves of a Chinese puzzle.

Marc didn't paw and pull and rush at her as Drew had done. Instead he undressed her as if he—they—had all the time in the world, as if she were someone important and precious and *worthy*. Once he got off the T-shirt, he undressed her button by button, sliding each seed stud through its loop, then taking hold of the zipper tab at the back of her dress and drawing it slowly down. Cool air brushed across her bare shoulders, the tops of her breasts, her torso. The dress whispered downward and then off, leaving her standing stripped down to her La Perla bra and panties.

"You're so damned beautiful," he said, staring down at her. Lowering his head, he sprinkled soft kisses along the swell of her breasts.

"So are you," she answered honestly. Overcome with gratitude and tenderness, she laid a hand along his cheek.

He looked up into her eyes and smiled. "I guess we both just have good taste, huh?"

Honey smiled back. "I can't speak for you, but I've finally started to develop some."

A chuckle greeted her too-true quip. Taking her face between his two hands, he kissed her forehead, her closed eyelids, and the tip of her nose before settling his mouth atop hers. His kiss was more urgent than before but every bit as gentle. A sweet, firm tongue probed hers, and then darted away, touching its tip to the roof of her mouth. Strong white teeth nibbled at her lower lip, followed by a thumb stroking across it. Honey sighed and sagged slightly against him. Reaching around, he unclasped her bra.

"Wait, I want to see you, too." She did. She also wanted to break free from the scenario of sex with Drew, the inevitable inequity of being stripped bare while he remained clothed.

He held his arms out from his sides, giving himself over to her. She slid both hands beneath the waistband of his sweatpants. Surprised and delighted to discover he wore nothing underneath, she took a moment to savor the smooth curve of his ass before tugging the garment down. Kicking free of it, he stood naked before her. He was beautiful, even more so than she'd imagined, leanly muscled with a washboard abdomen and powerful arms. She wanted to sip at those flat nipples, nuzzle the dark nests of his pits, bury her face in the bush of his groin and inhale him, take him all in, not because she was being bullied or paid, but because she wanted to. Because this was desire and it had been entirely too long, years, since she'd felt anything close to it.

He eased her down to sit on the side of the bed and floated to the floor, landing on his knees. Caught up as she was, it amazed her that such a big, muscular man could move with such agility and grace.

Unbidden, her thoughts switched back to her last time with Drew. The sullied soles of those expensive, bespoke shoes gagging her. The sharp, thrusting cock crammed down her throat, stealing her breath, her self-respect—her soul. Not satisfied with her kneeling, he'd had her squat instead, her legs open wide with muscles straining, his two fingers rammed up her ass, impaling her in place, prepared to punish her the second she ceased sucking him. None of what he'd done to her that time had left any discernible marks, and yet he'd scarred her as surely, as permanently as if he'd taken a knife to her.

She snapped her thoughts back to the present, this moment, and the beautiful near-naked man kneeling at her feet. At his own volition. For her pleasure! Even though she never once uttered, or even hinted at the dirty little ritual that Drew put her through, he seemed to know instinctively what she wanted—needed.

To be serviced.

"Lie back and let me take care of you."

No man had ever said that to her before, let alone come close to doing, that. Being an escort was the modern day equivalent of being a geisha, and geishas didn't receive pleasure. They gave it without conditions or complaints. Whether sucking cocks, licking balls, or tickling prostates, sex had always, always been work for her. Putting her personal preferences aside, she accommodated nearly every kink. Wall Street bred a tightly wound bunch—and when men like that gave themselves permission to let go, they didn't just unwind. They unraveled. She'd given enemas to those so desperate for release they were poised to implode and peed into the open mouths of those craving humiliation as though it was a new flavor of infused vodka. Still others she'd spanked and sodomized, flogged and "force" fed as they stood stripped down to their birthday suits or diapered as babies.

But what she'd never done before Drew was come. Once their honeymoon phase was over, he'd rarely gone down on her. In the early days he sometimes got impatient—*Babe, you're killing me. Haven't you made it yet?* Later on, he'd become petulant—*I work fucking hard all day. I don't have time for this shit. Can't you just buy a vibrator?* And of course in the last year, he'd become flat-out mean—*You have all fucking day to play with yourself. Now get down on your knees, or else!*

Regardless of his mood, the message was clear. Her body—her pussy—was for his pleasure, not hers.

But with Marc, she sensed things could be different and stay that way—good. If only she could manage to stay with him in the moment.

Honey lay back, stretching her arms above her head, dragging one of the pillows down toward her. Her vagina was the one orifice Drew hadn't in any way breached. Thankful for that, she tented her knees and let her legs fall open, waiting.

She didn't wait long.

Marc rose up on his knees, bracing his palms on either side of the mattress surrounding her. Suddenly his mouth was nowhere and everywhere—her tits, her belly, her mound. He slipped a hand beneath her. A dallying finger circled her anus. She tensed, not with pain but with . . . remembering.

"Stay with me," Marc whispered. "Forget him."

"I am. I *want* to."

"Easy, then, let me help you. Is it okay if I help you? Is that what you still want?"

As always, with Marc the choice was hers. Honey didn't doubt that, despite how far they'd gone, one word from her—no—would see him backing away from the bed and putting on his clothes. Only she didn't want him to go away. She didn't want him to go anywhere. She wanted to be with him, to feel him inside her. She wanted him to fuck her until she forgot she'd ever known a man named Drew.

Honey bit her lip, willing herself to forget the gagging taste of shoe polish and leather and city streets. "Yes, I want it." I want *you*.

Seemingly satisfied, he dipped his head once more. He sipped on her nipples. He stroked her ass. A teasing finger toyed with her anus, this time tracing tiny rings. He glided the finger of his other hand inside her front. A second and finally a third digit followed. It was that day at the IFC all over again, only better, so very much better. Heat pooled. The tingling built to a deeper tension. Flexing brought her bucking hard against his hand. He could have stopped there and coaxed her to coming, only he didn't. Instead, he dropped his head, brushing his unshaven cheek along her inner thigh. Spreading her wider, he blew on her clit. Hot shivers bolted through her. Her toes curled. Her pussy pulsed. Deft fingers sank inside her again, all three at once. A tongue's point probed her channel, touched the hood of her clit, swirled lavish circles around the kernel.

Honey bit her bottom lip, straining for release before he might tire and want to stop. "I'm sorry, I'm so close. This . . . I shouldn't take much longer."

He pulled his head up to look at her, his expression incredulous. "Take as long as you want. I could do this all night."

Boast though that no doubt was, he didn't seem to be suffering. Taking in his darkened eyes and wet mouth, she admitted he seemed to be enjoying himself.

"All night?"

"Okay, maybe not all night—I suspect you'd start to get pretty sore, and I do have morning rounds, so I'll have to sleep eventually—but how does the next forty-five minutes to an hour sound?"

"That sounds . . . " Honey broke off. Beyond *amazing*, she wasn't sure what to say.

"You want to spend that time talking or—"

Her clit fluttered. Her skin skittered. She was about to come. Marc sucked her into his mouth—and Honey imploded. Her buttocks clenched, her clit buzzed. Waves of dizzying release rolled over her.

Marc eased himself upright. In a moment of panic, she thought he might be headed for the sofa after all. She whimpered and reached for him, wondering what she'd done to turn him off or, worse, disgust him, relaxing only when she saw that his retreating steps took him no farther than the nightstand. A drawer slid out and then back in. He returned, tearing open a gold foil condom packet. She almost stopped him to say she was on the pill, but then she thought of all the times she'd been with Drew and held her peace. Who knew how many women besides his wife he'd been with over the years? Until she got tested, they'd better play things safe.

He sheathed himself, the condom gliding over a cock that wasn't only full and thick but beautifully, exquisitely shaped. Positioning himself over her, he fitted himself against her. Impatient, Honey lifted her hips, driving him inside her. Still wet from her orgasm, her body seemed to inhale him, welcoming him into her sticky heat. She groaned. She thought she was done with coming but suddenly she wasn't so certain. Wanting to take him as deeply as he could possibly go, she lifted her legs higher, wrapping them about his torso. Marc pulled out and thrust into her again—and again. Every time he left and reentered her, she was certain it would be the last, only it wasn't. He had amazing stamina, greater control than any of her previous partners. Perspiration filmed the backs of her knees. A bead of sweat slid between her breasts. She looked up into his eyes. Male pride shone from them, but she thought she saw something more there, too. Holding his gaze, she contracted and then released her inner muscles, cinching him tightly inside, squeezing him as if with a gentle, milking fist.

The sensation sent both of them over the edge. Marc groaned. Penis pumping, he released himself into the prophylactic. Honey wrapped her arms about his big, shuddering body and held him tight. The contractions ebbed, and he relaxed against her. Neither spoke. Other than their breathing and the occasional car driving by below, the room was silent. Honey stroked his back, her fingers slipping down his sweat-slick spine to his taut butt. With each caress, gratitude flooded her. Despite all that Drew had done to her, she wasn't ruined. She could still orgasm—multiple times, in fact. Her only regret was that Marc had to wear a condom. Now that they were finally lovers, she wanted him in every way, no holds barred. Having him spray inside her, going about her day leaking his essence, were primal pleasures predicated on her test results coming back clean. If they didn't, if she was positive . . . She couldn't let herself think about that, not now.

Instead she coaxed him to move with her to the top of the bed, where a bounty of pillows awaited. Light filtering through the window had them turning away onto their sides. Skin to skin, they tucked up together, their bodies fitting like two happy spoons. More content than she could ever remember being, Honey closed her eyes.

And fell almost immediately asleep.

❖❖❖ ❖❖❖

Later that morning, Marc propped himself up on one elbow and looked down at Honey. Makeup-free and hair a glorious mass of brown and butterscotch-colored tangles, she'd never looked more beautiful. "Okay, 'fess up. Honey Gladwell isn't your real name, is it?"

Lying against the banked pillows, she hesitated. "Why do you say that?"

They'd had amazing sex, the mind-blowing, soul-melding sort. The least she could do was to tell him her real name. "C'mon. Honey Gladwell and Holly Golightly are too similar for even a strictly action-adventure movie guy like me to miss."

She drew a long breath and blew it out. "Hortense Gustafson."

"Get outta here."

"I know it's not terribly lyrical. Hortense was my grandmother's name, and as for the surname . . . I'm mostly Scandinavian with bits of Polish and German thrown in." She lifted her face. "What about you?"

He got the question so rarely that he actually had to take a moment and think about it. Most people labeled him as African-American and left it at that. "My father's people were from Cuba. My great grandparents on my mom's side came from Barbados. At some point, everyone met up in Spanish Harlem and, well, here I am."

"That makes you—"

"An Ancestry.com nightmare?" He laughed.

She swatted at his arm. "I was going to say exotic."

"Exotic, huh? I like it. It sounds a lot more upscale than *mutt*."

She rolled her lovely eyes, puffy no more, though a few hours' sleep was all they'd gotten. "Well, don't let it go to your head."

"Which one?"

He grinned as she got the joke—and cut her eyes downward. Seeing the erection tenting his part of the sheet, she lifted her gaze to his and gulped. "Already?"

His short refractory period was nothing special, given his young age, but having spent the last six years with an alcoholic she probably wasn't used to quick comebacks. "Yeah, but if you're not . . . I mean that's cool. It's not a contest—or a race. We have time now." The last thing he wanted was for her to think he was some kind of sex addict, especially given all she'd been through.

She hesitated, moistening her mouth. "Do we . . . have time, Marc?"

Not really sure what she was asking, he nodded nonetheless. "Sure we do. I mean now that you're staying here—"

Her face lit. She pushed back from the pillows and sat upright. "I'm staying? Really!?!"

Granted, he might not be the greatest of communicators, but Marc had thought that much was settled. Honey was his girl, or at least after last night he hoped she would want to be. They'd spent months growing a solid friendship, fighting the sexual tension pulling at them. Now the stars were finally aligned, the timing right. Winterthur was history, a dark cloud already relegated to Honey's past. Finally free and clear to come together, they'd made love—not some furtive fondling in a darkened movie theater, but honorably, properly, *leisurely* in his home and bed. They'd even adopted a kitten together—well, sort of.

"Of course you're staying for as long as you like." Forever had a nice ring to it, but he feared saying so might well frighten her off.

"Are you sure? Because, I mean, I have some friends I could probably stay with."

As if after last night he was going to relegate her to spending weeks, maybe even months, couch surfing. He opened his mouth to say as much when it struck him. Other than the window dresser for Ralph Lauren, she hadn't mentioned any friends.

"Of course I'm sure. But you know, you've never told me about your friends. Maybe I could . . . meet them sometime." Although if they'd known about her living situation and the abuse she was taking, they didn't sound much like "friends" to him.

Her face took on that wary look he'd hoped last night might have banished. "Oh, I don't know about that."

"Why not? Ashamed of me?"

The question, though jokingly posed, was grounded in past hurts. She wasn't the only one who'd made herself vulnerable last night.

"Of course not! It's just that . . . I'm not sure you'd have all that much in common."

"Why is that?"

She bit her lip. "Well, for one, you're a doctor and you've always seemed like a pretty . . . straight arrow."

"And they're not?" He hesitated. She barely drank and he'd never seen any indication that she did drugs. Still, had he missed something?

"It depends on the definition."

He sat up straighter. "Why don't we start with your definition?"

"Well, they're not into drugs, if that's what you're implying."

That was a relief. "I'm not implying anything. I'm asking." He reached out, stroked a finger along her jaw, stopping at that sweet spot he couldn't seem to get enough of kissing. "Baby, we didn't just go to bed last night. We made love. I don't know about you, but I'd like to think that meant something."

"Of course it did—does. It's only . . . "

"Whatever it is, you can trust me."

"Liz, Peter, Brian, Sarah—they're all former adult entertainers."

Wow. Whatever he'd braced himself for, it wasn't that. "Okay. How um . . . did you meet?"

"Online."

Shit! "Like in a . . . chat room or something?" If so, what was she into?

She shook her head. "Not in the way you're thinking. FATE is a weekly meet up. We get together on Monday nights, have coffee, and talk about what's going on in our lives." She blew out a breath.

"But if they're all into . . . adult entertainment—"

"*Retired* from adult entertainment."

"Okay, retired, but then how do you fit in?"

For what should be a fairly straightforward question, she hesitated just a little too long for comfort—his. Finally she answered, "What do you think being a mistress means? You have an audience of one, but it's still an audience, and your livelihood depends on keeping him entertained."

Marc wasn't sure what to say to that. Instead he asked, "What do they think of Winterthur?"

"They only met him once, at Peter's wedding. I brought him as my date, and I think it's safe to say they all hated him."

That, at least, was in their favor.

"They think I'm a stylist."

"I'd still like to meet them—when you feel ready, of course."

"O-okay." The next several seconds were taken up with her plucking the pills from the worn blanket. "It's just that they don't know that Drew was ever anything more than my 'boyfriend.' They think I'm a stylist."

Few stylists Marc had ever met dressed like Honey did. Rather than burst her bubble and say so, he held his peace and let her talk.

"The group is for people who've left their pasts behind to live and work in the mainstream. Being . . . taken care of in that way is a major breach of the rules."

"Your secret's safe with me," Marc said, skeptical that Honey's "secret" was all that. If her friends had a brain between them, they must know. He reached for her hand. Carrying it to his lips, he turned it over and pressed a kiss to the soft palm. "You're safe with me, too, Honey. This apartment is your home for as long as you want it to be."

Big brown eyes searched his. "And Cat's, too?"

So much for returning the kitten to the rescuer in Union Square—like that was ever going to happen. "Yes, and Cat, too," he conceded, knowing it was useless to even try to appear to hold any lines with her. He was mush in her hands, and they both knew it. "Just be sure that whatever decorating you decide to do is kitten-proof."

"I get to decide!"

If things played out the way he hoped, in the future Honey would be deciding a lot of things to do with the both of them, starting with what kind of engagement ring she wanted. But for now . . .

"Of course you get to decide. I want you to decide things. I want you to feel like you have a say. So, are we good?"

Jubilant, Honey launched herself at his chest. Wrapping her arms around him, she angled her face upward and answered with a kiss. Drawing back, her brown eyes beamed into his. "Yes, darling, we're better than good. We're divine."

✳✳✳ ✳✳✳

Midway through their monthly Friday night supper, Marc's mother looked up from pouring more sweet tea into his glass and asked, "So when are you planning to fill me in on this new girl you're seeing?"

Marc froze in forking up his food. He'd known the question would come eventually, even soon—just not *this* soon. Stalling while he gathered his thoughts, he popped the bite of cornmeal-battered cod into his mouth even though he wasn't a seafood fan. Friday night suppers at his mother's always meant fish for the main course. A devout Christian, she'd been serving fish on Fridays since he could remember, long before "Meatless Mondays" had come into vogue or even been heard of. Thankfully she also served sides that he really liked, such as today's au gratin potatoes, creamed spinach, and sweet cornbread. Judging from the aroma wafting into the dining room from the open kitchen, he'd lay down odds that the pie she'd baked, from scratch, of course, was either sweet potato or rhubarb. The comfort food, invariably fried, doused in heavy cream, and drenched in butter, wasn't heart-healthy fare—he'd never in a million years recommend it to his patients—but it had an undeniably soothing effect on his soul.

"What makes you think I'm seeing someone?"

It was, admittedly, an undeniably feeble attempt to fend her off until he could figure out what answer to give. Maternal radar might not have much of any scientific evidence to support it, but Marc would swear his mother possessed a sixth sense so far as he and his elder brother, Anthony, were concerned.

She shot him The Look, the face that said, if not in so many words: *Boy, why are you messing with me?* It was an expression he'd seen countless times over the years. As always, being on the receiving end of it made him feel as if he was physically shrinking. Suddenly he was thirteen again, taken to the mat—and the principal's office—for cutting school to spend the spring day skateboarding with, according to his mother, his "shiftless, no account" friends. The principal had been circumspect, his mother less so. She'd made him toe the line—a hard one at that. Since he liked being outdoors so much, he could spend the next month of weekends helping with cleanup and plantings in nearby Fort Tryon Park. The skateboard, which he'd paid for with his own money, was promptly donated to their church's thrift shop. In its place, she'd given him a gift-wrapped stack of secondhand books, classic greats of American literature: Mark Twain's *The Adventures of Tom Sawyer*, Ralph Ellison's *Invisible Man,* and Maya Angelou's *I Know Why the Caged Bird Sings*. "You can take these to the park, sit yourself down on a bench, and read," she'd said, ruffling his hair.

Her steady stare brought him back to the present. "You're freshly shaven even though it's your day off, you look more at peace than I've seen you in years, and unless I'm mistaken, those are cat hairs on the front of your sweater—and I know for a fact you don't care for cats."

So maybe she didn't have extrasensory perception—maybe she was more of a mentalist. Surrendering, Marc set down his fork on the side of his plate. "What would you like to know?"

Done eating, she steepled her hands as if at prayer. "Why don't you start by telling me her name?" she suggested, expression softening now that she'd won her way.

A simple, straightforward question, easy to answer, or at least it should be. But with Honey, everything was the opposite of simple, complicated as hell, down to her name. Hortense Gustafson or Honey Gladwell—really, who was she?

"She goes by Honey."

Raised eyebrows met the admission. "Honey? It sounds like a name for a strip—"

"But her given name is Hortense." He grabbed for his iced tea glass and took a deep drink to ease his dry mouth.

Her eyebrows lowered and her eyes warmed. "That's a fine name. She should use it. You don't hear of all that many Hortenses these days. Her people must be very traditional."

Marc nearly spat out the sip of tea he'd just stared to swallow. "Traditional" in his mother's "book" counted as the highest praise. If she so much as suspected that Honey's "people" weren't blood relations but friends who were former adult entertainers, she'd "turn up her toes," as his Aunt Edna was fond of saying. Other than her mention of a mother, apparently still in Omaha, Honey hadn't spoken of any family. Her "FATEs," as she called them, sounded more like close-knit siblings than support group members. Marc was still waiting for an invitation to meet them. Maybe he expected too much too soon. She'd been at his place not quite a week. Still, he couldn't stop wishing she'd take the proverbial plunge and let him all the way in.

"You two serious?"

Again Marc hesitated. "Honestly, Ma, I'm not sure. I know I am."

Her mother gave an injured sniff. "She must know how fortunate she is to find you. Why, look at you: handsome, good-hearted, and God-fearing—at least you'd better still be—not to mention whip smart—a *doctor*! If she's looking for someone better, he ain't out there."

"It's not that . . . She uh . . . recently ended a long-term relationship."

He sensed rather than saw her shoulders stiffen. "She divorced?"

Marc hid a smile. Until recently, Honey had been the longtime mistress of a married man, but to his best knowledge she'd never tied the knot. "No, Ma, she's single, never married."

She relaxed visibly, her shoulders descending to their more or less normal position. "Well, that's a relief." She hesitated, turning a teaspoon over before adding, "What does she do for a profession?"

"She's a photographer," he answered without thinking.

Shit, he'd just lied to his mother. He hadn't meant to. Up to now, he'd prided himself on never having lied to his mother. Sure, there were things he hadn't told her, things that would have been inappropriate to relay and were none of her business now that he was an adult. But those were sins of omission, if even sins at all. Outright lying to the woman who'd borne and raised him was a big breach in his book. But the answer had slid out as if his brain was on autopilot and now it was too late to take it back. Thing was, his answer might not be true—it wasn't—but it *felt* true. With her keen eye for detail, for artistic composition, Honey *was* a photographer. She just hadn't owned it yet.

Evidently his answer pleased her. Her tentative smile spread into a broad one. "So when are you going to bring her around so I can meet her?"

It was yet another totally predictable, totally reasonable question for which he had no good answer, not even a good guess. "Honestly, I can't say right now. We're taking things slow."

That was the truth—mostly. He and Honey were taking things slow, in every way but in bed. The sex was mind-blowing; Honey an exquisite, mesmerizing lover. But even in the midst of grooving on all the good loving he was getting, he couldn't shake the sense that she was always acting out a role, playing some fictional part. Just once he'd like to take her in his arms, and to his bed, and know that it was the real *her* he was making love with, not some glamorized imposter.

"Let's . . . give it a while."

"All right, I won't push—for now. But know my door, and heart, are always open."

"I do know that, Ma—and thanks."

"Speaking of open hearts, I'm going to visit Anthony this week. Why not come with me? It's been . . . a while."

A while—two years and four months, not that Marc was keeping track. Anthony, his once adored big brother now doing prison time for possession with intent to distribute a Class A drug—crack—was a sore subject between them. As always, she bided her time before bringing him up—though she did usually wait to cut the pie first. His ongoing rift with Tony must be weighing on her mind.

"I don't think so but . . . tell him I said hi," he added, a pretty big concession since he hadn't so much as written since the conviction.

"Why not tell him yourself?"

"Because I have better things to do than spend my day off riding Metro North to go see someone I have absolutely nothing to say to."

The pained look she sent him was like a knife twisting in his gut, but Marc held firm. His mother's wasn't the only heart Tony had trampled on. Growing up, Marc had worshipped his big, athletic older brother, had wanted to be absolutely like him.

Not so now.

"Then maybe you could try listening instead."

Hungry no longer, Marc pushed his plate aside. "What, and turn the other cheek so he can slap that one, too?"

It was bad enough Tony had been dealing crack—on school property, no less! That he'd done so on behalf of one of Upper Manhattan's worst gangs made his actions not only reprehensible but unforgivable, to Marc at least. It was the same gang that had terrorized them as children, whose members had knocked down their Aunt Edna, stolen her grocery money, and left her passed out with a cut on her forehead so deep it had required stitches and an overnight hospital stay. The same gang that had blighted their multi-block area not for years but decades, shaking down local shopkeepers and terrorizing everyone in their radius, the elderly especially. They'd even taken credit for the torture and killing of several pets in retaliation against residents who'd filed complaints with the police. That Tony had allied himself with such scum of the earth—how could Marc possibly push past that and be brothers with him again?

"You're going to have to forgive him someday, if not for his sake, then yours. This anger you carry around inside you, it's not good for your body—or your soul."

She was right. Seething silence wasn't good for him. Maybe he would find a way to forgive Tony someday—but that day was most definitely not now.

He pushed back his chair and got up. "I have to get back. Hort . . . Honey's waiting."

She rose up beside him. "That girl's really gotten under your skin, hasn't she?"

Were it anyone else asking, Marc would have been vehement in his denial. He'd only known Honey for few months, a hiccup of time, and yet he was reasonably certain he was in love with her. That he couldn't tell how deeply her feelings ran held him back from saying so. Was he only a better alternative to Drew, or was he something, somebody, more? Somebody she might see herself making a life with?

But in this case, the person posing the question that wasn't really a question was also the one who'd diapered and disciplined him; who'd seen him through schoolyard bullying, an epic bout of chicken pox, and the hot hormonal mess of puberty; who despite working multiple jobs to make ends meet had somehow found a way to make it to nearly every spelling bee, school pageant, and science fair he'd ever participated in. Whether he was riding high or sinking low fast, his mother was always there to support him, dispensing wise words and warm smiles and huge hugs when he needed them most. And though she might not exactly have paranormal powers, her barometer for detecting bullshit was absolutely faultless.

Turning back, Marc knew better than to mince words. "Yes, Ma, she sure has."

Chapter Seven

"For me the only things of interests are those linked to the heart."
—Audrey Hepburn

Marc came home from his mother's to find Honey waiting. Only instead of the fabric swatches and paint chips he'd anticipated, she greeted him with candles, champagne, chocolate-covered strawberries— and her nearly naked self.

Draped across two chairs, she was topless except for a men's silk tie. Shoulders back, legs crossed, and gaze sultry, she greeted him with a slow, sexy scarlet smile. "Like it?" she asked, lifting the tie's tail and giving it a twirl. "I got it for you."

On the threshold of the candle-lit dining room, Marc stopped in his tracks, his mouth sucked dry of any saliva, his heart rate ratcheting. Along with the tie, she wore a black thong, black garter belt, black stockings, and black fuck-me pumps. Her hair was pinned high in the front but left loose in the back, waves cascading over one slender shoulder.

Like it? He'd never seen anyone more stunningly sexy in the whole of his life.

Moistening his mouth, he crossed into the room and moved toward her. *Play it cool, Sandler,* he counseled himself, feeling anything but. Fact was he'd never felt hotter—or hornier—in all of his life, and not only because a beautiful topless woman, Honey, presented herself for his pleasure.

Finding his voice, he finally managed to answer, "I'm not really a tie guy . . . but it certainly looks good on you."

"It's Hermès," she informed him, turning the tie so that it hung over her back, giving him an unobstructed view of those beautiful, rose-tipped breasts, breasts that he now knew fitted perfectly in his palms.

Mark swallowed—hard. No doubt about it, this girl was definitely getting under his skin. "Expensive?" he said, thinking not only of the tie.

"Very." Perfect half moon brows lifted. She inhaled and exhaled exquisitely slowly, no doubt knowing what the rise and fall of her diaphragm did to her breasts—and him. "I popped into their store on Madison today."

Jesus, when he handed her his credit card that morning, he had in mind a trip to Home Depot for housewares and maybe a toiletries run at Duane Reade, not a retail therapy excursion to fancy European fashion designers. "Just like that, huh?"

She nodded. "I had a gift card I've been saving for a special occasion."

In the midst of his horniness and hard-on, Marc stiffened. "Look, I appreciate the thought, but I don't want you buying me stuff with . . . *his* money."

A tiny frown appeared between her eyes. "The gift card was sent to me by a . . . previous employer. They send all the girls . . . employees, past and present, one every Christmas."

What kind of company sent that caliber of gift card to its former employees? "That's certainly . . . hospitable," he said, making a mental note to revisit the issue of finances, and previous "employers," later when he wasn't the only one with his clothes on.

For now, he checked out the prettily set table. A bottle of Veuve Clicqot had been opened and placed in a bucket of ice, two full fluted glasses at the ready, along with a pretty glass dish displaying the chocolate-covered strawberries.

Following his gaze, her smile widened. "I know you already ate, but I thought we could have . . . *dessert* together."

"Are we celebrating something specific?" he fished, wondering what occasion he might have forgotten. Valentine's Day had already passed. So had her birthday. His didn't come around for another several months, leaving . . .

"It's our one week anniversary."

Right, shit, their one week anniversary—and Marc had spent most of it having dinner with his mother. And now he'd come home empty handed without so much as a bouquet of bodega flowers. Obviously he had some serious brushing up to do in the boyfriend department.

But if Honey was pissed at him, she hid it well. "But there's more."

Taking in the scene, Marc didn't know how much *more* he could take. In just one week, he'd gone from living like a workaholic monk to coming home each night and indulging in hot, sweaty sex with a drop-dead gorgeous, relentlessly sexy woman who, he was increasingly sure, was the love of his life. And now that same woman sat with bare breasts and black stockings waiting on him to find his game and make his move. What *more* could he possibly want—let alone handle?

Judging from Honey's cat-that-swallowed-the-canary expression, he was about to find out. "I got my test results back today, and I'm perfectly healthy, totally clean."

Doctor though he was, she'd been more worried about it than he; still he was elated. There was nothing like a lab report to provide close to foolproof peace of mind. "Baby, that's great! I'm so happy."

"Me, too. And you know what it means?"

He did, or at least he was pretty sure he did. Still, not wanting to come off as crass, he held his tongue, waiting on her to supply The Answer.

"No more condoms!"

Marc grinned. *No more condoms* suddenly seemed like the three most beautiful words in the English language. "What are we waiting for?" He crossed to the table to pick her up—and carry her into the bedroom.

She stretched out a slender arm, staying him in mid-step. "Not so fast. We have time now, remember? Take a seat and have some champagne." She gestured to the remaining chair.

Once things had happened for them, they'd moved very quickly. She was right to expect a little romancing, and she'd already gone to a lot of trouble to set the scene. The least he could do was show up to the party.

Marc sat, his cock so noticeably hard he almost felt as if he did indeed have a third leg.

"Better," she said, her voice coming out almost as a purr.

Given that he was more or less on eye level with her breasts, and had a bird's eye view of the shadowed space between her slightly parted legs, a vigorous nod sufficed as his answer.

He picked up one of the champagne flutes and passed it to her, then took the remaining one for himself. "To the hands-down best week of my life," he said and meant it, saluting her with his glass.

She took a sip of the sparkling wine and set the glass aside. "The tie isn't the only thing I have for you."

Marc might not always be Mr. Smooth, but he had a pretty good idea of where this was going. "Oh, well, then I guess you'll have to show me."

"I will. It's more of a . . . performance art piece."

Marc grabbed his glass and downed half of it in one greedy, thirsting swallow. "I love performance art."

"So do I, though I'm more of an . . . exhibitionist than an audience member."

He swiped a hand across his brow. Jesus, when had it gotten so stuffy in here?

She took one of the strawberries from the dish and slowly dragged the peak of the fruit across her lips. "Hmm," she moaned, taking a tiny nibble.

Watching her, Marc felt his mouth drain dry. He was tempted to pour more champagne, but the "show" Honey was putting on deserved his full attention.

Candlelight flickered over her, accentuating the smooth porcelain perfection of her skin, not only her face but also her entire body. The slender hand holding the strawberry lowered to her right breast. Holding his gaze, she circled the fruit around her right nipple, again and again, leaving a faint chocolate stain. Watching her repeat the motion with her other breast, Marc felt his groin tighten and his heart rate ratchet to the roof.

Watching her, he got why suits such as Winterthur had paid top dollar for the privilege of passing a few hours between her legs—because she was worth it, so worth it. Gone was the frightened woman-child who needed someone to take care of her. In her place was a dark goddess, a *sex* goddess, capable of bringing mere mortals such as him to their knees with the lifting of one perfectly plucked and penciled brow. She wasn't only beautiful. She was a force of nature, impossibly, crazily charismatic, irresistibly desirable.

Tossing the strawberry into the glass of champagne, she looked over at him and asked, "Are you liking your present so far?"

God, *yes!*

Marc settled for a mute nod. Riveted, he couldn't take his eyes off her. He didn't *want* to take his eyes off her. Even with a pretty solid expectation of what was probably coming next, he found himself holding back his breath, on the edge of his seat.

Her long, stocking-clad legs parted. Inch by inch, she revealed a little more, and then a little more of herself. Feeling as though he were peeking through a portal to a sexy surreal reality, Marc leaned closer. Musk rose up to meet him. Though it was too dim for him to see, the peaty scent told him she must be not only damp. She must be drenched.

She widened her legs, stretching the tight wisp of covering black lace to what must be its limit. The split crotch spread open. Rose-pink nether lips revealed their glory. A budding clit seemed to beg for his tongue's attention.

Honey reached down. Holding his gaze, she parted the delicate folds, holding herself open as if for his inspection. "Do you like it? Is it all right?"

All right? It was beautiful, *fucking* beautiful, and so was she.

"Shall I show you more pink?"

Marc's mouth was so dry he could scarcely speak. Gathering what saliva he could, he managed to answer. "Yes, show me more."

She did, opening herself even wider for him, so wide he wondered that it didn't hurt. But then she was very wet and obviously very relaxed, entirely comfortable with her sexuality and her body. Milky moisture leaked from her channel. Mark yearned to bury his face between her legs and lap it up.

"Touching myself here feels so good, I don't want to wait any longer. Would it be all right with you if I play with my pussy a little?"

A little or a lot, either way Marc was on board. "G-go for it."

She did, sliding not one, not two, but three fingers inside. Making a mini fist of her hand, she worked them in deep. Suddenly she shuddered, her body thrown back against the chair, her head knocking against the wood though she didn't seem to mind or even notice. But then she wasn't putting on any show now, Marc was sure of it. Her reaction, her pleasure, was one hundred percent real.

Just as he was sure he couldn't hold off much—any—longer. His cock was so brick hard he couldn't say how he was going to get his zipper down without breaking it. His balls felt full to bursting. He shot up from the table, overturning his half finished champagne and sending it soaking into the cloth. Thinking it was a good thing they hadn't begun to redecorate yet, he didn't spare the precious time to right it. Instead he rounded the table to Honey. Her hand fell away, revealing cream-coated fingers, the same damp digits that she curved about his neck when he lifted her. Happy to have her mark him, he carried her over to the kitchen counter and set her down atop. Burying his face in her breasts, he tongued the chocolate from her nipples. But Marc had always preferred savory to sweet. Honey's pussy was the best he'd ever fucked or tasted. He lifted her right hand and slid her fragrant fingers into his mouth.

Honey's eyes widened, as did her legs. Stepping between them, he rolled his zipper down. His cock sprang free, so hot and hard it seemed to sear him. Sliding one hand beneath her as cushion, he used the other to guide himself to her. He pushed hard, loosing himself in pink lips and black lace, sticky wetness and musky heat. Unsheathed, his every sensation seemed amplified. He pulled out and entered her again— and again—each thrust carrying him that much closer to the Promised Land. And Honey as well. She leaned back, braced her weight on her palms, and banded her legs about him. The angle felt amazing; the knowledge that he would come inside her making it seem almost as if this were their first time. Torn, Marc couldn't wait to climax, and yet he also wanted to stretch out this moment to last forever.

But he was a mortal man made of flesh and blood, and watching her turn herself on had taken its toll. He couldn't hold out forever, or even much longer. As if reading his mind, Honey bucked against him, fast and hard. At the same time, her inner muscles wrapped around him, squeezing and releasing until he couldn't say where his body ended and hers began.

Not that it mattered. Just as their mouths had matched from their very first kiss, their bodies moved in perfect unison. Marc thrust hard and came, spraying his seed inside her, waves of pleasure breaking over him. Honey followed. Falling back onto her hands, she let out a scream. Even in the midst of orgasming, she couldn't seem to get enough. She pushed up with her pelvis, covering him to the hilt, her gyrating hips demanding nothing less than all of him. Marc gave it. Even after he'd spent himself, he stayed inside her, running his hands up and down her back, pressing kisses into the sweet curve of her neck and shoulder.

"Happy anniversary, baby," he said, laying his lips along her ear.

"It was, wasn't it?" Eyes closed, she snuggled against him, her arm loosely wrapped around his waist, her legs framing his.

More content than he could ever remember being, Marc lifted her off the counter and set her on her feet. "There'll be lots more anniversaries to come, I promise. For now, let's go to bed."

✳✳✳ ✳✳✳

Sitting in Liz's living room, her hands laced about a teacup, Honey sent her gaze on a circuit of her FATE group circle: Liz, Brian, Peter, and Sarah. Her attention lingered on the latter, formerly known as the international adult film sensation, Sugar. Now a bestselling author, devoted wife, and mom to Baby Christopher, the curvy, casually dressed blonde with the shining green eyes and soft smile scarcely resembled the stressed-out porn star who'd been on the lam from the press—and a stalker—less than two years ago. Seeing how Sarah had transformed since settling down with Cole was enough to turn even the most committed cynic into a believer in the power of true love.

And then there was the evidence of her own reflection greeting her in the mirror each morning. She might have left her pricey skincare products and cosmetics back at Forty-One Park, along with nearly everything else she owned, but the good loving she was getting from Marc seemed to more than make up for it. She glowed. She only hoped that, like Sarah's, her Happily Ever After in the making could withstand the test of time—and truth.

Knowing it was her turn to speak, she cleared her throat, mouth dry despite the tea she'd sipped steadily since her arrival. "Darlings, I'd like to start by sharing some really good—actually amazing—news. I've . . . met someone, someone wonderful."

Cheers, whistles, and high fives rolled through the room.

Sarah shot upright. "Where, how, *who*?"

"Anybody we would know?" Liz asked.

"Does this mean you broke it off with you know who . . . Jerk Face?" Peter piped up.

Struggling to stay afloat amidst all the enthusiasm, Honey grounded herself with a deep breath before answering, "Yes and yes. You don't know him but you know *of* him. Remember the snoopy doctor I mentioned last winter? Well, I've been . . . seeing him for months now."

"Months!"

"But only as friends until . . . "

"Until?" Brian prompted, mouth full of Oreo cookie, his fifth so far from the tray. With his beanpole body, he could afford the calories.

"Until I walked out on Jerk Face," Honey ended, relieved to get that much at least off her chest.

"Does this mean you'll stop having so many accidents now?" The question, matter-of-fact and yet eerily on the mark, came from Jonathan, Liz's precocious nearly nine-year-old. He must have snuck in a while ago, so quietly no one had noticed—until now.

The room fell silent. Talk about from the mouths of babes! Throat knotting, Honey forced herself to meet the boy's too-knowing eyes. "Yes, sweetheart, it does."

Jonathan shrugged. "Good, then I'm glad."

Liz frowned. "Jonathan, what have I told you about this being 'adult time'?"

He scraped the toe of one sneaker across the carpet. "Either I go to Mrs. Ritter's or to my room."

Liz nodded. "Right, and unfortunately Mrs. Ritter is in Seattle visiting her daughter, which leaves—"

"My room. Okay, okay, I'm going." Pulling a face, he turned to go and despite her discomfort, Honey hid a smile. When Honey first joined FATE, Jonathan hadn't yet turned seven. He was a little boy. At times like this, he seemed more of a miniature man. It was amazing the difference a year or two made to a child's development. She hoped one day to experience that progression more fully with her own child—hers and Marc's.

But as lovely as things were with them, any plans involving a picket-fenced cottage—or more likely, a Brooklyn brownstone—were entirely premature, albeit delicious to think about. They were still learning one another. Despite having been friends for several months, and now lovers, she knew little about Marc beyond the present. Other than his mother and "Aunt Edna," both of whom he obviously adored and respected, he rarely referenced his family. From the old photo album she'd found tucked away in a drawer, she knew he had two sisters, one married with a child, and an older brother whom Honey got the impression was a bit of a black sheep. At one point, he simply stopped appearing in family photos. Had he moved away or, worse, died? The brother was, for whatever reason, a sore subject. When she'd brought him up to Marc, his gaze shuttered and his sexy mouth flattened into a firm line. Honey's desire for secrecy about her own past kept her from probing. Whatever else she was or had been, she was no hypocrite.

Liz's voice brought her back from her reverie. "And no PlayStation until you finish your homework."

Jonathan's head shot up, shaggy bangs flinging free of his face. "Mom!"

Tone even, Liz said, "You know the rules."

"I *hate* rules."

Honey knew just how he felt. All her life she'd despised being told what to do. Ironic that she'd spent her eight years in New York living at the beck and call of others—men. Only recently had she acknowledged how her blurred boundaries had gotten her into trouble as well as kept her there, first as a paid escort and later as Drew's mistress. Both positions had begun with the promise of easy money and a luxurious lifestyle. Likewise, both had proven the adage that "all that glitters is not gold." There was no "gold" in being someone's paid sex companion, just emptiness and loneliness and, ultimately, isolation and fear. Thank God she'd gotten out in time—and had somewhere and someone safe to go to. Marc. Still, she sometimes caught herself wishing they'd met under "normal" circumstances—and more equal footing. Being the damsel in distress to his knight in shining armor had its upside, of course, but she worried he would always see her as someone in need of saving. She had so much yet to prove, not only to him but also to herself. Especially herself.

Trudging footfalls ferried Jonathan from their vicinity. The adults fell silent, collectively waiting for his bedroom door to close. They'd been meeting at Liz's for so long that they all knew her Soho two-bedroom almost as well as she did—the latch on the kitchen cabinet that the super kept promising to replace but never did; the toilet handle that had to be jiggled or else the tank would continue to run; the heat that for some mysterious reason never seemed to make it to a certain corner of the main room. In so many ways, Liz's felt more like "home" than Honey's Park Avenue apartment ever had. And as happy as she was at Marc's, as excited as she was to decorate, as many times as he swore she didn't need to ask his permission about a single detail but could do exactly as she liked, it still felt like "his" place rather than one they'd picked out and shared together. She suspected it always would.

Hearing the confirming click, Honey corralled her courage. "Now that I've shared my good news, I have something else to share: a confession."

Predictably that got everyone's attention. "I haven't been entirely honest with you. In point, I haven't been terribly forthcoming at all."

"About what?" Brian asked. Liz shot him a look and Sarah nudged him with her elbow. "What?" he demanded, darting a clueless look between them.

Rather than reply, Liz turned back to Honey. "Whatever you've done, we're here to help you work through it."

"Faith, *Acceptance*, Trust, and Enlightenment, that's what we're all about, remember?" Sarah added gently. "You certainly gave all those things to me when I needed them most."

"To all of us," Peter added. "So give us a chance to give them back to you."

Honey sighed. "But I've broken our cardinal ground rule, one of the few we have. And once I tell you, I'm afraid you may have a difficult time continuing to accept me as one of you."

They couldn't know it, but their unconditional compassion only made her feel more of a heel than she already did. Unlike her mother, stepfather, or Drew, unlike her previous "friends" and clients in the escort trade, the FATEs only ever saw the best in her. The only other person about whom she could say the same was Marc. He had a way of looking at her that made her feel like the most fascinating, most alluring woman in any room, be it crowded or only the two of them. When, if, she found the courage to come clean with him, could she honestly expect him to feel the same about the person she truly was: a high school dropout who'd whored herself, not once but innumerable times? She supposed that she should look upon this FATE session as a practice run for the total honesty she ultimately owed him.

"What's that?" Brian asked, reaching for cookie number six.

She braced herself with a deep breath. "I've lied."

Peter sent her a look as if to say, *is that all?* "Honey, sweetie, we've all lied. Adult entertainment comes down to the art of illusion, and illusion is all about creating lies and making our clients believe them."

She shook her head. Everyone's niceness really did make confessing that much harder. "Thanks, but what I mean to say is that I've been dishonest—currently—with all of you."

Brian's eyes bugged. "About?"

Suddenly overwhelmed, she was hardly certain where to start. "Everything. I'm a total phony, an unforgiveable fraud. I'm not really a stylist. I never have been." Back in Omaha, her mother had worked off and on as a beautician for various "beauty shops," and Honey had hung around enough to pick up on the basics needed to pass herself off.

"What kind of . . . work do you do?" Peter asked, sounding half afraid to hear her answer.

Honey hesitated. "Until a little over a week ago, I hadn't left the life, not really. Yes, I'd left the escort agency—that much was true. But I only left because one of my clients offered to set me up—as his mistress."

"The one you brought as your date to Peter's wedding?" Sarah asked.

Peter looked predictably appalled. "Jerk Face?"

Honey nodded. "One and the same—Drew Winterthur. For more than six years, he paid for my rent, clothes, food, all of it."

Liz's gaze sharpened. "Am I hearing past tense?"

Throat thickening, Honey nodded. "Things got pretty . . . intense, and I left."

Normally laid-back, Peter looked like he wanted to punch someone. "How intense?"

Honey drew a deep breath. "He has a . . . problem with alcohol—and major anger issues."

Sober for several years, Peter eyed her. "You mean he's an alcoholic?"

From being in the group together, Honey knew that Peter's one sticking point was that, when it came to substance abuse, he had zero tolerance for beating about the bush. He called the situation as he saw it, and he expected the same raw, no holds barred realness from his friends.

This time Honey didn't pause. "Yes, he is. When we first . . . got together, he drank, but no more than any of the other men I . . . dated. Gradually it progressed to the point where he doesn't ever want to stop. And he gets angry, really angry."

Voice gentle, Liz said, "Last winter, you didn't fall down the service stairs, did you?"

"No, I didn't. He . . . he threw me down."

"Oh, Honey!"

The four of them left their seats and closed in on her, not in condemnation but support. Liz stroked her back, reminding Honey of how good a mother's soothing touch could feel. Peter squeezed her hand, his kind blue eyes never leaving her face. Even Brian threw an awkward arm about her, a gesture so sweet and uncharacteristically demonstrative that Honey schooled herself not to mind the crumbs.

It wasn't until Sarah passed her the box of Kleenex that she acknowledged the wetness on her cheeks for what it was: tears. Anticipating their as-yet unspoken questions, she grabbed several tissues and blew her nose.

Tucking the used wad away in her pocket, she said, "I know, I know. How could I let things go so far? Why didn't I walk out at the first sign? I've asked myself those very same questions and there's no good answer other than I lacked courage. I screwed up."

"Hon, don't be so hard on yourself," Peter said, patting the back of her hand.

"He's right," Sarah said. "We're all human. We all see what we want and ignore the rest until something wakes us up—and usually it's not pretty. Believe me, I know a thing or two *thousand* about overlooking red flags. Failing to see what was right under my nose almost got me killed the summer before last."

"I've found that the best thing is to acknowledge the mistake, forgive yourself and anyone else involved, and focus on moving on," Liz added. "A big aspect of coming back from cancer is learning to release things in the past you can't change. Once you do that, it's a lot easier to be more present in the moment."

Honey nodded. It all sounded like great advice and yet . . . "It's just that it came about so . . . gradually. At first the . . . abuse was all verbal—mean-spirited remarks, put-downs in private and sometimes public. Later, we'd argue, and he'd backhand me to keep me in line or pin my arms to prove he could. It was degrading, there'd be maybe a bruise or two, but before last February, he'd never done anything to seriously injure me. I suppose I was only fooling myself, but honestly I never thought things would escalate to that point."

Liz wrapped her arm about Honey's shoulders. "Did I ever mention that this couch folds out into a bed?" She jerked her chin toward the sofa upholstered in zigzagging acid-orange stripes likely from the seventies. Like most of her furniture, it was salvaged from sidewalk throwaways or picked up for pennies from thrift shops. "With Jonathan and me using the living room as my home office, this isn't the quietest of apartments, but it's a safe space, and you're welcome to share it with us for as long as you like."

"My place is a studio and kind of a dump, but you can crash with me for as long as you want," Brian offered, shy-eyed.

Peter piped up. "Pol and I just finished renovating. We have an actual guestroom done all in Ralph Lauren—the fabrics, the paint colors, you name it—thanks to my discount. In the spirit of false modesty not being modesty at all, I outdid myself. It's scrumptious, and we'd love to have you."

Sarah chimed in. "Whoa, wait a minute. What are Cole and I, chopped liver?" She whipped her head back to Honey. "I don't know how you feel about taking a hiatus from the city, but our house in Bridgehampton is all yours for as long as you want it. With the baby and my deadlines, I don't know when we'll get down there next. For sure not before summer."

"Sarah, Peter, Liz, Brian, this is amazing of you, but I couldn't possibly—"

The blond beauty and new mom to Colvin Christopher Canning III dismissed Honey's protests with a flick of her fingers. "Puh-lease, of course you can—and should. Besides, you'd be doing us the favor. Between the baby, my book deadlines, and Cole's fundraiser schedule, we're lucky to get down there every other weekend in the summer, and we hardly ever get out there in the winter. I'll get you the keys and a ticket for the Jitney and you can have the place to yourself."

For the first time in her life, Honey got what must be meant by "an embarrassment of riches." Stunned into speechlessness, she realized she'd gone from having nowhere to stay to having a Soho co-op, Brian's studio, a Brooklyn brownstone, Marc's Washington Heights apartment, and a Hamptons beach house all at her disposal.

"Darlings, thank you! But the thing is, I already have a place to stay—with Marc."

"The dishy doctor?" Peter asked, eyes alight.

Honey nodded. "He's even asked me to help him redecorate."

Liz hesitated. "That's great, Honey, but isn't it a little soon? You just left one long-term relationship. Don't you think you deserve a break . . . from the living-together part, at least?"

Though Honey also worried about once more being wholly dependent on a man, having her bubble burst, even by friends with her best interest at heart, was a bitter pill to swallow. "Marc is the opposite of

Drew in every way imaginable. He cares about people, his patients, a lot more than he does about money or status. He has the loveliest manners and the biggest heart imaginable. And he hardly even drinks. Before you judge him, shouldn't you at least meet him? He's already asked about meeting all of you."

Liz eased back in her seat. "Marc sounds great and for your sake, I hope he is. But it's not him anyone's passing judgment on. Six years ago Drew swept you off your feet and you dove in headfirst. You seem to be following the same pattern with Marc."

Exasperated, Honey pitched her voice higher than she ordinarily would. "This is totally different. Marc isn't married. He isn't even dating anyone else. And we're in love—at least I'm pretty sure he feels the same. Is it so hard to believe that a really good guy might fall for . . . someone like me?"

A chorus of "no!" answered. Sarah intervened. "Look, I get it. Sometimes when you meet the right person, you just *know,* and everything falls into place very quickly. At least that's how it was with Cole and me—well, at least once we stopped fighting our feelings. Still, Liz makes a good point. It's never a bad idea to look before you leap—and living together is a pretty big leap."

Liz nodded. "All I'm saying is to take some time and think things over. And of course we'd love to meet Marc." She paused, running a hand through her curly black hair, gloriously grown out to shoulder-length since the chemo treatments ended a year and a half ago. "Does he uh . . . know about FATE and why it was formed?"

Honey hesitated. "Yes and no. I told him about the group, but I sort of . . . left out the part about me working as an escort. He thinks I got in because of being a mistress, that you all stretched the rules or something." Okay, so maybe she wasn't as free from hypocrisy as she'd like to think.

Quiet greeted the admission. "When the time is right to tell him, you'll know," Liz finally said. "In the interim, we're here for you. Always."

Honey had thought she was finished with crying, but her suddenly misting eyes told her otherwise. "Knowing I have all of you in my corner means everything, truly it does. I don't know how to thank you, what to say."

"Say you're never going near Jerk Face again," Peter said, vehement.

"That you're finished with him—that's pretty much all I need to hear," Sarah agreed.

Drew's barrage of text and voicemail messages, teetering between berating and apologetic, had been nonstop that first week. Clearly her radio silence was doing little to dissuade him. It was time to stop being nice, to take off the gloves and hit him where it hurt, really hurt—his wallet. She'd messaged that she wasn't coming back, not ever. If she received even one more text or phone call from him, the next call she made wouldn't be to him or even the police. It would be to his wife. Katharine. Small surprise, she hadn't heard from him since.

She sent a watery smile on a circuit of the room. "That, darlings, is one promise I can absolutely make."

Chapter Eight

"The best thing to hold on to in life is each other."—Audrey Hepburn

Coming into her second week at Mark's, Honey acknowledged she couldn't put it off any longer. She'd have to return to Forty-One Park and pack her things. Once she took stock, she'd get movers in to carry out the furniture she chose to hold onto, assuming she could afford short-term storage. Afterward she'd turn in her key to the doorman and close out that chapter of her life once and for all.

They arranged to go on a morning when Marc's schedule allowed him to come with her. He insisted it wasn't safe for her to go alone or with another woman such as Liz and as much as she disliked admitting it, he was probably right. She doubted Drew would come around during a weekday morning but then again he was a wildcard. She couldn't bee too careful, especially now that she had so very much to live for.

Stepping inside the silent unit, she gasped, grabbing at Marc's forearm. "Oh, no!"

Drew's final revenge: her beautiful clothes, the fruits of more than six years of canvassing vintage clothing stores and flea markets throughout the city's five boroughs, littered the floor in torn scraps. Her hats had taken it too, the crowns crushed, the ribbons and scarves, rosettes and other embellishments torn off. Pearls spilled everywhere.

Mr. Pinky's head was torn off, the stuffing bleeding out onto the bed-spread. The sight, a tangible reminder of Drew's viciousness, brought tears to her eyes. The stuffed animal cat, a gift from her mom, was her last link to Omaha and her childhood. Thank God she'd gotten the real-life Cat out in time.

Following her gaze, Marc crossed to the bed and picked up Pinky, scooping up the remains in his big, gentle hands. "I'm pretty sure there are people who specialize in repairing stuffed toys."

"Thanks, but it's okay. I have a real cat now." *And you. I have you*, she almost added but bit back the statement. She didn't want her declaration of love to take place amidst Drew's destruction.

He set down the mutilated toy. Hands fisting, he shook his head. "There is nothing about this that comes close to okay."

"You're right, there isn't," she conceded. "But clothing and jewelry can be replaced. Living creatures can't. I hate what happened here, but I'm also really grateful to be safe, to have Cat safe—to have you safe."

He set his hands on her shoulders, their reassuring warmth seeping through her Ann Taylor linen trench coat, one of a very few clothing purchases she'd allowed him to make for her. Though new and off the rack, it reminded her of the trench Audrey had worn throughout *Breakfast At Tiffany's*. Like Holly Golightly, she'd escaped from her past choices in the nick of time.

"I know that look. What else is on your mind?" Marc asked.

"I've been thinking about our . . . my living arrangements. Once I pass my GED and get some sort of job, I should start looking for a place of my own—just for a while."

His face fell and his hands slid away. "I know Washington Heights isn't exactly Park Avenue, but I have plenty of room and with a little practice, I can probably get my dirty socks into the hamper on the first shot. And Cat's already used to it—and me."

His offer warmed her but the more she thought about what Liz and Sarah had said in group, the more right her friends seemed. She needed some space on her own to figure things out. She still hadn't scraped together the courage to tell him about her call-girl past. That was a lot for any man to accept. Marc cared for her deeply. She could feel it, see it in his eyes. He might even be on his way to loving her. But in love as in life, there were no guarantees. Once she admitted to going on "dates" with men for money, he might not feel the same about her.

"Darling, thank you, but I'm afraid I—"

"Can't accept," he finished for her, looking unhappy yet resigned. "Mind telling me why?"

It would be all too easy to cast aside any plans of her own and slip back into the pattern of allowing a man to take care of her. But if the past six years with Drew had taught her anything, it was that the easy way out wasn't so easy at all. If she and Marc were to have a shot at a future, preferably one that led to a real-life Happily Ever After, first she was going to have to do the hard work involved in coming to him, and into their relationship, as an equal.

"I've never really had a place of my own. Before Drew, I was sharing a one-bedroom in Union Square with three other girls, and back in Omaha I lived at home with my mom and stepfather. I need to make it on my own . . . for a little while at least. Please try and understand."

He hesitated and nodded. "I think I do. That doesn't mean I have to like it—or stop trying to change your mind."

Honey found her smile. "I'd be disappointed if you did."

Could she really be this happy? Could her life be working out despite all the mistakes she'd made?

"I have to run some errands but will you at least let me buy you lunch later? Despite all this, I feel like we should celebrate."

"New leaves and new beginnings?" Honey suggested, the familiar words having a bitter ring.

"I was thinking more along the lines of a whole new book. Marc lowered his head and brushed his mouth across her. Pulling back, he smiled. "C'mon, let's get out of here."

✳✳✳ ✳✳✳

"Honey Gladwell?'

Outside of Forty-One Park, Honey froze in her tracks. Another "friend" of Drew's? Or perhaps a former client? Unsure which was worse, she spun around. A tall, slender man in a dark suit, crisp white shirt, and black wingtips stood on the sidewalk before her. Short-haired, clean shaven, and square jawed, he might have been in finance except for his suit, clearly off the rack. That and the dark tinted sunglasses gave him away; the latter were cheap as well but effective in completely hiding his eyes.

Her heart hammered. Perspiration broke out on her forehead despite her side of the street being all in shade. The urge to bolt was huge. She'd run in heels on plenty of occasions to catch a cab or the crosstown bus, only her legs seemed to have turned to Jell-O. Should she cry out for help instead, scream at the top of her lungs? But help from what—*who?*

Finding her voice, she managed to answer, "That depends. Who are you?"

"Special Agent Carlson. FBI." He whipped out a badge, holding it low and cupped in his palm so that only she could see. "And you are Honey Gladwell, or Hortense Gustafson."

Jesus, he really was with the FBI. Despite the bright sunny day, the scenario suddenly took on a film noire quality, a sense of sinister expectation dimming the lights and adding an inner chill to the otherwise soft spring breeze. The last time she'd felt this same frightening sense of helplessness, had such a foregone surety of defeat, Drew was dragging her into the stairwell.

"What if I am?"

Whatever was going on must have to do with her escort days. What else? Just as she'd always feared, her past was coming back to bite her. The timing of her retribution couldn't be more ironic—or tragic. Just as she set her feet on the proverbial straight-and-narrow, just as she was finally getting her life together, hell was raining down. It was almost biblical. It *was* biblical. It seemed her mother had been right all along.

She was destined to come to a bad end.

Only it wasn't only her anymore. There was Marc now. She was poison fruit. She could only hope the tastes he'd so far taken wouldn't end up ruining him along with her.

Agent Carlson's monotone brought her back to the moment. "We need to talk."

Fresh panic flared. If she could buy some time, a day, she could maybe manage to get away, on the next bus out of New York. They'd catch up with her eventually, of course, but hopefully not before she'd managed to put some significant mileage between herself and Manhattan—and most importantly, Marc.

"I'm afraid I'm just on my way—"

"I need an hour of your time—in private."

Despite her pounding pulse and almost out-of-body sense of disorientation, a smattering of reason wended its way into her buzzing brain. Admittedly prostitution was illegal, but it also had to be proven. Even if they had her dead to rights, she was a small fish in an altogether enormous pond of nefarious activity. Other than spreading her legs in exchange for money, most of which had gone to the agency, not her, she hadn't been party to any crimes. She didn't do drugs; certainly she never sold them. Surely the FBI had weightier matters to address than rousting a retired escort, especially one who'd taken herself out of the game six years ago.

"My past is in the past, and I prefer to leave it there. Unless you have a warrant, I can't imagine why I should speak to you."

Honey wasn't certain law enforcement actually needed a warrant to interview someone but the words had popped into her head, likely the legacy of watching so many *Cagney & Lacey* reruns when she was little and, well, on the fly, it had *sounded* good.

His stone face assured her that her scripted response carried absolutely no weight. "You're in a lot of trouble, Miss Gustafson. It's in your best interest to cooperate. I'm going to need you to come downtown with me."

As if on cue, a black SUV rolled up to the curb, stopping in front of them. Carlson took possession of her elbow, steering her toward the rear door. "Get in the car, ma'am."

Panic climbed her throat. She whipped her head about to face him, the sharp motion knocking her hat askew. "And if I choose not to?"

Unsmiling, he stared back at her, or at least she imagined he did. His lenses were so tinted she couldn't really tell. "Then I'd say you can count on wearing orange in your near future."

He released her, reached for the door handle, and opened the door. Heart in her throat, Honey climbed in.

✳✳✳ ✳✳✳

Honey was late. Not fashionably late, or Manhattan late, but late-late—by more than a half hour. Seated at one of the coveted tables by the open ceiling-to-floor windows of Il Cantinori, Marc checked his cell phone yet again. Still no message in response to his, no text, voicemail, or email, but then she was bad about letting her phone battery run low. It was the perfect spring day, perfect romantic restaurant, perfect wine list and menu—all perfect except for the one absolutely essential missing ingredient: Honey.

The bottle of champagne he'd ordered bobbed in its metal bucket of melting ice. He was on his second glass of tap water and his third slice of bread, and the server who'd started out so obsequious stood giving him the hairy eyeball from the vicinity of the bar. On his last tableside visit, he'd made a point of mentioning that lunch service stopped at 2:30. Marc didn't blame him. He was a last-minute reservation taking up coveted table space without ordering, and he wasn't anything close to a regular. In fact, it was his first time here. In the Manhattan top-tier restaurant trade, second to stiffing a server, table squatting was the closest thing to a sin. Be that as it may, he sure as hell wasn't about to order lunch without Honey, not at these prices.

Where was she?

Could she have gone to the wrong restaurant? El Cantinero, a Mexican restaurant, was nearby. The names were similar enough for someone like him to get them confused, less likely for Honey. She was a walking *Zagat's* for Manhattan fine dining establishments. He seriously doubted she would make such a mistake. Still, everyone had an off day once in a while, and seeing her belongings destroyed and her former apartment trashed had to be traumatic. Even for a sicko such as Winterthur, beheading her childhood stuffed animal was a seriously low blow. Though she seemed fine when he left her, it was possible she was having a delayed reaction, maybe even a mini meltdown.

Or maybe she really was waiting at El Cantinero, staring into her plastic basket of tortilla chips wondering why he was such an asshole? To be safe, he tapped out one last text message, this one containing his coordinates.

I'm still at Il Cantinori, 10th between Broadway & University. Champagne's chilling. Where ARE you?

✳✳✳ ✳✳✳

The conference room was windowless, featureless and neon-lit; the tea tepid, from a bag, and served in the sort of white Styrofoam cup that

Honey hadn't known they even manufactured anymore. Sandwiched between two federal agents in an interior conference room on the twenty-third floor of 26 Federal Plaza, Honey tamped down the temptation to go back to gnawing at her nails.

Not for the first time since she'd sat down twenty minutes ago, her thoughts went to Marc. He would be wondering where she was. Worse, he'd assume she'd stood him up. A smart girl would have text-messaged him an excuse, preferably one that was believable. With luck, he would even buy it. But she'd promised them both that she would never lie to him and despite the odd—horrendous—circumstances, it was a promise she was doing her level best to keep. Besides, Honey wasn't feeling particularly smart at the moment; ditto for lucky.

She divided her gaze between Agent Carlson, seated at the conference table across from her, and his associate, the SUV driver, Agent Wilkes. Ten minutes into their interrogation, their good-cop bad-cop routine was already wearing thin. "I think it's time you told me exactly what sort of trouble I'm supposedly in; otherwise I'd like to leave. I have a luncheon engagement," she added, not that she expected them to care but because (a) it was true and (b) a luncheon was a far more respectable activity than how they probably imagined a former call girl passed her time.

The agents traded glances.

"If this is about my past, I can assure you that when I left the . . . service, I left that life behind. I don't have any communication with anyone from those days, not the other girls, not the former clients, and certainly not the agency owners."

"It's not about your past . . . employment. It's about your boyfriend."

She hadn't expected that. "My . . . " Marc, what could they possibly want with Marc? He was as straight as straight arrows came. Though she hadn't known him all that long, not really, she'd stake her life that he wouldn't dream of doing anything remotely illegal.

Apparently reading her confusion, Agent Carlson quickly cut in, "Not the doctor, the other one—the finance guy, Andrew Winterthur."

Staring down into her tea, which Agent Wilkes, a.k.a. Good Cop, had insisted on providing, she willed herself to relax. If Drew had gotten himself into some sort of trouble with the feds, that was too bad but it wasn't her worry, not anymore. "I broke it off with him several weeks ago," she said, never happier to admit the truth in all her life.

"Is that why we found you standing outside of Forty-One Park, the building where he's put you up for the last six years?"

"How long have you been following me?"

Carlson's gaze shuttered. "Answer the question, ma'am."

"Very well, I was there to collect my belongings."

"And yet, other than your shoulder bag, you walked out empty handed."

A mental picture of the apartment in the aftermath of Drew's rampage leapt to mind. Even though she had bigger worries now than replacing her ruined things, a lot bigger, anger swelled, squeezing out the fear—for now.

"That's because he didn't leave me anything to pack. If you don't believe me, then maybe you'll believe this." She opened her Prada purse and pulled out Mr. Pinky's remains, stuffing spilling from the severed head. In a last weak moment, she'd scooped him up in the hope he might be salvaged after all. "He slashed or smashed every piece of clothing, every memento, every photo I'd left in the apartment. Other than the clothes on my back, a few toiletries, and my rescue kitten, I have nothing left."

"I'm sorry." The two agents exchanged looks. As much as Honey wanted to believe they were expressions of sympathy, she was too smart for that degree of self-deception.

"Is there any chance he might take you back?" Wilkes asked.

"Take me back! He put me in the hospital last February. He could have killed me. He broke my wrist. I shouldn't have gone back to him after that, but I did. I certainly wouldn't be so stupid, or self-destructive, a second time."

"You may not have a choice," Carlson said.

"I beg your pardon?"

"How much do you know about the Wolfgang Fund?"

"I've never heard of it."

"What about HG Enterprises—that ring any bells?" Carlson persisted.

Stunned, Honey stared up at him. With the sunglasses removed, she saw that his eyes were blue, weary-looking and bracketed by lines. He probably wasn't much more than forty, and yet he had the mien of a much older man. And suddenly she got it. He and his partner might be gaming her, but only to a point.

She really was in a serious lot of trouble.

"Other than that it's my initials, I've never heard of it," she answered honestly. *Drew, what the hell have you done now?*

Carlson's gaze bore into hers. "Sure about that? I should remind you that lying to a federal agent brings a penalty of up to five years in prison and a $250,000 fine."

"Of course I'm sure!" Lowering her voice, she added, "Drew never spoke to me about his business dealings."

"Never? Do you mean to say that in six years, there was no pillow talk ever?"

The thought of drinking more tea gagged her. She pushed the cup aside. "Beyond the general complaint here and there, there wasn't. Look, I was his mistress. When he visited me, it was for sex, not to gather my opinions on the latest market trends."

It was the truth—but would the truth be enough?

"In that case, allow me to enlighten you. HG Enterprises is one of several dummy corporations Winterthur and his partner, Frank Dawes, set up almost six years ago. Like the others, it's a ghost corporation—it doesn't exist anywhere but on paper."

She fitted a hand to her forehead, pounding apace with her heart. "I don't understand. Drew is a partner at his firm. I may not know anything about finance, but I do know it's a very well-respected private equity firm with offices not only in New York but worldwide."

"That's true, but it seemed your boy was feeling entrepreneurial—and greedy. He set up the Wolfgang Fund as a shadow syndicate operating within his private equity firm. Right now it looks like he and Dawes are the only insiders involved, though it's too soon to be conclusive. Most of his marks are middle-class folks from out of state looking to make some scratch for their kids' college funds, time share properties, supplemental income for retirement, that type of thing. When he cold-calls from his interior office line, his firm is what shows up on their caller IDs—perfectly legit, or so it would seem to the average Joe."

"But that's—"

Carlson cut her off. "Fraud, Ms. Gustafson—securities fraud, and we have reason to suspect money laundering, too. Like it or not, you're implicated. He set up that dummy corp in your name, using your social security number and what looks an awful lot like your signature. Are you telling me it's not, that it's a forgery?"

He nodded to Wilkes, who slid a stapled sheaf of papers across the conference table toward her. Feeling numb, Honey picked them up and began flipping through to the final page.

"Oh my God." The signature was unmistakably hers, down to the thick blue-felt pen she used.

She remembered that pen as well as the day. Certain she was embarking on her fairy tale future, she'd stepped over the threshold of 6C, Forty-One Park for the very first time, hand-in-hand with Drew.

"Like it?" he asked, leading her about the empty apartment.

She turned to him, her mouth tiring from all the smiling she'd been doing. "Like it? Darling, I adore it."

They made love on the air mattress he'd just happened to have waiting and inflated. Afterward, while sipping champagne in bed, a lease document (or so he'd told her at the time), had materialized along with a pen.

"Babe, I need your social for the lease. No need to read it, baby, just fill in your SSN and sign on the dotted line; I'll take care of all the rest. This way if anything happens to me, I've got you covered."

I've got you covered.

Honey replaced the top page and slid the stapled document back to Carlson. "No, it's not a forgery. I thought . . . He told me I was co-signing the lease on our apartment."

"You know what, Ms. Gustafson, I believe you. Agent Wilkes, you believe her, don't you?"

"Sure I do."

Carlson turned back to her. "We believe you, ma'am, but whether or not a jury buys your story, well, that's another matter."

"A jury!"

The two agents nodded. Carlson answered, "Whatever promises Winterthur made you, the bottom line is that he's a married man and you're the other woman, and not just the other woman but a former escort who was paid for her . . . services. You're not going to have much luck playing the sympathy card with a jury, not in this economy." Yep, definitely the Bad Cop.

"You're arresting me!" So much for one hour of her time! Had she traded one prison for yet another impenetrable one?

"Not yet," he admitted, "but there's a pretty high probability it's going to come down to that—unless you cooperate."

"Cooperate how? I've told you everything I know, which is nothing. What more can I possibly do?" she added, half-afraid to find out.

Wilkes regarded her over steepled hands. "Winterthur's holding an Investor Day at the Waldorf Astoria this Friday. It seems the natives are getting restless—it was a suspicious investor who tipped us off. He's past year five, the year when investors expect a liquidation event to occur, only there's nothing to sell or take public. To cover his ass and buy more time, he's flying in his top investors from as far away as Ohio for a day-long dog-and-pony show at the Waldorf, a razzle-dazzle play to make them feel important, special. Little do they know it's all smoke and mirrors, and they're footing the bill for all of it—the venue, the booze and food, even the hookers. Apologies, ma'am, no offense intended."

As much as she hated to, Honey thought back to her last night with Drew, to the early part of the evening before Frank showed up and things went from weird to crazy bad.

"Remember I told you about that Investor Day I wanted to throw? Well, the funding came through and it's happening: a blowout bash at the Waldorf for my key out-of-town investment clients, and I want you there."

And later Frank had said, *"If he wants me to cover his ass on Investor Day, he knows he has to keep me happy . . ."*

At the time she'd been too terrified to think beyond getting herself and Cat safely out of there and to Marc's, but in retrospect the veiled exchanges made stunning, sickening sense. Drew had used her yet again, only instead of emotionally and physically battering her, he'd set her up as his patsy. Unless she "cooperated," whatever that meant, she might well end up going to prison for him.

It seemed her mother's prophecy was to be proven true after all. She really was about to come to a bad end.

Carlson's voice called her back to the current moment. "Text him and say you've thought things through and you realize you've made a mistake. Play to his ego. Tell him you want to come back—and to prove it, you'll be at the Investor Day as promised—only what he won't know is that you'll be wearing a wire."

Honey shook her head, which was drumming apace with her heart. "But I told him I never wanted to see him again. I threatened to call his wife if he didn't leave me alone. Obviously he believed me, otherwise he wouldn't have destroyed all my things. If I contact him out of the blue, suddenly willing to forgive and forget, won't that make him suspicious, even spoil your investigation?"

This time Wilkes took the lead on answering. "Ego is always these guys' downfall. They operate on the assumption that the rules don't apply to them. They think they're always the smartest guy in the room and though that's often the case, eventually they trip themselves up. Jeffrey Skilling, Bernie Madoff, Jordan Belfort—history repeats itself again and again. Right now Winterthur figures he's covered his tracks. We've given him no reason to suspect otherwise. Play your part well and there's no reason he will."

"Don't you think you're giving me too much credit? After all, I did sign incorporation papers thinking they were a co-op lease. I'm not exactly Mensa material."

Carlson stared at her askance. "I think you can play dumb with the best of them when it suits your purposes, as it does now. Sure, at the time it was easier to go along and not look too closely at the fine print, but that time is past. If Winterthur isn't stopped, a whole lot of people are going to lose a whole lot of money, some of them their life savings."

Honey bit her lip. Until now, she'd told herself the only person her poor life choices had hurt was herself. Now she was forced to see that wasn't so.

"What makes you so certain he hasn't moved on to some other girl already? He may not have prostitutes on his payroll, but I promise you he'll have hired models as servers. He can be funny and charming when he wants something—or someone. Finding a girl to take my place at

Forty-One Park won't be hard. He may have one in mind to move in already."

Once, the prospect of Drew replacing her would have prompted panic and thrown her into a total tailspin. Now she could only hope that he had. If she reached out to him and was rebuffed, would she still be let off the hook? Even in the midst of all the unknowns she suddenly faced, she paused to appreciate how far she'd come. In these last few weeks, she'd evolved to a better place—thanks, once again, to Marc.

Carlson didn't exactly roll his eyes, but he looked like he wanted to. "Don't be so modest, Ms. Gustafson. Like all rich guys, Winterthur can have—buy—anything and anyone he wants, and yet he picks you. And not only does he pick you, but he sticks with you for six years, puts you up on Park Avenue, no less. A guy like that doesn't go to that kind of trouble and expense, not to mention risking his marriage, unless he feels he's getting a good . . . return on his investment. Obviously, he thought you were worth it. You're the one who broke things off, not him."

"But he—"

"Knocked you around and wrecked your stuff, I know, and I'm sorry for your suffering, I am. But you, Miss Gustafson, had to have some idea of who you were . . . getting into bed with. Joe and Judy Smith from Cleveland don't know who they're dealing with. What happens to them when they realize HG Enterprises is a bust and they're looking at living out their supposed golden years with next to no savings? Do you want that on your conscience, ma'am? Because I surely don't want it on mine."

"If he finds out I'm betraying him, he'll kill me, Mr. Carlson. I know I'm no better than a hooker to you, but still, do you really want my death on *your* conscience?"

"He'll never touch you, you have my word," Wilkes, the Good Cop, broke in. "We'll be in a van parked a few blocks away, listening

161

to every word. The moment things get too hot to handle, we'll get you out."

"You really think he'll take me back?"

"I don't think—I *know* he will," Carlson answered. "How do I know? I know because Andrew Winterthur is obsessed with you. Even more so than his ego, you're his Achilles' heel—and I intend to use that, *you*, to put him away."

Honey bristled. "And if I won't be used?"

All her life men had been manipulating her, telling her what to do and when and how to do it. Her stepfather Sam, the paunchy thin-haired "suits" who'd paid for her favors, Drew, and now Carlson and company—they all seemed to be cut from the same cloth. They'd all been out to take as much from her as they could—a piece of her ass, her self-respect, her future. The one exception was Marc. Other than trying to save her from going back to Drew, he never asked anything of her other than to be herself, to be "real" with him. And he'd given her so much—friendship, a safe haven, superlative sex—all without expecting anything in return.

Carlson's eyes, weary-looking no longer, drilled into hers. "With or without your help, eventually I am going to get this son of a bitch. And when I do, I'm going to put him away for the next twenty-five years, not to mention the millions of dollars in restitution he's going to have to pay to the government and SEC. The only question is whether, when I do, you go away too or stay free to live your life. It's your choice, but I need you to make it now, this minute. Are you in or are you out, Ms. Gustafson? What's it going to be?"

Honey swallowed hard. "Choice" in this context was really an egregious misnomer. There was only one path left open to her. Her "choice" came down to taking it—or not.

"I'm in, Agent Carlson. Only, under the circumstances, hadn't you better start calling me Honey?"

Chapter Nine

"I believe in being strong when everything seems to be going wrong."
—Audrey Hepburn

Honey returned to the apartment that night in what Marc could only call an agitated state—restless, hypersensitive, and altogether on edge. It made total sense that she would be upset, even devastated, about Drew's trashing the apartment and destroying all her belongings, and yet all things considered, she'd seemed in good spirits when he left her.

Not so now.

Pacing the apartment's four corners, she couldn't seem to settle. Was she maybe experiencing a delayed reaction to the trauma? When he asked what had happened to her at lunch, she responded with an obviously manufactured excuse—something to do with her interior designer friend calling about a sample sale in Brooklyn, poor cell reception, and a generally lost sense of time. Marc wasn't buying.

Unable to take it any longer, he put down his tablet and rose from the couch. "Damn it, woman, look at me. *Talk* to me."

She folded her arms. "What do you want to talk about?"

"What do I . . . It's not like I have a script. Just be real with me. Tell me whatever's on your mind. It's obvious something is."

Her eyes shot arrows at him. "And if I don't feel like talking?"

"Honey, please, work with me here. We're trying to be a couple."

"Perhaps we're trying too hard."

First she didn't feel ready to live with him, and now this. What was going on with her? "You don't mean that."

"So are you going to start telling me how I should feel about things, too?"

"Of course I'm not."

"I need some air." She pivoted away and grabbed her bag as if to go.

"Hold up, I'll go with you."

"Thanks, but I'd rather be alone."

"It's eleven o'clock at night. It's not safe."

"I'll be the judge of that, but thanks for your concern."

Thanks for your concern—seriously? He caught up with her at the door. "I can't let you leave like this."

She whirled on him. "What are you, my keeper now?"

"Of course not."

"Then stop acting like it."

He placed himself in front of her. To get to the door, she'd have to go through him—and he wasn't budging. "Look, you've had a hell of a day. What you faced in that apartment would be pretty traumatic for anyone. If you'll just try to relax, have some tea, and get a good night's sleep, everything will look brighter in the morning."

She let out a raw laugh. "I promise you, nothing will look brighter tomorrow. Now step aside."

"I won't. I care about you too much to let you leave in a mental state where you might get hurt. Do you even know where you're going?"

"I hear Paris is always a good idea."

Paris is always a good idea—yet another Audrey quote, this one from *Sabrina*. Marc had had enough.

"Damn it, Honey, this is real life—yours and mine—not some old movie we're re-enacting. So skip the script and speak to me like a real person. Be real with me, baby. It's all I've ever asked from you."

"What makes you so certain I'm not? I have a perfectly good airline voucher gathering dust and only another few months to use it. From everything I've read and heard about Paris, mistresses are an accepted part of the culture, almost a tradition. No one gives it a second thought, not even the wives. Who knows, maybe I'll marry some terribly rich old Parisian man who'll dote on me. Only promise you'll take care of Cat."

"That's not funny."

"Who's being funny? I'm being practical. I'd take him with me, of course, but with the quarantine laws it wouldn't be fair. I'd say I was only loaning him to you, but I really can't say when I'll be back—or if I'm coming back—so it's probably best to make it a permanent adoption."

Drew stared at her aghast. "You're going to up and leave? Throw everything away? What about us?"

She had the gall to shrug.

"Damn it, Honey, I'm in love with you."

Silence greeted the declaration.

"Did you hear what I just said? I *love* you."

Her gaze narrowed. "Tough beans."

He grabbed hold of her shoulders. "Honey, please."

"You can either let me leave or knock me down—those are your choices."

"I would never be violent with you."

"Never—that's a very long time. Here, let me get the ball rolling." She hauled back—and slapped him.

Cheek stinging, Marc stared at her. "Jesus, what the hell is wrong with you?"

"Not a thing. I feel great. Now it's your turn. C'mon, you know you want to."

"Maybe I do, a little bit, but then I want a lot of things—four weeks of vacation, funding for a new trauma center, oh yeah, and world peace. But if I can live without those things, I guess I can forgo the pleasure of blackening your eye." Just the thought made his stomach sick.

"Great, then don't wait up."

"Okay, you're angry, I get that. You have every right, but you can't keep carrying it around. You've got to get rid of it. Give me your best shot. All that anger, take it out on me."

Honey didn't need to be told twice. She sent her slender hand singing across his jaw, the strike a blur of slender fingers tipped in pink-painted nails. A real slap this time. The sting made his eyes water—and his cock thicken.

The adrenalin rush reminded him of his first tracheotomy performed as a lowly intern. The patient was a construction worker with bad airway burns from inhaling scalding steam from a burst pipe. He was on oxygen when the paramedics brought him in; Marc had scarcely had time to touch him when he began gasping beneath the oxygen mask. Protocol had dictated he page his attending, but he knew for a fact that Denison, the doc pulling night duty, was getting up close and personal with the pretty new nurse in the break room and had left word that anyone who interrupted him was putting his or her ass on the line, and yet . . . Four to six minutes without oxygen was all it took for permanent brain damage to occur. Already they must be nearly two minutes in; any longer and you were looking at coma or death. After those first few fraught seconds, Marc was resolved. Fuck protocol, fuck Denison, and fuck the possible malpractice suit his going rogue might well bring down on both Denison, under whose license he was practicing until he passed his boards, and the hospital. His every instinct had screamed to snap up that scalpel and go for it—and he had. The patient was obese with poor neck landmarks; he found the inferior border of Cricoid cartilage mostly by feel—and luck. Once he had it, he made the cut, a centimeter horizontal incision. Seconds later he recalled that vertical, not horizontal, was the latest recommended approach, and likely he'd gone too far down—*fuck!* But it was too late to turn back. The clock was literally ticking—whatever he did, right or wrong, it was up to him to see it through, find a way to make it work. There hadn't been time to reach for a kit; instead he used his fingers to pinch open the slit. He inserted the tube with shaking hands, bent over and breathed into it, two sharp, quick breaths. *Pause five seconds, then give one breath every five seconds*—wash, rinse, and repeat. The surreal several seconds of standing back and waiting to see if it had worked, the sweet rush of relief and gladness—joy—when the newly made stoma started sucking down air. Afterward Denison had bawled him out pretty badly, insisting it was a botch job worthy of a rookie paramedic. On the positive side, he'd avoided severing any vocal chords. The patient would sport a wicked scar for the rest of his days, but his brain and future were intact. He'd live as a fully functional adult, not as a vegetable nourished through tubes. Despite all the flak he'd fielded, he'd left the hospital that night feeling good about himself, even a little bit proud.

"Proud of yourself?" he finally asked Honey.

Breathing hard, she managed a nod. "I've always . . . always wondered how it must feel to get angry and . . . not have to hide it, to be . . . the one who does the hitting."

"So how does it feel?'

Her pupils were dilated, her cheeks flushed. If he didn't know her, he'd think she was on something. But he did know her and the rush she was experiencing was due to skyrocketing adrenalin. "I'm not . . . sure yet. Powerful, I guess. Free."

In staging the devastation at the apartment for her to find, Drew had once again hurt her and, once again, he'd gotten away with it. Unfortunately, he wasn't around to be slapped or told off. But Marc was. What Honey needed most right now was to get the built-up, buried rage out of her. For that, she needed a surrogate. She needed . . . him.

"You're pissed off about your stuff being trashed, so use it. Use *me*." He grabbed her and tugged them both down to the hardwood floor, bringing her on top of him. "Hit me, fuck me, whatever you want. I'm here for you. I can take it."

She reared back, shifting so that her legs straddled him. Grabbing hold of his shirt with both hands, she tore it open, sending buttons popping. Bending her head, she suckled his nipples, then dragged her mouth upward and bit hard into the side of his neck.

Marc moaned. Laving at his bruised skin brought him bucking. He lifted the hem of her linen dress to her waist and anchored his hands to her hips. Now that the striking had stopped and the fucking had started, he hoped he was more than a stand-in for her ex, but for now he would be whoever and whatever she needed him to be.

Moving upward, she straddled his face. Levering herself slightly above him, she tore open her panties' split crotch. A petal pink vulva bloomed above him, his personal Georgia O'Keefe canvas. Too caught up to await any cue, Marc buried his nose and mouth in her moistness. She smelled like the park did after a shower, earthy and yet scented with freshly mowed grass and spring flowers. He breathed her in, senses overflowing, the room spinning like a carousel. Brine coated his mouth, stinging his split lip. He found her clit and circled. He licked and lapped, nipped and nibbled. Honey ground against him. Glancing up at her, he confirmed that hitting him again was the farthest thing from her thoughts. Her head was thrown back, her eyes closed. Her thighs quivered. Her arms shook. On the cusp of coming, she pulled back, heavy eyelids lifting. Holding his gaze, she glided downward. She took his penis in hand, positioned herself over him, and came down—hard.

Her small hands bit into his shoulders, holding him to the floor, at least in theory. He lifted his torso and hips, driving as deeply as he could go.

Honey groaned and rocked against him. Her hands slammed into his shoulders, pushing him back to the floor, her nails raking his already scored skin. She pulled back and sheathed herself yet again. Marc thrust upward, sharp and deep.

He knew the exact moment when her orgasm hit. Her eyes dilated, her mouth opened, and her skin flared. Her nails scored his skin. Like a velvet fist, her pussy pumped him, the contractions rhythmic and powerful. Marc gave in, coming hard. Penis pulsing, spunk spraying, the only words that sprang to mind were the very ones she wasn't yet ready to hear.

I love you.

✳✳✳ ✳✳✳

Honey rolled off him and onto her side. Now that her adrenalin was ebbing, her conscience made a comeback. "Oh my God, look what I've done to you." She lifted a hand to her mouth, and then stopped when she realized she wore his skin beneath her nails.

"I'll live."

Marc sat up stiffly. Sucking his cut lip, he pulled up on his zipper. His shirt was rent to ribbons, his skin shiny with sweat and sticky with blood. The bruise at the side of his neck looked as though she had gored him. Even when called upon to play the dominatrix in the past, she'd never hurt anyone, certainly not like this. And Marc wasn't anyone. She was someone whom she cared for deeply, maybe—probably—even loved. A lot. And yet she had gotten off on hurting him just like . . . Drew?

Starting out, she hadn't expected to orgasm—but she had, oh how she had. The pleasure had ripped through her, wave after breaking wave. Until now, even with Marc she'd always held a part of herself back, inwardly bracing for the strike that, with him at least, had never come. Now she knew it never would.

The reassurance exacted a precious price. She might not have taken a pound of his flesh, but she'd taken several good-sized chunks of it. His split bottom lip still bled and his cheekbone still bore her handprint, along with several scratches.

He draped an arm around her back. "Hey, calm down. It's okay. You didn't dish out anything I couldn't take."

"But I—"

"Wanted to see what it felt like to be on the giving side of sexual violence. Now that you have, I hope you won't make it a habit."

"Never again, I promise."

She had never willfully hurt another being—until now. And once she'd let loose, she hadn't wanted to stop.

She struggled to her feet, tugging down her dress. "Let me get you cleaned up." She stretched out a hand.

He started to protest. "You don't have to baby me. You didn't do anything I didn't let you do."

Rather than debate him, she kept out her hand. "Then humor me. Please, it's the least I can do."

"Okay."

He got up and they went into his bathroom. Honey took inventory of his wall-mounted medicine cabinet, shockingly bare. A tube of Neosporin that had nearly run dry, a few dusty-looking cotton balls, and one measly Band Aid pretty much summed up his first-aid supplies.

"For an ER doctor, you're not exactly stocked. You don't even have any alcohol."

"Alcohol stings."

"Baby." She squeezed the Neosporin for all it was worth and began dabbing the cooling cream on the scratches cross-hatching the tops of his shoulders.

"Before you, I pretty much came home to sleep and shower. Those are usually pretty safe activities—at least they used to be."

Honey swallowed hard. "I've never been on this side before. I'm not sure how to go about making amends. A diamond tennis bracelet, dinner at Eleven Madison Park, a weekly blow job for life? What can I do? Tell me, please."

"You can stay here with me."

Given what had just gone down, Honey couldn't believe she'd heard him right. "Are you sure?"

Bruised and bedraggled, he still looked very much like a man who'd made up his mind. "Stay here with me. A few more days, months—or forever, it's up to you."

He lifted her onto the chipped marble-topped vanity, the granite hard and chilly. Her dress rode upward. Marc pushed it higher and parted her thighs.

Honey glanced down, then up at him. "W-what are you doing?"

Hands on her knees, he opened her legs wider and stepped between. The gleam in his eye made her feel entirely desired and entirely safe. "You've had your alpha moment. We're doing things my way now."

Honey answered with a wordless nod. She'd tested him—hard—and he'd passed with flying colors. Now that he'd proven she could trust him, really trust him, she could hardly wait to explore their mutual limits. Knowing Marc would never take things too far made the prospect of kneeling at his feet and fellating him feel exciting and sexy, not degrading and frightening as it had for so long now.

He leaned in and kissed her. Honey gave in. Caged by his strong arms, caught between his body and the wall mirror, she moaned into his mouth.

"This time I get to see you—all of you." He reached between them, and began tugging at the buttons fronting her dress.

It fell open, baring the tops of her breasts. Caught up in kissing him, Honey barely registered him unhooking the front clasp of her bra. The lace cups fell away. He took her in his hands. "You're so beautiful," he said softly, flicking his thumbs over her nipples.

Honey shivered. She glanced down. She'd always thought of herself as small-busted. Back in her escort days, she'd briefly considered augmentation. Now that she looked, really looked, she saw she wasn't only petite, but pleasingly firm and prettily shaped. Pink nipples stuck out as if begging for attention. Marc gave it, rolling her between his thumbs and forefingers. Pleasure struck her, not only in her breasts but everywhere.

He bent his head and fitted his mouth over one throbbing point. Heat hit Honey—everywhere. She gasped and arched against him, seeking to bring them closer. As amazing as his mouth felt on her breasts, she craved his kisses and touch lower. A lot lower.

Marc must be a mind reader. Taking a step back, he took hold of the hem of her dress. Gliding his palm upward toward her waist, he ferried the fabric with him. Chilly air touched the tops of Honey's stocking-clad thighs, the gooseflesh a stark contrast to the heat pooling inside her.

Looking down, he murmured, "So pretty," and traced the top of her torn La Perla panties with a single finger.

Honey honestly thought she might splinter. Though she'd climaxed mere minutes ago, her body, all her being, was building toward another release.

Marc slid a hand between her thighs and palmed her through her panties. Musk rose up between them. Honey didn't need to look down to know that she was wet, her juices seeping through the split silk.

He stilled his stroking. "Do you trust me?"

A sob caught in her throat. "Y-yes."

"Enough to tell me where you really went today?"

Tempted as she was to rest her head against him and confess every-thing so that he might help her find a fix, she couldn't, mustn't, give in. "HG Enterprises" and the fraudulent investment scheme Drew was perpetrating in her name wasn't his problem to fix. It was hers.

"I had some things to take care of. Let's leave it at that, okay?"

He eyed her. "Tell me this much—did you go to see him?"

By *him*, he meant Drew, of course. Honey studied him—the high forehead that might be called "noble" in an earlier era, the earnest eyes, and the stubborn set of his square jaw—and inwardly admitted that she could never lie to this face. Never. "I absolutely did not. I haven't set eyes on him since the night I left." It was all true and yet so much less than honest. "Okay?"

He sent her a spare nod. "Okay . . . for now."

He followed the line downward to the cleft parting her inner lips, and Honey held her breath. The intimate touch carried her to the edge of the counter and the brink of orgasm. Wetness blanketed the insides of her thighs. Her pulse skipped; her flesh frissoned.

Slipping in her slickness, he slid a finger inside her. A second fol-lowed. Rhythmic scissoring nearly sent her over the edge.

Honey lifted herself against his hand, her bottom leaving the coun-ter. But Marc refused to be rushed. His fingers circled her clit. His dark head brushed her lower belly as he angled his mouth to her sex. Honey spread her legs. The bottoms of her feet anchored to the shelf of his broad shoulders. She leaned back on her palms and prepared to give herself up to the pleasure.

All these weeks he'd used gentleness as a weapon—and Honey finally admitted that it had worked. She was hooked—on the hot sex, the fun, easy conversations and, above all, him. He could make her laugh like nobody's business. His smile, his eyes, his touch all could melt her.

Apparently intent on torturing her, Marc scattered soft kisses inside one thigh and then the other. His deft fingers spread her. Warm breath fell upon her sensitized flesh. A tongue's point probed her slit.

"You even taste like honey," he murmured, licking damp lips.

He fluttered his tongue until Honey was certain she would die of pleasure. Only she didn't die. She exploded. Her engorged sex rocketed, setting off a starburst of spasms. Keening sobs tore forth from her throat.

Even so, she couldn't seem to get enough. With Marc, she wasn't sure she ever would. She lifted herself against him, her body beckoning him back.

Finally the salvo faded. Breathing hard, she tugged down her dress, and then looked to Marc resting back on his heels on the floor. Sweat dampened his shirt, molding the material to his broad shoulders and tapered torso.

"You're amazing," she said, though she suspected that wouldn't exactly come as news to him.

As much as she had always fantasized about a man putting her first, right now she didn't want chivalry. She wanted sex. With Marc.

Chest heaving, he got to his feet. Sliding an arm about her, he looked from her gaping dress into her eyes. "I meant what I said earlier. I want you to stay with me. I swear you won't be sorry."

He might not be sorry yet but once he found out about her unawares involvement with Drew's fraud scheme, he would be. Even before being picked up by Carson and Wilkes, she was a hot mess. She wouldn't know how to go about having a healthy adult romantic relationship if Prince Charming rode up on his white horse and bit her on the fucking ass. Her only models, her stepfather and Drew, were both brutes who used fear and fists to win their way. Poor Marc; he might be brilliant, a doctor, but when it came to her he didn't have a clue what he was in for.

She laced her hand with his. "I may not be sorry, but I only hope you'll be able to say the same."

"I will," he said, his surety tearing at her heart—and her conscience.

Laying a hand on either side of his face, she dragged him back down to her. Their mouths met. Their tongues sparred.

Marc answered with a groan. Spreading her folds, he positioned himself over her channel. One quick, clean thrust carried him inside her. The emotions of the day made restraint seem foolish. They came hard, fast, and together, their urgent breathes and unbridled cries filling the bathroom.

✷✷✷ ✷✷✷

Marc couldn't put it off any longer. A recent heart surgery patient complaining of dizziness had been brought in by his panicked wife, and he'd ordered a CBC, Complete Blood Count, to rule out markers that might indicate bleed-out from the surgery or infection. The labs should be back by now. As great as his hospital-issued tablet was for triaging vitals, patient reports were still solely accessible through the hospital's central computer system.

Fortunately it was a slow night. All but a few of the triage gurneys were empty. Hoping his luck would hold, he headed for the central staff area known informally as the Pit. As usual, it was a mess, the small central table littered with soda cans, open bags of junk food, and assorted takeout containers. A half-eaten pepperoni pizza congealed in its open cardboard delivery box. Blue-bound patient charts spilled across the surrounding countertops and took up several of the plastic and metal chairs. Three of the six computers were taken, two by staff members with whom he worked on a fairly regular basis. Fortunately they were busy typing, their backs to him. The other, a good-natured if gabby senior nurse whose name he remembered was Wilma, crammed a fistful of cheese popcorn into her mouth while filling out a requisition form. Hospitals, like most workplaces, were hotbeds for gossip. Marc had never given anyone cause to say two words about him—until now.

Keeping his head down, he gave Wilma a broad berth, tiptoeing toward the open terminal farthest away. With luck, he'd look up his results and be in and out before she or the others spotted him.

"Good Lord, what happened to you?" Wilma asked, covering orange-stained fingers over the phone receiver.

So much for luck.

Before Marc could come up with a plausible lie, one of the nursing assistants swiveled around on his seat, his jaw dropping when he saw Marc's face. "I bet it was one of those delivery dudes on the bikes. Motherfuckers will mow you down and keep pedaling."

"No, it wasn't anybody on a bike."

"Don't tell me you got in a fight?" Wilma persisted. "Not you, of all people."

Not exactly sure how to take that, Marc shook his head. "No, I wasn't in a fight—though I did box in college," he added to salvage his pride.

Their knee-jerk disbelief that he might be a badass on his off-duty time wasn't wholly flattering. It took him back to his prepubescent beanpole days when he seemed to be a magnet for every bully on the block. If it hadn't been for Tony having his back, Marc wasn't sure he would have survived to make it to college. The unexpected thought prompted a painful pang.

Wilma waived a chubby hand, several fingers stained orange from the snack. "Oh, I'm sure you can handle yourself. It's just that you've got to be the most laid-back resident on the floor."

So much for his having no game—and no poker face. If they thought he was relaxed, there was only one explanation. He must be an ace actor. That was both the plus and minus of being both passionate and an introvert—few people ever got to glimpse the storm raging inside you.

But these past few weeks he'd let Honey see inside him, not all the way but more in-depth than any other women he'd dated. It struck him that maybe she wasn't the only one of them addicted to playacting roles rather than keeping things real. With her carefully curated vintage couture and retro hair and makeup, as well as the Audrey quotes sprinkling her speech, she was at least honest about it. Marc suddenly realized that he couldn't lay claim to the same.

Wilma's voice drew him back to the present. "Hmm, hmm, hmm. I'd lay down money it's a woman that made those marks." A fat finger pointed toward his left cheek. "That's a scratch, and as a general rule men don't fight with their fingernails." She turned to the other nurse. "Doctor Sandler here has woman problems."

"I don't have . . . " Mid-denial, Marc stopped himself. Woman problems summed up his situation with scary accuracy, not that he meant to admit it. "Let's just say a friend was going through a rough time the other night and leave it at that, okay?"

Seeing her and the assistant nurse trade smirks, Marc felt his face burn.

Wilma looked him up and down, her glowing gaze suggesting she was seeing him in a new light. "Hmm, hmm, hmm," she intoned again, sucking salty fake cheese from her thumb as if giving it head. "Suit yourself, Romeo—or should I say Doctor Fifty Shades?"

✳✳✳ ✳✳✳

Honey tried again, studying the paint chips fanned out over Marc's dining room table. It was no use. The various hues of pale blue blended together, no doubt because her tired eyes burned. She'd hoped the previous night's hot sex with Marc might settle her mind, but instead it only emphasized how very much stood at stake for her to lose. Marc. Ever since Carlson and company had swooped into her life, a future together no longer seemed like such a sure thing. She'd spent most of the night and early morning lying awake beside him listening to the sounds of his breathing. Thankfully he was pulling a double shift at the hospital. Hearing his phone alarm go off, she'd quickly closed her eyes and pretended to be asleep rather than face him.

She pushed the samples aside and picked up her cell phone. "Liz, it's me. Honey. I know it's late but do you maybe . . . have a minute?"

As a freelance graphics designer, Liz often worked late into the night. She swore she got her best work out of the way when the apartment was silent and Jonathan sleeping. "Of course. Actually you just saved me from emailing."

"I did?" Either Liz had major telepathic powers or they were on totally different pages.

"Did you get my e-vite?" Liz asked.

Honey hesitated. "I . . . I didn't see it."

That was, strictly speaking, the truth. She hadn't checked her email in days, not even from her phone. Ever since the other day when she'd texted Drew her "apology," with agents Carlson and Wilkes looking on, she'd been walking around in a semi daze. To her dismay, he'd accepted. Far from her slipping off the FBI's hook, "Operation Moneybags" as she thought of it was going forward full steam and taking her, and her future, with it.

"No matter," Liz said, pulling her back to the present. "How would you feel about bringing your hot doctor over for drinks this Friday? Nothing fancy, just a cheese platter and some two-buck chuck, but I already checked and Peter and Pol can make it. Brian hasn't gotten back to me yet, but Sarah and Cole are coming by with the baby. What do you say?"

"Actually this Friday isn't . . . good for me—us." Friday was Drew's Investors' Day and thus the sting operation.

"Oh, that's too bad," Liz said, sounding disappointed and maybe a little miffed, too. "Another time, then. I'll leave it to you to let me know when you're free." She made as if to end the call.

Heart pounding, Honey shocked herself by saying, "Liz—wait!"

"What is it?"

Honey hesitated, weighing her words. Though she'd resisted the temptation to tell Marc anything about the FBI's plans for her, she needed to confide in someone. If things went poorly, if something happened to her at Drew's hands, she didn't want her friends, and most of all Marc, left thinking she was a brainless bimbo who'd betrayed them all by going back to her abuser.

And she could use, if not advice, certainly a sounding board. Liz was one of the smartest and most grounded people Honey knew. Ever since joining FATE, she'd looked up to Liz not only as a mentor but also as the big sister she'd always wanted. The courage with which Liz had faced cancer was a testimony to her inner strength. Above all, she could trust Liz to give her straight talk—even if the answers weren't always ones Honey wanted to hear.

"That promise I made last Monday night, I'm afraid I'm going to have to break it."

Liz paused and Honey could all but hear the wheels turning as she thought back to their last FATE session. "Honey, why? He's a violent sadist. He's hurt you before. There's no telling how he might retaliate this time, especially since you've rejected him. What could you possibly have to gain by getting back with him? Why would you even consider coming within ten feet of a guy like that?"

How about because I look dreadful in orange? "I . . . " Honey stopped herself from saying more. What if the FBI had tapped her phone? To her best recollection, the cell hadn't left her hands or her sight, not even during her FBI interview. Still, if she was wrong, she risked dragging Liz into her mess, and above all Liz had her son to consider.

"Honey, for God's sake, say something—anything."

"I . . . Is there any chance I could come over for a few minutes?'

Chapter Ten

"There are certain shades of limelight that can wreck a girl's complexion."—Audrey Hepburn, *Breakfast at Tiffany's*

The message Marc received from Liz, one of Honey's FATE friends, had come from out of the blue. When she asked to speak to him in person rather than over the phone, he knew something serious must be up. Pulling a twelve-hour shift as he was, the hospital cafeteria was the best he could manage, given the short notice. She agreed to meet him there on his morning break.

Sighting a built brunette wearing a visitor's badge and eying the diners, Marc pushed his plastic chair back from the cafeteria table and stood. "Liz?"

She nodded, looking relieved. "It's so nice to finally meet you. Honey's told us quite a lot about you."

Taming his curiosity as to what she might have said, he gestured to the lines leading to the hot and cold food bars. "Can I get you some breakfast?"

She glanced down to the paper cup she held. "I'm good with coffee, thanks." She slid into the seat across from him. "I really appreciate you making time to meet, Doctor Sandler."

"Please, call me Marc, and I'm the one who's grateful to you for accommodating my work schedule. I know a hospital cafeteria probably isn't what you had in mind, but the coffee here isn't half bad."

She shrugged. "I've had more than my share of hospital food in the last few years, so no worries. I consider myself almost a connoisseur at this point."

Rather than pry, he said, "Honey's mentioned you two are in some kind of a group together, but I don't know much else."

She hesitated. "I can't really speak about the nature of our group with you—that would be up to Honey and what her comfort level is."

"Of course." He glanced at his phone, checking the time. He had to be back on the floor in ten minutes. "I'm afraid I can't stay long."

"I know you're busy but this was too important to let go and—" she leaned forward, lowering her voice "—I wasn't entirely comfortable discussing it over the phone."

"I think you'd better tell me what's on your mind."

She sighed heavily. "Are you aware that the other day when Honey went back to pack up her . . . old place, she was picked up by the FBI?"

The FBI! "No, I was not. That night I noticed she was in an off mood, but she wouldn't tell me what was wrong. What could the FBI want with Honey?"

"It's not Honey they're after, but Jerk Face—sorry, Winterthur. Drew Winterthur is the man who—"

"I'm familiar, yes."

"The feds suspect him of stock fraud but they need more proof—his recorded confession—and they want Honey to get it for them. He's holding some kind of big bash at the Waldorf for the investors he's swindled, and Honey is supposed to get it then."

He'd always known Winterthur was a boozer and a brute. What he hadn't realized was he was also a real-life Gordon Gekko.

Thinking back to the trashed apartment, Winterthur's handiwork, he said, "Can't she just say no?"

Liz hesitated. "Unfortunately Jerk Face set up one of his dummy corporations in her name and got her to sign the incorporation papers by making her think it was the apartment lease. If she doesn't do what they want—"

"They'll indict her, too." Marc gripped the edge of the table. It was eight years ago all over again, history repeating, only the loved one involved on the wrong side of the law wasn't his drug-dealing brother but Honey, the woman he loved. And unlike Tony, she was innocent. "Thank you for telling me. I know it can't have been easy."

"It wasn't, but from everything she's told us about you, you seem like you genuinely care for her."

"I do. I haven't known her all that long, but I love her."

Her tense expression eased. "Then my telling you was the right thing to do."

He nodded. "It was. But what I don't understand is why Honey didn't tell me herself."

Sure, he'd been working a lot that week, but the other night when she'd come home in a mood, he'd given her ample opportunity. Instead of telling him the truth, she'd talked nonsense about taking off to Paris. After all the progress they'd made these last few weeks, the barriers they'd broken down, could it be she still didn't totally trust him?

Liz hesitated. "She's afraid you'll interfere."

Damn right he was going to "interfere." FBI or no FBI, no way was he letting her go back into the lion's den alone.

"Believe it or not, she's trying to protect you."

Marc didn't need protecting, but after this was over, Winterthur well might. Rather than say so, and risk Liz clamming up, he asked, "When is this all going down?"

"Tomorrow starting at noon."

D-day, Operation Moneybags, dawned cloudless and mildly warm—a stark contrast to the storm taking place in Honey's mind. One worry at least had proven unfounded. Getting Marc out of the house had been surprisingly easy. Thank God for his early morning staff meeting, which had allowed her to get ready unobserved. Pulling off the charade of getting back together with Drew didn't allow for half measures. Full makeup, big hair, and lots of cleavage had, until recently, been a way of life, but now she felt as though she were slipping back into a costume.

Standing in the back of the FBI surveillance SUV, she stared into the dressing mirror and asked herself yet again if Carlson's trust hadn't been misplaced. Until a few weeks ago, she'd been trapped in a long-term abusive relationship with an intimate partner. Before that she'd been an escort and, earlier, a runaway. Despite all the marvelous changes she'd made since meeting Marc, she still didn't have her GED. Was she truly "asset" material?

And then there were the logistics of the operation, which truly boggled her mind. Surveillance in the wireless era seemed to be part *Star Trek*, part *James Bond*. Given the slinky dress Drew would be expecting her to wear, where could she conceal a wire?

As it turned out, the digital device, no bigger than a pen cap, was sufficiently sophisticated to record not only sound but also high-definition video, streaming it live to a remote computer. In her case, it was disguised as a bejeweled clip and affixed to the hair fascinator she'd be wearing. It seemed her penchant for vintage fashion had a practical application after all.

But technology, no matter how advanced, could only take you so far. There was, as always, the human factor to consider. Marc.

Liz had counseled, even pleaded, for Honey to come clean with him, but Honey had held firm. He'd never go along with her putting herself in such danger. He might well try to stop her. Who knew, but he might go all Sir Galahad on her and follow her inside the Waldorf. Interfering with a federal investigation carried a stiff penalty, including jail time. Ever since they'd met, he'd put himself out on the line for her, starting with the morning she checked herself out of *his* ER and he showed up at her apartment to make sure she was safe. The days of her putting him on the line were past.

She looked between Carlson and Wilkes; the latter had just completed a sound check. "Are we done?"

Carlson shook his head. "Not quite. You'll need a safe word."

Even under these circumstances, Honey couldn't resist. "A safe word? I wouldn't have figured you for the type."

Carlson's ears turned bright pink. "Something you can easily work into the conversation in the unlikely event that things go south, and we need to get you out of there."

Small surprise, the first word that came to mind was a name. *Audrey*.

And why not? The actress was the closest Honey had ever come to having a patron saint. Knowing that invoking her name would bring her the necessary aid and exit strategy made her feel watched over and safe—or at least as safe as someone concealing a recording device to entrap her violent and apparently felonious former lover could be expected to feel.

She only hoped she wouldn't need to use it.

"Audrey?" He looked predictably puzzled.

"Trust me, Drew hearing me say 'Audrey' will be the most natural thing in the world."

"Remember the script we went over," Carlson counseled. We need him to incriminate himself explicitly."

Honey nodded. "Assuming he doesn't throw me up against a wall on sight, I'll get you your evidence."

Carlson cracked an actual smile, the first she'd so far seen. "You're confident, that's good."

"Of course I'm confident. Men like Drew live and breathe to do one thing when they're alone with a woman like me."

Blushing, the agents traded sheepish looks.

Taking pity on them, Honey supplied, "Brag."

❊❊❊ ❊❊❊

Eyes on the parked Con Edison truck, Marc pulled up the hood of his gray sweatshirt and fell back, blending in with the other pedestrians packing the city sidewalk. Dressed to the nines, Honey descended from the vehicle's rear, walked over to the curb, and flagged down a taxi to take her the few blocks to the Waldorf. Standing back as she got in was one of the hardest things Marc had ever had to do. Playing dumb earlier while she'd continued lying to him hadn't proved any picnic, either. Instead of going to work as he'd told her, he'd hung around, staking out his building. As soon as she'd left, he'd followed her.

Now he waited for the cab to whisk her away and then made his way over to what must be the FBI surveillance SUV. Reaching it, he rapped his knuckles on the rear passenger side door. A couple more knocks brought the heavily tinted window rolling down.

A dark-haired man wearing sunglasses poked his head out. "Can I help you with something?"

"I don't know, can you? I'm looking for my girlfriend. I just saw her step out of this van."

"Sorry, pal, you've made a mistake."

"I don't believe I have. My name's Sandler, Doctor Marcus Sandler." He reached up and dropped his hood.

The guy's eyes bugged. "Jesus, did anyone see you? Never mind, get in!"

Marc didn't have to be asked a second time. He grabbed the handle, slid the door back, and climbed inside.

He glanced around, giving his eyes a moment to adjust from the sunlight. The vehicle's interior looked like a compact version of the bridge of *Star Trek*'s USS *Enterprise*. Though he'd known they were setting up a sting, the sheer quantity of surveillance equipment took him aback. Closed-circuit TV monitors lined the console. Six side-by-side cameras afforded a 360-degree panorama of the hotel block as well as its interior. Videotape decks, video printers, a power periscope, motion detection and logging devices galore—if Honey's safety hadn't been at stake, Marc might have geeked out on the sheer coolness of it all.

Feeling eyes on him, he turned back to the agents. "Which one of you is Carlson?"

The dark-haired man stepped forward. "I am."

He and his blond partner were both in dark suits. A third man, shaggy-looking and wearing headphones and a zip-up jacket, sat with his back to Marc, gaze glued to the monitor before him. "I've got her coming outta the elevator."

Glancing over the guy's shoulder to the screen, Marc saw Honey step off a hotel elevator and head down a carpeted hallway. Based on the way she kept patting one side of her headpiece, it was a pretty good bet that's where the recording device was concealed—damn!

"How much do you know?" Carlson's question had him dragging his gaze away from Honey.

He straightened and turned around. "Enough to know you're trying to nail Winterthur using my girl as bait."

The blond agent spoke up. "Until a few weeks ago, she was Winterthur's girl."

"That was then, this is now."

Marc thought back to the foiled fancy lunch meant to celebrate the start of their future together and a wave of regret washed over him. Since meeting Liz and learning of the sting, he felt almost as if he and Honey were star-crossed lovers from an Edith Wharton novel. As with Ethan Frome and his Mattie or Newland Archer and his Countess Ellen, Fate with a capital "F" always seemed to find a way to drive him and Honey apart.

Only Marc wasn't having it.

He looked back to the nearest monitor as Honey approached a busy banquet room. "If you won't pull her out, then put me in, too."

Whatever happened, Marc was determined that Honey would know it wasn't only her FATE group friends she had to rely on. She had him.

"I'm afraid that's out of the question. We're professionals, Doctor. We've got this."

"But, I'm a veteran at this. I've worn a wire before."

"How so?"

Marc hesitated but only for a moment. "My brother was dealing drugs, and I turned state's evidence against him. Because of me, he's in prison."

Until now, Marc had never admitted that to a living soul. He was pretty sure his mother at least suspected, but they never spoke of it, not directly. Even though betraying his brother had been in the service of doing "the right thing," a part of him had never fully forgiven himself. Every time he saw his mother's gaze list toward the empty chair at the dining room table, he felt another chunk of his soul chip away.

The agents exchanged looks, no doubt impressed at what a heartless SOB he was. Marc tensed, waiting.

"Okay, but you can't go in like that. Nobody's going to buy that you're an investor."

Marc glanced down at himself. Along with the hoodie, he wore track pants and his running shoes and carried a backpack. For once his fashion failure was in the service of stealth. Had he left the house in a suit, Honey would have surely noticed.

"And Winterthur's already met you at the hospital fundraiser in February."

Jesus, how long had they been following Winterthur and, by extension, Honey?

"So, set me up with a disguise." Marc looked over Carlson, the taller and more broad-shouldered of the two. "What suit size are you?"

The agent blanched.

"I am the captain of my fucking universe!"

The voice, Winterthur's, had them staring at the monitors once more. He stood at the front of the thronged banquet room, screaming his "greed is good" shtick into the microphone. Judging from the rapt faces in the audience, he had his "investors" right where he wanted them. Marc scanned the image, studying the setup. Attendees sat at eight-top tables or hung out by the platform steps or at the bars set up in back. Servers, skimpily clad and masked, ferried drinks from the service bars to the main table. So far as Marc could see, they were all women—but did it necessarily follow that they *had* to be?

Carlson broke in on his thoughts. "Tell me, Doctor Sandler, just how do you imagine we're going to get you in there now without jeopardizing this whole operation? Why should we even try?"

Despite the dire circumstances, Marc managed a smile. "Because I have a very special set of skills, agent."

"Right, you're a doctor. If someone chokes on a chicken bone from the buffet, I guess we're all set."

Marc looked up. "I wasn't speaking about medicine."

"No? Then what?"

"I waited tables in college."

✳✳✳ ✳✳✳

"Do you see what I see? Because I see a lot of wealth in this room!"

Standing onstage in front of the logoed backdrop, microphone in hand, Drew stoked his audience's enthusiasm. Roars rose up from the floor of round-top tables. In reserved seating nearest the stage, Honey resisted the urge to cover her ears.

"*Feel* it. *Own* it. Say it with me: I am the captain of my fucking universe."

Obediently the room chorused: "I am the captain of my universe."

He'd been drinking heavily since she'd shown up two hours earlier, slugging back scotch between the other presentations. Sweating out his Macallan 25, he scowled. "No, not just universe—your *fucking* universe. Say it again."

Louder this time, the shout rose up: "I am the captain of my fucking universe!!!"

The back-and-forth reminded Honey of the evangelists who used to come to town in the summers, pitching their tents and portable bleachers on the fairgrounds, selling salvation at ten dollars a ticket. Drew was cut from the same cloth, only he was worse, much worse. The tenters had hired local kids to put flyers on car dashboards, but Drew and his flunkies used their phones to invade people's homes, sinking in their hooks, not letting go until they'd siphoned off their money—and their dreams.

"Whew, that's better." Drew paused to wipe his forehead, not with the silk handkerchief folded in his suit pocket but with the back of his hand as if to show that he was no snob, that though he might be a fancy Manhattan "wealth manager" he was still a man of the people. "I don't know about you, but all this shouting's making me thirsty. You folks thirsty?"

One of the relatively few attending female investors, a fiftyish woman in a polyester pantsuit, turquoise bowtie blouse, and with an asymmetrical nineties-era bob, lifted her beer bottle and shouted, "Hell's to the yes!"

Drew let out a laugh. "That's the spirit. Drink up, everybody. You've earned it."

Sipping her Pellegrino from a champagne flute, Honey conceded that was the one true statement he'd so far made. Every investor in the room had paid for the "privilege" of their presence with blood, sweat, and tears. Unless she succeeded in getting Drew's confession on record, they'd be paying permanently.

The current event alone must cost a small fortune. Bankrolling it with his investors' money, Drew had spared no expense. Upon arrival, each "guest" had been given a lavish goody bag of high-end booze, bath products, and tech gadgets. Models circulated between tables wearing elaborate feathered and bejeweled masks, beaded bikini-style tops and bottoms, stilettos—and nothing else. The earlier brunch buffet had included seafood, carving and omelet stations, as well as limitless Bloody Marys, mimosas, and Bellinis.

Later on the agenda came a sit-down dinner in the famous Starlight Room. He'd also reserved the Presidential Suite for the after-party. It was conspicuous consumption, decadence done to the extreme, a smoke-and-mirrors ploy that sickened Honey. How she could ever have consented to be part of this, not the pump-and-dump scheme—she honestly hadn't so much as suspected—but the lifestyle, a world where things were done because they could be gotten away with, regardless of whether they were right or wrong, good or bad, healthy or polluting?

Drew's voice riveted her back to the stage. "Are you with me, people? C'mon now, let the Drewster hear you say it."

"Yeah, Drew, we're with you!"

Drew glanced Honey's way and grinned. Playing the proud girlfriend, she plastered on what hopefully passed for a bedazzled smile and raised her glass to him.

Seemingly satisfied, he turned back to the audience. "Good. Now we're going to take a well-deserved break. Those bars on either end of the room are open for a reason, so go get yourselves another cocktail because when we start up again, I have a very special surprise for you.

So if you haven't already, check your boundaries at the door because, ladies and gentlemen, you are in for one helluva show."

Honey spied a few nervous looks and self-conscious smiles, but after several hours of boozing, most attendees had drunk the Kool-Aid along with everything else the open bars had to offer. Scanning the sea of flushed faces, Honey wondered if the whistleblower was among them. If so, he—or she—must be feeling much as Honey did. The possibility made her feel somewhat less alone.

Nursing her pretend champagne, she watched Drew descend the side stage stairs. Glad-handing a path through the tables of investors, he made his way toward her.

Frank Dawes grabbed a fresh drink from the tray of a passing server and joined him. She hadn't set eyes on him since the night he'd come close to raping her—with Drew's blessing, no less. Beyond shooting her a few fuming looks, he'd so far kept his distance. They drew up at her reserved table, Frank eyeing the empty seat on either side of her.

"You're looking good, Honey," he said, checking out the cleavage revealed by her low-cut dress.

Honey sent him an openly icy stare, grateful that her deal with Carlson and company didn't require cozying up to her would-be rapist. "And you, Frank, unfortunately, look exactly the same."

His fat face twisted into a frown.

"That's enough, you two," Drew intervened, sliding into the seat beside Honey. "Frank, mind finding the catering manager and telling him to send over another bottle of Macallan? We're running dry."

Frank lobbed Honey a seething stare. "Why not send little Miss Hepburn here? Maybe she can blow him and get us a discount—a *deep* discount."

Aware of Carlson's surveillance team listening in, Honey felt her face heat. Refusing to rise to the bait, she held her head high, her shoulders back, and her smile in place.

Drew draped a proprietary arm about her, and she resisted the urge to move away. "Seriously, buddy, I need a few minutes alone with Honey."

"Suit yourself, but don't say I didn't warn you." He speared Honey with another look. "I'm watching you, bitch." She opened her mouth to answer but before she could, he strode away in a huff.

"Don't listen to him. He gets this way when he's stressing." Drew leaned closer, his scotch-stale breath blowing across her face. "I want you to know I'm glad you're here."

"So am I," she lied. Mindful of her mission, getting Drew's recorded confession, she fished, "W-what is Frank stressed about? Everything seems to be going so well. Isn't it?"

"Of course it is. Everything's going great. Look, I even got my girl back and looking more gorgeous than ever."

He gave her yet another appreciative once-over, and Honey forced herself not to fidget. Though the Stella McCartney dress wasn't her usual style—the figured black lace showed through to a thigh-high cream-colored underskirt—it was a perfect choice for the occasion, suggestive, even teasing, a dress designed to whet appetites, not sate them. Though the FBI was prepared to foot the bill, to avoid arousing Drew's suspicions, she'd agreed to purchase the dress with his credit card. Once tonight was over, she planned to give it away, perhaps to Liz.

His gaze finally left her legs and returned to her face. "But I gotta say I was surprised to get your message. I really thought you were gone for good."

Thinking how close she'd come to free, Honey swallowed against her throat's thickening. "So did I."

One sandy eyebrow lifted. "What changed your mind?"

She shrugged, though his arm still banded her. "I suppose I . . . hadn't counted on how different life would be without you." Different as in glorious, liberating, spectacular.

His lips lifted in a smug smile that her palm itched to slap away. "Yeah, well, now you know, so no more running away. And threatening to blow the whistle on me with my wife—that wasn't cool. I'll admit it, you really had me by the balls there."

"I'm sorry." The apology, though empty, tasted bitter nonetheless. She took a sip of water, wishing she might rinse her mouth. "Since I'm here, maybe you could explain how all this . . . stock business works. HG Enterprises sounds so grand. I hadn't realized you'd named a company using my initials. That's really . . . lovely of you. What does it do, exactly?"

He opened his mouth, as if to answer, and then closed it again. "Don't worry about it," he finally said, reaching for his drink.

Clearly he needed more scotch—and a little push. "HG Enterprises doesn't do anything at all, does it? It's a made-up company, isn't it? What is the term? I just learned it the other day." She paused, pretending to ponder. "Oh yes—*dummy corporation*. Isn't that what it's called?"

His arm fell away but not before she felt him tense. "Lower your voice!"

"Sorry, but I'm right, aren't I?" She'd better be, because so far she'd been the only one of them doing any talking for the record. "The stocks you're selling aren't even penny stocks, are they? They're worthless."

"Since when are you so interested in my business dealings?"

For a few frozen seconds, Honey's heart stopped. She'd gone too fast, been too brash, too transparently obvious. Drew was many things—violent, vindictive, and apparently as crooked as they came—but he was far from stupid.

She slipped on a smile. "In the spirit of 'new leaves and new beginnings,' I thought I should take more of an interest in what you do, that it might . . . bring us closer."

Saying the latter nearly brought up her breakfast. The moment she got his incriminating admission on record, she meant to clear out as fast and far away as she could. Once she was free and clear, she promised herself she'd tell Marc everything, not just about the sting operation but about her past, too. He deserved the truth from her, regardless of what he chose to do about it.

Drew reached out, pulling her closer. "That's sweet, baby, but to be totally upfront with you, I've never been all that interested in your mind. Now that hot body of yours, on the other hand . . . " He reached over and palmed her breast.

"Drew, please, not here." She tried moving his hand away, but he wasn't having it.

He brought his mouth brushing her ear. "You've been a seriously bad girl, Honey, a real little bitch. At some point, I'm going to have to punish you. You realize that, right?"

"Wasn't destroying everything I own punishment enough?" Try as she might, she couldn't entirely keep the archness from her voice.

Fortunately it seemed he was too tripping on ego to notice. "I'm thinking of something more . . . creative." He reached out and traced her mouth with his thumb, and Honey braced herself against her sudden terrified trembling.

"Scotch, sir?"

That voice, it sounded like . . . *Marc!* Honey whipped her head around and looked up. *Oh . . . my . . . God.* It *was* Marc! Even wearing a black satin mask and an old style fedora, he was impossible not to recognize. A bow tie—no jacket, no shirt—and a pair of black tuxedo pants that looked like they'd been painted on summed up his server's "uniform."

But what was he doing here? Did he know about Operation Moneybags, or had he simply followed her here thinking she'd really gone back to Drew? Either he saw her as a serial cheater or a FBI patsy with a shady past—Honey couldn't decide which scenario was worse.

Offloading the bottle of Macallan and clean glasses from the tray, he snagged her gaze. "Another champagne for the lady?"

"N-not right now, thank you." She cast a quick, sideways look at Drew, but his attention had already wandered to the stage, where several hotel staff members were setting up for his "surprise." He was so all about himself that a doctor he'd met briefly months ago wouldn't make a lasting impression—or so Honey hoped.

Drew turned back to her. Beneath the table, he grabbed her hand—and laid it on his crotch.

Aware of Marc hovering, mask-framed eyes murderous, she dropped her voice and said, "Drew, please, not here. We can't—"

"Sure we can. This is my party, and I'll come if I want to," he shot back with a snort, clearly pleased with himself for his perverted paraphrasing of the sixties pop song.

Marc broke in. "Shall I pour now, sir?"

Drew lifted his gaze from Honey and glared. "Don't bother. Just leave the bottle and go."

Marc reached for the scotch. "It's no bother, sir. It's my job."

Drew made a grab for the bottle as well. "I told you, just leave it."

The tug-of-war ended in Marc's favor. Taking possession of the bottle, he bent to pour the liquor into Drew's glass—and doused his lap instead. To any onlooker, it would appear to be an honest accident, only Honey knew it was purely on purpose.

Looking up from his drenched pants front, Drew exploded. "You cock-sucking, ass-rimming piece of shit! I'll make sure you never work another event in this city again."

"So sorry, sir," Marc apologized, sounding sincere and lackey-like, though Honey saw the way his mouth tightened and the telltale muscle jumping in his jaw. "I'll get you some club soda," he added, backing away.

Drew turned to Honey. "I have a spare suit in the suite. Hang out here. I'll be back soon."

Relieved for the reprieve to gather herself and rethink her strategy now that Marc was here, Honey nodded. "Of course. Don't rush on my account."

He bent and planted a peck on her lips, his breath stale with booze. Honey forced herself to bear it though she wondered how, and why, she'd chosen to for all those years.

But at least he hadn't suggested she join him in the suite, not yet. That would come later, of course. Watching him hurry toward the nearest exit door, she acknowledged she needed to get him to confess before he either passed out or tried taking her to bed—or both. But first she had to find Marc and convince him to leave. As soon as Drew cleared the ballroom, she popped up from her seat and went in search.

Fortunately his height and clothing, or lack of it, made him easy to spot. She met up with him by the service bar, where he was offloading the dirty glasses he'd collected into a busboy's bin.

Seeing her approach, he finished clearing his tray and, in a carrying voice, asked, "Changed your mind about that champagne after all, ma'am?"

Aware of the two bartenders and several guests and servers nearby, she didn't explain that she wasn't actually drinking. She'd intended to stay sober and clear-headed but, still reeling from the shock of seeing Marc as she was, one real drink might not be so bad.

"Y-yes, I have."

Marc shook his head. "Dishwasher's backed up, and we ran out of champagne glasses. I'll go into the kitchen and get some," he added, casting a look to a swiveled side door.

Honey nodded. "Great, thank you. I'll . . . come back in a bit."

She waited for him to get a bit ahead and then followed him over. Sliding the empty tray under a brawny arm, he took hold of her elbow and steered her into the kitchen.

Inside, the noise was near deafening, the back-and-forth between servers, busboys, dishwashers, prep people, and line cooks making it hard to find a spot where no one would bump into them. On the plus side, everyone seemed too fraught to bother giving them more than an annoyed look in passing.

Knowing she didn't have much time until Drew returned, Honey started in. "Oh my God, what are you doing here? And dressed like . . . that?"

Even in the midst of processing her shock, now that they were away from Drew, she felt her body reacting. Just looking at Marc had her nipples peaking and her panties' crotch dampening. Despite having seen him naked on several occasions now, having him here, like this, had her salivating.

Mindful of the wire she wore, she added, "You don't know what you've stepped into the middle of. You need to leave—now."

He shook his head, adamant. "Not happening." Dropping his voice, he added, "I know you're wearing a wire and I know why, and I'm telling you flat out I'm not setting foot outside this hotel without you."

"But Drew's *met* you, remember? Just because he hasn't recognized you yet doesn't mean he won't."

"He met *Doctor Sandler*. I doubt he'll press pause long enough on his activities to connect the dots from ER doctor to—"

"Male model?"

A deep blush answered. "I was going to say drinks mule, actually. Apparently a few of the investors are gay."

Trust Drew to cover his bases, in this case expanding the eye candy to include a little beefcake. Marc was a serious serving of both. But there would be plenty of time later for ogling, or so she hoped. For now . . .

"How long have you known? How did you even find out?"

He blew out a breath. "The postmortem will have to wait until later. Suffice it to say, you're a seriously bad liar. I knew the other day you didn't miss lunch because of any sample sale. Now I know the real reason: you were being interrogated by the feds."

Honey swallowed. He must have spoken to Liz. Unless he had been tailing her along with Carlson, it was the only explanation. "I believe they prefer 'interviewed.' It comes off as less confrontational."

He shrugged. "Semantics. Had you trusted me with the truth, I would have put you in touch with a buddy of mine, a criminal defense attorney, who might have come up with an alternative to sticking your neck out like this. Since you didn't, since we're here, I'm going to make sure you stay safe until you get what the FBI needs to close this case. How close are you?"

"Not very," she admitted, acutely aware of Carlson and company listening in. "I think he may suspect something. As soon as I started asking questions about the money, he clammed up."

"Then don't ask anymore, not directly. We have some time. I'll keep the scotch flowing. He may not incriminate himself to you outright, but you might catch him saying something to his partner."

For a self-avowed straight arrow, he certainly seemed savvy on the subject of sting operations. Wondering about that, Honey asked, "If you knew everything, why'd you deliberately spill scotch on him?"

His gaze shuttered. "What makes you so sure that wasn't an actual accident?"

She tossed him a look.

"Okay, I saw his hands all over you, and I . . . maybe went a little crazy for a minute."

Honey felt her heart turn over. A hot hunk with a brain *and* a heart of gold—she couldn't imagine what she'd ever done to deserve him, but whatever it was, she meant to keep doing it. He was the polar opposite of Drew and Frank and all the other users like them. She only hoped that once she came through this, *if* she came through, he'd still be willing to stick around so she could make it all up to him. She opened her mouth to say . . . something when a canned gong sounded. Together they turned toward the exit.

Marc pitched his voice above the din. "You'd better get back to your table. Sounds like it's showtime."

✳✳✳ ✳✳✳

Seated back at the table with Drew, Honey watched the stage surge with models. Pulled off the floor and temporarily relieved of drinks' duty, they performed a loosely choreographed collective striptease to the tune of the Human League's "Don't You Want Me?" Who knew their sparkly costumes were tear-offs? Tasseled pasties quivered from the tips of bouncing breasts. G-strings bisected gyrating bottoms. Perspiration glistened off spa-sculpted bodies.

Drew lip-synched the lyrics, pantomiming crooning into an invisible microphone. Honey forced a smile and made a show of singing along too, though the kicky eighties pop tune only underscored her regrets. She might not be "working as a waitress in a cocktail bar," but otherwise the parallels to her former arrangement with Drew weren't lost on her. Drew had indeed picked her out and turned her around—turned her into someone new. Only the person she'd become at his behest wasn't someone she liked terribly much.

Getting him to confess—brag—was proving trickier than she'd thought. What if he didn't? Would Carlson still honor the spirit if not the letter of the deal he made with her?

She couldn't afford to think about that now. Her best bet was to get him alone or in a smaller, more intimate setting of his peers where he'd be more inclined to speak freely. The rub was that the only real peer he had with him today was Frank. Insulting him earlier had felt good at the time, but now she saw it for what it was: a serious tactical error.

The music segued to hip-hop. The sea of spinning females parted, the dancers exiting the stage by way of either set of side stairs. A tall man shrouded in gray hoodie, baggy sweat pants, and wearing white high tops swaggered to center stage. The performer flipped back his hood and Honey's breath caught on a gasp. It was Marc. Pushing drinks in a skimpy uniform was one thing but this—stripping on stage—could he really pull it off? The one time she'd suggested they go dancing, he'd sworn he had two left feet.

But the sex machine strutting the stage's four corners was an entirely different entity from the conservative persona he projected in public. Sure, she'd seen the super sexy side of him in private, but what he was about to do—put himself out there, literally *out* there—was about as public as you could take things.

His routine began with breakdancing. A few moves into it, she saw her worries were unfounded. He more than knew what he was doing. Back flips, spins, cartwheels, flares, even hand hops—he performed all in perfect time to the music. She knew he was in amazing shape. After years of sleeping with an alcoholic who sometimes went soft or nodded off, she had reason to appreciate his stamina in bed and out of it, but this . . . How did he keep it up? And where had he picked up those moves?

And he didn't just have the choreography down. He also brought . . . *attitude*. Sending smoldering looks out into the audience, lingering on the face of each woman regardless of her appearance or age, he knew how to connect, how to make her feel as if she were the most beautiful, desirable female in the room. Until now, the only woman Honey had ever seen him look at that way was herself. Even though she knew the act was necessary to his cover, Honey couldn't help it. She felt jealous.

And then his clothes started coming off, and she forgot about being jealous—or breathing.

He started with the hoodie, bringing the zipper down in one slow, smooth slide. A few more acrobatic moves and then the sneakers went by the wayside. Somehow he managed to slip them off without fumbling, even though they were at least loosely laced—there must be some trick to it but still, *impressive!* He peeled off the wife beater and pulled it off over his head, treating the audience to a view of beautifully sculpted biceps, impossibly firm pectorals, and six-pack abs. Skimming off the sweatpants sent every woman in the audience, including Honey, swooning. Powerful thighs, molded knees, and muscled calves—how had Honey missed that his legs weren't only athletic but unbelievably beautiful?

But it wasn't only his torso and legs that the wild-eyed crowd ogled. It was his package. Encased in a red G-string the color of sin, he was long and thick and at least semi-hard. Recalling the amazing texture and taste of him, the exquisite pressure of all that unrelenting maleness moving inside her vagina and at the back of her throat, Honey caught herself licking her lips. Catching Drew watching her, she slipped her tongue back inside her mouth and tried to remember that, in public at least, she'd always acted as a lady.

But then Marc turned so that he faced away from the crowd and— wow! Like his legs, his ass was a marvel of masculine beauty. Staring at those firm quivering cheeks, the curve from back to buttocks a purely perfect arc she longed to lick, the lobes taut as barely ripe melons, Honey reached for her glass and downed most of the remaining sparkling water in a single, thirsting swallow. A few booty shakes sufficed to bring the audience surging to its feet—and a few members dropping to their knees. Given the gyrations he was keeping up, Honey was amazed the scarlet G-string didn't snap.

Eyes popped. Mouths fell open. Squeals and shrieks ricocheted around the room. Several women, and a few men, fanned themselves. Honey couldn't be one hundred percent certain, but based on the deep, throaty exclamation, she suspected the woman two tables away had come.

Honey couldn't really fault her. Marc was wickedly mesmerizing, insanely sexy. Even with Drew seated beside her, his arm draped along the back of her chair, she couldn't help being seriously turned on. Her breasts budded. Her pussy pulsed. Tingling heat pooled in her lower abdomen. Stickiness seeped through the crotch of her panties, blanketing her tightly cinched inner thighs. Once she rose, she wouldn't be surprised to see that she'd left a stain on the seat. At one time, the possibility would have mortified her. Not so now. If she'd thought she could get away with it without Drew questioning her, she would have risen and headed for the nearest restroom, not to put out a panicked SOS to Carlson but to step into one of the stalls and masturbate away the tension.

The medley segued to Maroon 5's clubby hit, "I've Got the Moves Like Jagger," and Marc picked up pace. Gaze glued to him, Honey acknowledged that he did indeed have the moves. Hips flexed, muscles rippled. A broad-backed hand did a horizontal slide across his powerful, glistening chest.

Well lubricated from several hours of free liquor, the audience responded with unbridled enthusiasm, their frenzied state far surpassing their earlier response to Drew's "greed is good" pep talk. Right now, the only "money maker" anyone cared about was the thick ridge bulging from Marc's G-string.

From somewhere in the audience, a female shrieked, "Show me your meat, mister!"

Honey looked over her shoulder in the vicinity of the voice. Ms. 1992, it had to be. There were so few women present that the dozen or so in attendance were easy to spot. Staying in her seat was a major test of Honey's willpower. If she'd had her druthers, she would have gotten up, gone over to the horny heckler, and shaken her until her bonded teeth rattled.

But whatever Marc was doing, he was doing it for her. In putting himself under cover, he'd taken himself out of his comfort zone, though he certainly seemed at home. He looked as though he'd invented dirty dancing.

All but one of the other women and a few men rose to their feet as well, some dancing in place, most waving fistfuls of bills and beckoning Marc over.

"Here—here!"

"C'mon baby, let's see what you've got."

"Damn, he's so fine."

"Fine? He's fucking *hung*."

"Shake your beef, baby—shake, shake, *shake* it!"

Sweat streaked his sides, and despite their dire situation, Honey longed to catch the salty droplets on her tongue. She supposed she shouldn't be so surprised. Though washed-to-death T-shirts and old-as-dirt jeans were his usual off-duty ensemble, Marc always carried himself like a king. No matter how many hours he spent on his feet in the ER, that straight-backed stance never wavered.

The sensation of being watched had her dragging her gaze back to Drew. Out of the corner of her eye, she caught him scowling. Apparently entertainment was one thing, competition entirely another. Ripped, hung, tall, and gifted with moves Drew could only dream of, Marc was an instant sensation, the man of the moment, a big fish. Drew, in contrast, seemed a mere minnow.

Frank returned. He passed Drew a fresh bottle of scotch and whispered something into his ear. They both stared back at the stage—and Marc.

Drew's face twisted into the mean mask Honey had seen too many times to ignore. Instinctively her stomach tightened. "Get him the fuck off—now!" he said to Frank.

Frank looked dumbstruck. "But the song's not—"

"Just do it!"

Honey's heart froze. Helpless, she watched Frank walk over to the DJ and motion for him to kill the music. Burly bouncers from the private security firm Drew had hired stepped up onto the stage from opposite sides. Meeting in the middle, they took Marc by either arm and led him off.

Honey strained to see where they were taking him, but the crowd closed in. Boos burst through the banquet room. Someone, likely Ms. 1992, hurled a beer bottle toward the now empty stage. Bits of food from the buffet followed. The room no longer rained men, or in this case "man." Instead cherry tomatoes, buffalo shrimp, and chicken wings pelted the front of the room.

Throat tightening, Honey turned to Drew. Too worried for Marc to be frightened for herself, she demanded, "Why did you do that? He was only doing his job."

He glared at her. "Why are you suddenly so concerned about some no-name male model? Or do you maybe know him after all?"

Had he recognized Marc after all? Doing her best to play it cool, she said, "O-of course not. Until he brought over the drinks, I'd never seen him before."

He eyed her. "Yeah? Well then, you must have gotten acquainted awfully fast."

A chill slid along her spine. "I don't know what you're talking about."

"According to Frank, there's security footage showing you and Magic Mike huddled up close and personal in the kitchen."

He had her. That was the bad—okay, awful—part. On the positive side, it seemed he hadn't recognized Marc, at least not yet. There was nothing to do but brazen it out.

"Oh, right, that," she said, waving a hand as though flicking away a fly. "After you went to change, I realized I had scotch splashed on my dress. I went to see about getting some club soda."

"From the kitchen? Why not the service bar?"

"They . . . ran out of glassware."

He stared at her askance. "You really are a crap liar, you know that."

"I'm not lying. Frank is. I wouldn't sleep with him, and now he's out to get me. You heard what he said earlier. Why not have him show you the footage and then you can decide which of us is lying?"

The captured conversation probably looked pretty damning, but the playback would lead her to Frank—and Marc. Confession or not, until she found him, the word "Audrey" wasn't leaving her lips.

"Maybe I will . . . when he gets back."

"Back from . . . where?" she asked, worry ratcheting to something more—panic.

"Back from entertaining our dancing friend." Lifting his hand as if to consult the expensive wristwatch, a grin cocked the corner of his mouth. "Right about now Magic's being taught the lesson of his life."

*** ***

Standing in an inner courtyard, Marc glanced between the bullet-headed bouncers flanking him like bookends—seriously scary book-ends. "Hey, if your boss didn't dig my routine, he doesn't have to pay me. Sound fair?"

It had been years since he'd danced and, until now, always with his clothes on. It was Tony who'd taught him. Back in the day, they'd ride the subway down to Union Square, set up shop on the 14th Street entrance, and breakdance until their feet, knees, and elbows bled.

But once Tony had been convicted and sent away, Marc had put away his dance moves as he'd put away his love for his brother. Both were still there, but buried deep in storage. As he had Tony, he probably should have left any dancing well alone.

Neither guard so much as cracked a smile. "Jesus, at least give me my stuff and let me get dressed."

Once again there was no response. No doubt about it. He was about to get an ass whipping, just as soon as whomever they seemed to be waiting on arrived. So long as they stuck to fists, preferably bare and not brass-knuckled, he'd probably come through okay. With their shaven heads and shiny suits, they struck him more as bouncers than hit men—though with a psychopath like Winterthur, it was hard to say who he might have on his payroll. Either way, fighting fair probably wasn't in their vocabulary—if they even had a vocabulary. So far, neither had let a single word slip since "escorting" him from the banquet room.

The door opened. The heavyset suit, Frank Dawes, stepped out. He lumbered up to them and held out Marc's backpack, which Marc had left in the staff locker room. His other hand was wrapped around a baseball bat. "What the fuck are you doing here?" he demanded of Marc.

"What kind of question is that? The agency sent me. Look, if you have a problem with my performance, take it up with them." He reached for the pack but Dawes held it out of reach.

"Yeah, really? Which agency?"

In hindsight, a vendor list would have been a really good thing for Marc to get from Carlson. Only with Honey already inside, and him chomping at the bit to go in after her, there'd barely been time to figure out a plausible cover, let alone do extensive background prep.

"You should know. You contracted with them."

"The models we hired were all women."

He tried for a shrug, but with Mutt and Jeff weighing down his arms, it wasn't happening. "I guess I missed the memo. Anyway, I didn't hear a lot of complaints back in there." He jerked his chin toward the door.

Frank unzipped the backpack. Fortunately Marc had had the fore-thought to leave his driver's license back in the FBI van, but what had he forgotten? Frank's smug look suggested he'd already searched the bag and found . . . something.

Sweat trickled between his shoulder blades. Unlike Honey, he wasn't wearing a wire. He could shout "Audrey" at the top of his lungs, but Carlson and his agents wouldn't come running. But what really scared the shit out of him was what Winterthur might do to Honey. Marc's whole purpose in forcing his way in earlier had been to protect her. So far he'd done a pretty shitty job of it.

Frank dug around in the bottom of the bag and pulled out a wallet-sized laminated square: Marc's state medical license. It must have dropped out of his wallet earlier when he took out his other ID. *Damn!*

Dawes held the license up to the light. "If you're moonlighting, Obamacare must be a real bitch, huh, *Doctor* Sandler?"

✷✷✷ ✷✷✷

Honey sat through the dinner service, though she barely choked down more than a few forkfuls from each course. "Seriously, you can't just have someone taken away and beaten up because I talked to him for five minutes. There are laws."

Sliding a bite of steak into his mouth, Drew smirked. "Laws are for the mindless masses that follow them. It's a nation of sheep, baby, and every herd needs a shepherd."

"I'm serious, Drew. The male model, what have you done with him?" She articulated the question for the FBI's benefit. Marc had gone missing, and they needed to know.

Drew's derisive laugh assured her that her concern had landed on deaf ears. "Screw him, he's nobody."

Honey swallowed against her throat's thickening. "Everybody's somebody."

Marc wasn't only somebody. He was the finest man, one of the best human beings, it had ever been her privilege to know—and love. And like everyone she'd ever loved, she'd let him down. Badly.

Drew scoffed. "Do you really think a guy like that could ever give a materialistic little whore like you the lifestyle you're used to? Sure, he has a big dick but when it comes to Manhattan, a man's wallet is the only bulge in his pants that matters."

So that's what this was about. What she thought of as Drew's Napoleon Complex had once again reared it's ugly *little* head.

But she still had a job to do. She needed his confession, not just for her sake, but also for Marc's and the future she still hoped they'd have together. So long as she wore the recording device, she was protected to a point. All she needed to do was work "Audrey" into a sentence and federal agents would swarm the place—or at least that's how it worked on TV cop dramas and in police procedurals. Marc, however, had no such safety net. They could be waterboarding him in the basement, and unless she found him first, no one would know until it was too late.

Drew gestured with the tines of his fork to the room at large. "Look around you. All these shmucks with their polyester suits and bad haircuts and petty little dreams turn over their money to guys like me because they're too fucking lazy and stupid to figure it out for themselves. See that guy over there—I know for a fact his big dream is to buy a timeshare in St. Pete's Beach in Florida. And that f-ugly bitch with the huge honking beak is planning to spend her payout on rhinoplasty and a boob job. And see that grandfatherly guy with the salt-and-pepper hair, horn-rimmed glasses, and crazy bad cardigan? His wife of thirty years doesn't have a clue, but he has a 'mister' on the side. He's hoping to feather a homo love nest for the both of them with the windfall from his return—good luck with that."

"So I wasn't wrong earlier. What you're saying is HG Enterprises and the others, they're all shell corporations. They don't actually provide any services or make any products? They're just . . . pretend?"

He set the fork on the edge of his plate. "No, I didn't say any of that. You did."

Beneath the table, Honey ran a damp palm down her designer dress. "But I'm right, aren't I?"

He poured more scotch into his glass. "Tell me again why you're suddenly so interested in finance?"

"I'm not. I'm . . . interested in you."

His eyes stabbed into hers. "No, I don't think you are."

She opened her mouth to protest when his cell beeped, signaling a new text message had landed. He picked it up from the table. Heart in her throat, Honey watched and waited.

Sliding the phone into his jacket pocket, he looked over at her. "Frank's figured out who your boyfriend is." He shook his head as if she were a child who'd disappointed him. "Fucking the ER doctor—that's low, even for a lowlife whore like you."

Denial was pointless. Heart rate ratcheting, Honey shoved back her chair and stood. "Where is he? What have you done with him?"

Drew rose up beside her. Heedless of any onlookers, most of whom were too drunk to notice much anyway, he pulled her roughly against him. Squeezing her head between his hands, he kissed her, scotch-soaked tongue delving into her mouth. The suffocating embrace raised every survival instinct she'd spent the past six years burying. Flinging free, she opened her mouth to scream "Audrey!" when her hair fascinator went flying.

It landed on the tabletop. She grabbed for it, but Drew snapped it up first. "You know, it occurs to me I've never seen you wear anything like this before. It looks like it's from the flapper era. Your precious Audrey wasn't born yet."

Breathing hard, she held out a hand for the accessory. "Lots of people change their style."

"Maybe—but not you."

Honey stayed silent.

"Don't ever play a player, baby—you'll lose every time."

She willed her choppy heartbeats to calm. So far the worst he thought was that she'd cheated on him with Marc. He was still in the dark about Operation Moneybags, and Honey hoped to keep it that way. As dangerous as Drew's jealousy could be, it paled compared to what he'd do to her if he found out she wore a wire with the intention of sending him to prison.

He unclipped the bejeweled butterfly from the headband and cracked it against the side of the table. The case opened, revealing the recording device.

His gaze flew to her face. She expected him to berate her, curse a blue streak, but instead he laid his forefinger across his mouth, and said absolutely . . . nothing. He pulled his fancy fountain pen from an inner jacket pocket and reached for the table tent. Flattening the card stock, he scratched out a single sentence in big block letters. When he finished, he held up the paper so only she could see.

KEEP YOUR MOUTH SHUT OR MAGIC MIKE DIES.

✳✳✳ ✳✳✳

They brought Marc up by way of the service elevator, taking it to what he figured must be a private penthouse floor. With his right eye swollen shut, it was tough to tell much of anything for certain. They stepped off, Dawes leading the way toward a door at the end of the hall. Braced between the two thugs, he felt himself being buoyed along.

Downstairs in the atrium they'd worked him over pretty hard. With the two tough guys holding him pinned, Dawes had gotten in a few punches, but even in a one-sided fight, the man was too out of shape to keep things going. Sweaty-faced and fighting for breath, he'd been only too happy to turn Marc over to the hired muscle. They took turns holding his arms while the other pummeled him. Blows to the head, face, solar plexus, and stomach followed, so many that Marc lost count. A baseball bat to his right knee was saved for the finale. Though he was no orthopedist, he was pretty sure that strike to his patella had ended his breakdancing days.

Feet dragging along plush corridor carpeting, Marc fought against throwing up. "Where are you taking me?" he asked, swollen lips slurring the question.

Dawes shot him a smile over one beefy shoulder. "To a party, and this time, you get to be the guest of honor."

That didn't sound good.

Ahead, the suite door opened. "Welcome, welcome," Drew called out from inside.

They released him and shoved him through. He shot a hand out to the wall, catching himself at the last minute before falling on his face and sliding slowly to the floor though his right knee refused to bend. A gasp sent his head shooting up. He cracked open an eye, the one that still opened, and saw her. "Honey."

White-faced and wet-eyed, she ran to him. "Oh, my God, Marc." She sank down on her knees beside him. "This is all my fault."

He shook his head, or at least he tried to. The effort doubled his vision and sent his senses swimming. "Y-you look really . . . pretty. Meant to tell you earlier but I . . . forgot."

"Oh, Marc." Gentle hands, Honey's, slipped over his shoulders. She braced him against her, her light floral fragrance cutting through the stench of sweat and blood.

Holding his head up felt like a feat but somehow he managed it. Regardless of whether or not she'd gotten Winterthur's confession on record, and judging by the stricken look of her, he didn't think she had, she needed to save herself.

"G-get . . . get yourself out of here. Forget . . . *everything*. Just say the word and . . . go."

She shook her head. "I can't." She touched her hair, and for the first time he noticed what was different about her. The fancy headband was gone, and with it, the wire. *Shit.*

Expensive wingtips sidled up to them. "So, Doctor Sandler, we meet again. Pardon me for not recognizing you with your clothes off."

"What do you want?"

"For starters, I want to know why Honey was wearing a wire—and why you were helping her."

The inside of Marc's mouth tasted coppery. His saliva was the consistency of paste. He spoke slowly, focusing on enunciating the words without spitting blood or drooling. "She didn't have a choice. The feds are on to you, Winterthur. They may not get you tonight, but they'll get you eventually."

Drew paused as if considering. "Maybe . . . but I doubt it."

Kneeling beside Marc, Honey lifted her tear-streaked face to her tormentor. "I knew you were a bastard, but even I underestimated just how far gone you are. You have plenty of money, more than you know what to do with. You could retire today and never have to work again. Those people downstairs, all those people, you don't need their money, so why? Why do all of . . . this?"

Straightening, Drew shrugged. "It's what I do."

Marc felt Honey stiffen. Shoulders back and head high, she didn't seem so much frightened as furious. "What . . . you do? Wreck people's lives? You're proud of that?"

He let out a laugh. "Sure, why not? I don't build anything. I've never wanted to. What I do is trade in dreams—fucking castles in the air." His mouth curled in disgust. "Every sucker down there is a loser with a capital 'L.' They're born to be screwed, and guys like Frank and me—" He gestured to Dawes hanging back by the door "—were born to do the screwing. People like them don't deserve money. They don't have the first idea of what to do with it. The way I look at it, keeping wealth in the hands of the One Percent of us who know how to use it is performing a public service."

Disgusted, Marc spoke up. "So you got what you wanted. What's left?"

"Oh, that's where you're wrong, Sandler. I want a lot of things. Maybe Honey hasn't mentioned it, but I'm a man of big appetites." He slanted her a sly look, and despite feeling like a scarecrow that had the stuffing knocked out, Marc wanted to murder him.

Drew squatted down beside them. "Right now what I want is for us to play a little game. Honey here is going to suck my cock and then Frank's cock and then Frick and Frack's cocks, and maybe to liven things up, we'll bring in a clit and she can suck it, too. But here's the catch. Every time she stops, every time she so much as thinks of taking a break or a breath, a breath that doesn't have cock or pussy in it, you doc, are going to get whacked with that bat." He flung an arm out toward the bouncers, the one brandishing the bat. "Everyone clear on the rules? Great, I'll take that as a yes. Okay kids, let's get started."

Marc snagged Honey's gaze and shook his head. So much for him being her knight in shining armor. So much for thinking he could keep her safe. "Honey, don't do it." He'd let himself be bludgeoned to death before he saw her sacrifice herself in that way.

High on booze, power, and God only knew what else, Drew bounced about the room. "Oh, she's going to do it all right, and the best part is, you're going to watch. Pretty cool, huh?"

"No, she's not." Lowering his voice, Marc twisted toward Honey. "Baby, please, hang tough, if not for me, then for *Audrey*."

With the wire gone, saying the name aloud was pointless so far as rescue went, but invoking Honey's role model might just jar her into remembering who and what she was. With or without him, she needed to get her GED, go to college, have a life she could feel proud of—a life that didn't include scumbags like Winterthur.

She sent him a pitying look as though he must not quite understand. "The wire, Marc, he found it."

Winterthur broke in. "That's right, I did. You two can scream your stupid code word to the rafters, and it's not going to help you. The cavalry isn't coming, Sandler, so do yourself a favor and sit back and watch the show. In her escort days, Honey here commanded a grand per date."

Her escort days! Marc's Cyclops gaze flew to Honey—but for once, she couldn't look him in the eye.

Smug-faced, Drew sallied forth. "Don't tell me she failed to mention she spent two years as an escort—or a call girl, as you people would say. I can't say I know how she fucks when it's for free, but when there's money involved, believe me, she works her ass off."

"Yes, it's true," she finally said, saving Marc from asking. "I was going to tell you eventually, tonight actually. I came to New York as a runaway with no diploma and no money, and being paid to wear pretty clothes and go on 'dates' with professional men seemed exciting, even glamorous. Once I realized what was . . . involved, I told myself I'd stop as soon as I figured out something else to do, only—"

"She met me," Drew finished for her. "You would have thought I was Prince Fucking Charming the way she looked at me back then."

Marc swallowed hard. "It sounds like you took advantage of a desperate situation."

Drew snorted. "Believe me, I didn't have to twist her arm. A few shopping trips to Tiffany's, and she couldn't get enough of sucking me off—or whatever else I wanted. The first time I had her lick my boots, she came so hard I thought I was going to have to call 911."

Honey snapped back as if struck. She shot to her feet and whirled on Winterthur. "Kill me if you want, but you don't own me, not now, not ever again!" Arms outstretched, she dealt Drew a pretty impressive shove.

Only goading guys like Winterthur was a seriously bad idea. Adrenalin sent Marc surging to his feet. He took his first hobbling step, determined to do whatever he could to defend her. Maybe if they were busy beating him, she could slip out and escape.

The door to the suite flew open. "FBI, freeze!"

The three federal agents burst into the room, weapons drawn, Carlson at the front. The baseball bat clunked to the carpet as the two thugs and Dawes all lifted their hands high.

Marc sagged against the wall. "You took long enough."

"What can I say? I can't resist a grand entrance," Carlson deadpanned. Holding his gun on Drew, he shouted, "Hands in the air, Winterthur—now!"

Marc's relief was short-lived. Drew grabbed Honey, shoved her in front of him, and grabbed her in a chokehold, the blade of his arm cutting across her windpipe.

"Anybody make so much as one fucking move toward me, and I'll break the bitch's neck."

Carlson trained his cocked pistol on Drew. "It's over, Winterthur. Let her go. You're only making things worse for yourself."

Perspiring profusely, Drew shook his head. "Whatever you think you've got, it'll never hold up in court. It's entrapment, pure and simple."

"In that case, why not turn yourself in?" Carlson reasoned, edging toward Drew and Honey.

Wilkes moved closer, covering his partner. "He's right. Guys like you have their lawyers on speed dial. Surrender now and maybe you can cut yourself a sweet deal."

Supporting himself on his good leg, Marc launched himself at Winterthur. Focused on Carlson and the other agents, Drew didn't see him coming. The sideways strike knocked him back, loosening his grip on Honey, who slipped free. Though the beating he'd taken had been brutal, fortunately they hadn't gotten around to messing with his hands. Making use of them now, Marc grabbed the slighter built man and slammed him into the wall. Drew screamed, the back of his skull smashing into drywall.

"How's it feel to be on the receiving end of being beat, big man?" Marc hissed.

Holding him pinned, Marc hauled back—and swung. His fist smashed into Winterthur's nose. Blood spurted. Beneath his knuckles, cartilage crunched. He drew back, prepared to keep going.

Carlson's shout cut through his craziness. "That's enough, Sandler. I said *enough!*"

Marc unfurled his fist, dropped his arms, and backed away.

Chest heaving, Winterthur folded to the floor. "Don't just stand there. I need a doctor."

Weapon lowered, Wilkes walked up to him. "Yeah, yeah, we'll see about it," he said, slapping on the cuffs. "You have the right to remain silent . . ."

Honey rushed over to him. "Oh, darling, we have to get you to a hospital," she said, wrapping a steadying arm around his waist.

Adrenalin ebbing, he realized he didn't feel well at all. Pain pulsed through him. Woozy, he turned toward her—and reeled. Dark dots danced. A tunnel loomed ahead. Freed from the harness of gravity and fear, he felt himself being sucked toward it. Frantic voices rose up around him, but he was too far gone to answer. Honey's was the last he heard before he disappeared into the blackness.

Stay with me, Marc. Please, darling, I love you.

It was all for nothing.

Honey watched through a waterfall of tears as the two paramedics lifted Marc from the board onto the gurney. His face was a mask of bloodied cuts and bruises. Whatever skin wasn't lacerated and swollen was the color of ash.

Standing aside while they strapped him in, she smoothed a hand over his arm. "I love you, Marc."

Like the foiled sting operation, the declaration was pointless. Unconscious, he couldn't hear her. At least she didn't think he could.

Weapon holstered, Agent Carlson came up beside her. "You did good, Ms. Gustafson."

"So I've fulfilled my obligation to the Bureau even though—"

"You have."

"I want to ride with him in the ambulance," she said, still looking at Marc.

"Of course," he said. "We'll follow you to the hospital and take your statement there."

Honey jerked her gaze from Marc to Carlson. "That's fucking generous of you, agent, but unfortunately I'm not feeling especially thankful at the moment." Despite her past, she made it a point never to curse, certainly not in public, but the day's events called for an exception.

"You're in shock."

"Damn right I'm in shock! The man I love is lying unconscious on an ambulance gurney. He may have internal bleeding and God only knows what else, but that's not even the worst of it. The worst of it is I put him there—me, no one else. When he wakes up, *if* he wakes up, he's probably going to hate me. *I* hate me."

"I know it's hard to see the bigger picture right now, but what you did today has saved a lot of people not only money, in some cases their life's savings, but their futures."

She slanted him a look. Could a FBI agent really be that naïve? "Granted, you've got Drew for assault and battery and whatever other charges go with having the crap beat out of someone, but you have to understand, he can afford a team of top lawyers. He'll pay a stiff fine and maybe do some community service or a few months in an anklet under house arrest, but in the long run he'll be fine—and back to running his next scam." Marc, on the other hand, might not walk right ever again. Was that really justice? Honey didn't think so.

Carlson stared at her for a long moment. "You don't know, do you?"

Honey swiped a hand through her hair, a wreck like the rest of her. "Know what?"

"Winterthur, we got him."

"Yes, yes, he's in police custody for now, but what I just said—"

"His confession. On record. We got it. He's not just getting a wrist slap. He's likely going away for a while."

"But I don't understand. The bug you planted in my hair fascinator, he found it. Whatever he said, confessed, afterward, I'll testify to, but it's his word against mine and I'm . . . a former prostitute."

"Every successful undercover operation always allows for the unexpected."

Honey paused. Hope could be a dangerous thing. It sucked you in, spitting you out when life didn't come through. "Are you saying you had some sort of . . . backup plan?"

Carlson smiled, actually smiled, his mouth stretching so wide Honey marveled his face didn't crack. "We didn't only rely on the wire in your headpiece, Ms. Gustafson. We also bugged the suite."

of her classes had a few continuing education students who were even older than her—thank God!

Since enrolling in SVA, she'd come to know the work of Depression-era photographer Dorothea Lange, whose photographs of migrant workers had often been captioned with words from the workers themselves, and Richard Avedon, the first staff photographer for *The New Yorker*. It was Avedon who'd famously said, "What I hope to do is photograph people of accomplishment, not celebrity, and help define the difference once again."

Inspired by their legacy, Honey had focused her first student show on portraiture. By far her own worst critic, even she had to admit that the poignant black-and-white photographs of children and adolescents living in the Marcy Houses in Brooklyn had turned out better than she'd hoped, well worth the past few frenzied months of shooting, culling, editing, matting, and framing. Once home to the rapper Jay-Z, the low-income city housing project was notorious for its crime statistics. During the shoot, Honey had felt herself tearing up on more than one occasion, but she'd also found plenty of hope amidst the despair, especially reflected in the eyes of the children.

Pursuing the project had quickly become about more than academic credit. If even one of her photos motivated someone, be it a private person or public official, to prioritize working on better solutions for the Marcy House kids and those living in similar circumstances throughout the five boroughs, she would view the show as a success regardless of what grade she got.

But among her "fan club," as Marc insisted on saying, she'd already earned best in show. Nearly everyone she currently knew in New York had turned out to support her, as well as a few people she was just now meeting, and one very special guest . . .

"Hortense, these are just wonderful. I am just so gosh darn proud of you."

Epilogue

"I have learnt how to live . . . how to be in the world and of the world, and not just to stand aside and watch."—Audrey Hepburn

One year later, School of Visual Arts, Manhattan

Marc: "I'm so proud of you, baby."

Peter: "I knew you could do it, Honey."

Liz: "This is beautiful work, seriously stunning."

Sarah: "I'm doing a non-fiction coffee table book on raising kids in NYC. Would you consider being one of my contributing photographers?"

Brian: "Awesome!"

All the praise had Honey's face heating. "Thanks, everyone, but I've still got a long way to go before I graduate."

"On the flip side, look how far you've come already, and in just a year," Liz said, arm draped around Jonathan.

As usual, her friend made a good point. Thanks to Marc helping her cram, she'd passed her GED on the first try and began taking summer courses for college credit. Starting her freshman year at the ripe age of twenty-eight seemed almost sitcom material, but her worst fears had proven overblown. So far, everyone had been super nice, and several

Honey turned to her mother. Betty's once-brunette hair was salt-and-pepper now, her eyes and mouth bracketed by fine lines; still she looked more vibrant and relaxed than Honey ever remembered seeing her. Small surprise, the key to her rejuvenation had been deep-sixing Sam. Honey's running away had been a wakeup call. Religious principles notwithstanding, once Sam had bragged aloud about using his fists to keep not only his wife but also his stepdaughter in line, "'til death do us part" or not, her mother was done with him. A restraining order, a divorce, and a small business loan had secured her a fresh start as the owner of her own hair salon.

But Honey—Hortense—remained lost to her. In reading the news about Drew's indictment, she'd seen Honey's picture in the paper and, though the name was different, the face undeniably belonged to her baby. There'd been the first tentative reaching out on Facebook, followed by phone and Skype chats; still nothing could prepare Honey for standing face-to-face with her mom after almost a decade.

She'd flown in four days ago, a blowout surprise orchestrated by Marc. Once the initial awkwardness faded, they hadn't been able to stop touching—or talking. Ironic how the woman to whom Honey had worried she wouldn't have two words to string together was the very person to whom she couldn't seem to *stop* talking. Then again, they had a lot of years to catch up on—and considerable mutual forgiving to do.

They weren't the only ones.

Marc's older brother, Anthony—Tony—had been released on parole in time to attend the event. Living with their mother for now, he too had come by earlier to meet "Marc's girl" and wish her well. A hulking, soft-spoken man with sad eyes, he didn't much match Marc's memory of his brash, big-talking older brother. Seeing the siblings embrace for the first time in eight years had been an emotional moment for everyone, especially their mother; the latter had greeted Honey with the now habitual hug.

Happier than she could remember ever being, Honey reached out and squeezed her own mother's hand. Even after four days, she still couldn't quite believe she had her mom back in her life. "Thanks, Mama, but I couldn't have gotten this far without Marc. He spent all his days and evenings off last summer helping me cram my basic coursework so I could apply in time."

They'd moved in together that previous spring into an apartment occupying the first floor of a converted Brooklyn Heights brownstone that accepted tenants with pets. Honey still had a hard time grasping that she lived in New York City with an actual backyard.

Marc shook his head. "You didn't need my help. You were doing just fine on your own."

Honey shook her head. "In the science part, I so did need your help."

"Okay, well, yes, that's true. In science she did."

Grinning, Peter's husband, Pol, piped up, "Will you look at them. Bickering like an old married couple already."

Honey caught Marc's eye and hid a smile. Considering what they'd done in the shower that morning and on the kitchen counter the night before, they were still solidly in the "honeymoon" phase.

Peter caught her hand. "Ooh, I see someone's gone and put a ring on it."

Feeling shy suddenly, Honey nodded. "Marc was so sweet. He waited for Mama to get here and then he proposed."

"Asked my permission like a proper gentleman," her mother put in.

Pol sent her a teasing smile. "And do you mind telling us all what answer it was you gave, Betty?"

Resting fisted hands on her still slender hips, Betty replied, "What do you think I said? Look at him—smart, polite, easy on the eyes—and a doctor! I told Honey if she didn't marry him, I sure as heck would."

Marc broke into a blush. Fighting laughter, Honey shook her head. "Oh, Mama, you said no such thing."

"Maybe not," her mother conceded, "but I thought it."

The others crowded around to ooh and aah and generally admire the ring. The modest diamond set in white gold might be a mere chip compared to Sarah's multi-carat rock, but Honey couldn't imagine a more perfect symbol of their love—or a finer man to commit her life to. That Marc wasn't only incredibly kind-hearted and principled but also brilliant, sexy, and, well, an actual doctor, still sometimes overwhelmed her. She felt like Cinderella—and though she didn't have a fairy godmother, collectively and individually her four FATE friends more than filled that role.

"It's perfect," Liz said.

Sending Marc a sideways smile, Honey nodded. "It is, isn't it?" she said, not only thinking of the ring.

Marc carried her hand to his lips and kissed the top. "I did good?"

"I think I'll keep it—and you." Standing on her toes, Honey brushed a kiss across his smoothly shaven jaw.

Other than a tiny scar topping his cheekbone, he'd healed without a trace. Though his knee had required arthroscopic surgery, it too had mended. He still pleaded pain whenever Honey suggested they go dancing, and yet he was back to boxing and playing basketball. Go figure.

"When's the big day?" Sarah asked.

Honey and Marc exchanged smiling glances. He held back, letting her take the lead on answering. The small gesture spoke volumes. He wasn't interested in controlling her. When the time was right, they'd formalize their relationship in a church of their mutual choice, but for now, whether engaged or married, it was no less true—they were equal partners, a team. Having never had anything close to a true romantic partnership before, Honey recognized their relationship for what it was: more precious than platinum.

"Once we set a date, you all will be the first to know—promise."

Jonathan piped up, "Me, too?"

Laughter made the rounds. Smiling, Honey reached down to wipe cookie crumbs from one corner of his mouth. "Yes, darling, you especially." She lifted her eyes to Liz, and added, "Right now I'm just really focused on school."

After Marc's, Liz's opinion probably mattered to her the most. Though her life was her responsibility and no one else's—she got that now—knowing Liz was proud of her felt good.

Liz and Sarah exchanged smiles. "Smart girl," Liz said.

"Getting there." She slanted Marc a look. "I like to think Audrey would approve."

He leaned in and brushed his lips along the arc of her cheek. Even though they were in public and the kiss was a chaste one, still Honey felt the familiar tingling heat building—the sensation that suddenly had her counting the hours until they could be alone at home once more.

"I'm sure she would, sweetheart. I'm sure she would."

Publisher's Note

Intimate Partner Violence (IPV) affects more than twelve million Americans annually, according to the Centers for Disease Control and Prevention. Four in five IPV victims are female. IPV can assume several forms—domestic violence, dating violence, sexual assault, and stalking. The good news is that help is available.

The National Domestic Violence Hotline (www.thehotline.org) is reachable 24/7 at 1-800-799-7233. Calls are anonymous and confidential.

WomensLaw.org maintains a database of state-specific information on laws governing IPV, shelters, and related issues and resources.

LoveIsRespect.org promotes and raises awareness about dating abuse and helps promote healthy relationships among tweens, teens, and young adults.

Pets are often collateral damage in abusive relationships. Seventy-one percent of victims entering domestic violence shelters report that their abusers threatened, injured, or killed a family pet, according to the American Humane Association.

The Humane Society of the United States maintains an online Directory of Safe Havens for Animals, shelters that will temporarily board pets of domestic violence victims, at: http://www.humanesociety.org/issues/abuse_neglect/tips/safe_havens_directory.html

SafePlaceforPets.org and Pets911.com both allow site visitors to search for animal shelters, rescue groups, and emergency veterinarians by zip code.

RedRover, formerly United Animal Nations, offers various grant programs to enable victims to leave their batterers without having to leave their pets behind; http://www.redrover.org/redrover-relief-domestic-violence-resources.

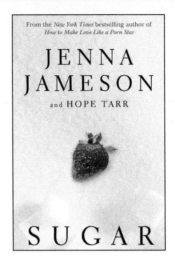

Sugar

by Jenna Jameson and Hope Tarr

"A novel of heart and heat . . . the multiple sex scenes, with or without BDSM, are spectacularly kinky and hot." —*Romantic Times*

New York Times bestselling author Jenna Jameson (*How to Make Love Like a Porn Star*) teams up with romance author Hope Tarr for this wild erotic novel—the first of the FATE series.

Fleeing Los Angeles and her scarlet past, former porn star Sarah Halliday returns to her New York roots hoping to lose herself in the crowded city streets, protected from the paparazzi's reach . . . or so she thinks. A chance encounter with a returned war hero—now prominent executive Cole A. Canning—is the very last thing she wants or needs, or is it?

When the handsome and deliciously kinky executive shows her that there are other ways to satisfy her needs (and he knows all of them), she finds herself in the middle of a sexual awakening, a true romance and a happily ever after. This is a rollicking must-read for all fans of *How to Make Love Like a Porn Star*.

$22.95 Hardcover • ISBN 978-1-62636-101-0

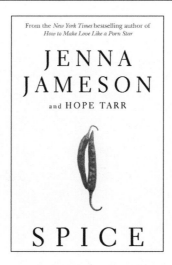

Spice

by Jenna Jameson and Hope Tarr

As the adult film sensation known as "Spice," Liz Carter was celebrated for her sultry looks, sexy curves, and natural DDs. Years ago, a surprise pregnancy prompted her to leave porn and LA for her native New York, where she launched a new life as a single mom and graphic designer. Staying single and solo is a lonely path, but it's also easier—and safer—than risking being recognized. To fill the void, she forms FATE, a group for former adult entertainers who find themselves in need of a supportive, safe environment where they can speak freely.

FATE is just a few months old when Liz learns she has breast cancer. The multiple surgeries and chemotherapy are grueling, but with the help of her fellow FATEs, she comes through. Cancer-free for more than a year, Liz runs across a Facebook message from a former male stripper seeking to join the group. A coffee meet-up to screen the potential newcomer proves to be more than Liz bargained for. Tall, dark, and Irish American, Sean has her seriously rethinking her "single and solo" status.

But Sean is not who he claims to be. Stumbling across the FATE group page one day, Sean, who is actually a tabloid news reporter, realizes he's hit pay dirt. What better way to break out from working the lowly gossip and obit sections than with a juicy exposé on a hidden enclave of Manhattan-based porn peeps? There's only one flaw in his plan: the group leader, Liz. Not only is she really nice and really smart and really sexy, but watching her mother not only her son but everyone else in the group twists up his insides. But he has a story to write—so why does he keep finding excuses to put off finishing it?

$22.95 Hardcover • ISBN 978-1-62914-492-4